Loving LOGAN

JANICE WILLIAMS

Primix Publishing
11620 Wilshire Blvd
Suite 900, West Wilshire Center, Los Angeles, CA, 90025
www.primixpublishing.com
Phone: 1-800-538-5788

Published by Primix Publishing   01/27/2022

ISBN: 978-1-955177-80-1(sc)
ISBN: 978-1-955177-81-8(e)

Library of Congress Control Number: 2021925799

Contents

Prologue vii

Chapter 1.   California. 1
Chapter 2.   California. 6
Chapter 3.   Colorado 26
Chapter 4.   Missouri. 35
Chapter 5.   Illinois 51
Chapter 6.   New York. 65
Chapter 7.   Washington DC. 83
Chapter 8.   California. 102
Chapter 9.   Hawaii 108
Chapter 10. The Wedding. 133
Chapter 11. Japan 145
Chapter 12. Indonesia 153
Chapter 13. Thailand 167
Chapter 14. Singapore 176

Epilogue 189

Prologue

At the young age of eighteen, I escaped my home, family, and friends. I was born and raised in Marin, California, a prestigious area north of San Francisco. Coming from a family of significant wealth, every girl's fairytale, I had money, clothes, cars, everything money could buy, but I wasn't happy. My dad was a workaholic, my mom was an alcoholic, and I was utterly miserable. Their constant fights were legendary. However, I had an insatiable itch to reconnect with the love of my life, Logan James, a famous rock icon. I knew him before the world ever knew his name. Leaving everything behind, I set out on a journey that changed my life.

My insatiable itch had to be scratched. Yes, as unbelievable as it might sound, every word is true. Leaving home was the best thing I've ever done, and the following months were the best of my life. Don't prejudge my decision. I think my story will convince you.

Chapter One

California

I woke to excruciating screams resonating from the downstairs living room. My parents, Charles and Amanda, were at it again. Fighting had become a daily ritual. Didn't they know the effect they were having on their children? Crawling back under the covers, I pulled the lavender duvet over my head. I was determined to escape the mental torment which had become my life. Finally, I was getting out, and unfortunately, my plan of escape didn't include my younger brother, Charlie.

Deciding to leave a note, I grabbed a pen and paper. I didn't deserve the wrath of my parents convincing me to stay. I was eighteen and more than capable of making my own decisions. There was no way my leaving home was open for discussion. After reading the note below, I wasn't there to hear their ensuing conversation. Still, I can easily imagine the following drama and their dialogue as depicted.

"I'm sorry. I don't expect you to understand my reasons for leaving, but if you're both honest with yourselves, I'm sure it will be an easy guess. Please don't try to contact me. I'll call when I feel the time is right. College isn't the answer, at least not now. I have to do this for myself. Please tell Charlie I love him and that I'm sorry for not letting him know."

"Charles, Charles," I'm sure mom screamed like a banshee running into my dad's office. "Oh my God, Charles, Jade is gone." Then, frantically wiping her eyes, she handed him the note.

"Woman, calm down. What do you mean? I'm sure she's upstairs."

Stroking his day's growth of gray stubble, my dad lounged back in his leather chair. He was amused.

"Really, Amanda, this is Jade doing what she does best, being dramatic, and I wonder where she gets it from? Certainly not me. It's just another one of her crazy antics. But, trust me, she'll be home before dark," he vented.

"Charles, how can you sit there and not take this seriously? She's not answering her cell phone," Amanda exclaimed. "You're wasting time. We need to find her."

"I'm busy. Do whatever you want. I don't have time for Jade's silliness. I've got business to take care of, and I'm meeting two clients later this morning. Why don't you ask Fran if she knows anything? Check the garage. I'm sure this is a joke, and you'll find her Mercedes parked in its usual spot. Now leave. I've got to make a few phone calls. Business-related," Charles snapped. Noticing the worried look on mom's face, he was sure she would want him to contact the police. The last thing dad needed was our family squabbles plastered all over the San Francisco Chronicle. It wasn't conducive to a prominent attorney or his law firm. However, I was eighteen and capable of making my own decisions even if they disapproved.

"Charles, you're going to regret this if anything happens to her. Do you understand?"

"Close the door and leave me alone. You're delusional. Your constant screaming and drama around this house are enough to drive anyone away. Take a close look at yourself," Dad fumed, tossing the note into the wastebasket. "If my mother were a raging alcoholic, I would leave too."

"Charles Dupree, you're going to wish you hadn't uttered those words. You're a workaholic. You spend your entire life in this office," mom raged, slamming the door shut as she raced to the garage.

Waiting for her exit, dad immediately checked my college funds. If I were serious about leaving, it would be a dead giveaway. Getting online, he held his breath. The blood drained from his face as he stared at the computer screen. A zero balance instantly reflected the seriousness of the situation. He had argued more than once with mom that keeping the account joint with me wasn't a good idea. No kid in her right mind should have easy access to such funds, not even at eighteen. Noting a recent photo of me, which dad had sitting on his desk, he picked it up, once again lounging back in his chair.

Slowly running his fingers through his thinning, salt and pepper hair, he contemplated my reasons for leaving. Reaching for his lighter, he lit a cigar. He was pissed mom had allowed such lunacy. He thought I was exactly like her and that we were both crazy. However, the truth was that I was more like him. I'm sure he thought my brother, Charlie, was the only sane one in the family, even at the young age of twelve. He had been grooming his only son from birth to one day becoming a partner in the family law firm. I was a lost cause, just like mom. Even though the loss of nearly a half-million dollars was hard to swallow, dad could easily make it back within a few weeks. He was picking up some wealthy clients later that day. The only thing on his mind was keeping our family antics out of the newspapers. Savoring a long draw on his cigar, he walked over to the bar. Reaching for a bottle of Blanton's Bourbon, he poured himself a drink. Tossing back a huge gulp, I'm sure he only wished that mom had left too. We were enough to drive him over the edge. He could easily raise Charlie alone with the help of Fran, our longtime housekeeper.

Suddenly pulled from his thoughts, Dad wasn't surprised to hear mom's screams as she once again bounded into his office. "Charles, her Mercedes is not in the garage."

"Amanda, I told you, I'm busy," dad furiously interjected. "I've got no time for this. I'm taking my work to the corporate office downtown, and I don't want to be disturbed. Do you understand? Jade isn't stupid. She knows what she's doing."

Reaching for his cell phone, he called Alistair, his chauffeur. Then, hurriedly stuffing folders into his briefcase, he was out the door, leaving mom alone to deal with the ongoing dilemma. Deciding not to mention that I had drained my college funds, he wanted her to stew in a mess of her own creation. Dad had quickly tired of mom and all the problems associated with her. The fact he had been considering divorcing mom forever might now become a reality. The loss of his daughter was a small price to pay to be free of the women in his life. Dad smiled. Charlie was all he needed, and a new start in life seemed too good to be true.

Chasing him out to the curb, mom relentlessly screamed.

"Oh, you're going to regret this, Charles Dupree. Runaway, that's all you've ever done. I'm calling Ron. I want a divorce. You're a bastard. Do you hear me?"

I'm sure the word divorce was music to his ears as he stepped inside the limo.

Now that you've been introduced to mom and dad, I think you can easily justify my reasons for leaving. Let me give you a more detailed description. They were both trust fund babies and threatened to divorce since they repeated their vows and said, *I do*, inside Grace Cathedral in San Francisco.

Dad is exceptionally handsome by any stretch of the imagination. It didn't take a rocket scientist to understand why mom fell in love with him. Tall, statuesque, with jet black hair and steel blue eyes, his chiseled features could have easily graced the cover of GQ Magazine. He was the only heir to a conglomerate called Dupree Holdings and the managing partner in a prominent law firm in San Francisco. This fact was the icing on the wedding cake as far as my mother was concerned. Unfortunately, however, dad was a workaholic and never home.

Enter mom. Her stunning slim, hourglass figure, long, platinum blonde hair, and azure blue eyes could easily rival the goddess Venus. Her undeniable charm and wit had easily caught my dad's attention. Likewise, her gorgeous petite profile provided him with the perfect arm candy. Even though there was a ten-year age difference between them, my dad being the eldest, they had a lot in common. Mom came from a family of significant wealth. Grandpa Jack had made millions in the oil fields of Southeast Texas. Meeting during a winter ski trip to Aspen, they had fallen in love at first sight. Even though I'm sure they appeared like Ken and Barbie, it didn't take long for the smoldering embers of love to cool.

I was born only a few months after their wedding, which gave me cause to doubt their motives for marital bliss. My brother, Charlie, followed six years later. I suppose the responsibilities of raising two young children without their father at home were brutal. My dad hired Fran early on to help with household chores. Fortunately, I inherited my mother's gorgeous appearance, tall, thin, with long, blonde curls. We mirrored each other. Unfortunately, I had my dad's stubborn, innate ability to be a free thinker. I'm sure looking back, I wasn't easy on my parents. However, they both adored my younger brother, Charlie, named after my dad. His appearance didn't reflect a strong family resemblance. Surprisingly enough, Charlie had flaming red hair and freckles. He was cute for a twelve-year-old and resembled our great grandfather Harvey. That was my mom's story, and she was sticking to it. However, the truth be known, our handsome gardener had flaming red hair, and my dad always brought up that fact in their arguments when Charlie wasn't around.

Now back to how it all began. After leaving the note on the kitchen island where it would easily be seen, I hurriedly ran to the garage. Jumping into my new silver Mercedes convertible, my high school graduation gift, I quietly backed out of the driveway and let the top down. It was June, the sun and fresh air felt invigorating. I had no regrets, taking one last look in the review mirror at the sprawling stucco mansion. I was on my way to the City of Angels to see my favorite rock band, Riot Storm. Crossing the Golden Gate Bridge, Marin soon became a distant blur. Blasting the radio, I felt free.

Los Angeles was approximately an eight-hour drive south on Interstate 5. Stopping for gas and snacks, only my best friend, Zoey, knew my destination. She was sworn to secrecy, and I knew she could be trusted. I wanted no contact with either of my parents even though I did feel a bit sad leaving Charlie without an explanation. However, there was no way I would burden him with my problems at his age. He was too young to understand my reasons for leaving. Hopefully, one day in the future, I will tell him.

Chapter Two

California

Driving above the speed limit, I kept a close watch for the California Highway Patrol. The last thing I needed was a speeding ticket. The concert started at 7:00 p.m. with an opening band, and I would be right on time with a bit of luck. The guys usually went on stage around 8:00 p.m.

Stopping for gas, I checked my cell phone. Mom had left more than a dozen messages. None of which I had the slightest bit of interest in hearing. However, I finally decided to text a reply. Knowing my dad, I knew he would convince my mom to let me go. We were a lot alike, stubborn, and strong-willed. By now, I'm sure he was aware that I had drained my college funds. Whether or not he chose to disclose the fact to mom, he knew there wasn't any real reason for worry with this amount of money under my control and with my street smarts. However, I'm sure mom didn't share his thoughts on the situation.

Calling Zoey, my best friend, another reason for driving to Los Angeles, I wanted her to have my arrival time. Zoey and I had grown up together in Marin and attended the same high school. Our parents were prominent socialites and always together. However, Alan Zimmerman, Zoey's dad, had since relocated to Los Angeles to be closer to the recording studios taking Zoey and their entire family. He was now managing Riot Storm.

Zoe and I had agreed to meet outside the arena. Even without a ticket, I knew she had our backs as far as gaining entry. Her dad wouldn't let us down as far as tickets were concerned. Alan had managed Riot Storm for years, and I was obsessed with the lead singer, Logan James. No, I take that back. I was in love with Logan James. We attended the same high school. He was three years older, and two summers ago, we were inseparable until he graduated and joined the band on their overseas tour. I was devastated when he left and determined to rekindle what we once had. Unfortunately, we had not been in contact since he left Marin. But, I had to make this work. Going home was not an option.

Quickly paying for a cold soda, a bag of chips, and pumping gas into the car, I was soon back on the interstate and only two hours away from Los Angeles. I couldn't fathom my luck that Riot Storm was stateside and that I would soon be reunited with Logan up close and personal. I said a prayer that he still felt the same towards me. He was all I ever wanted, and it had been two long years since he left to join the band on their overseas tour.

Finally, after what seemed like an eternity, I reached the section of Interstate 5 referred to as the grapevine. Jamming out to the band's latest hit, *Daytime Nightmares,* I entered the steep grade of the Tehachapi Mountains. Soon leaving the curved roads behind, the sprawling outskirts of the greater Los Angeles area came into view. Suddenly stopped in rush hour traffic, I panicked. We were moving at a snail's pace. Finally, after almost an hour, the arena came into view. Finding a place to park in a nearby multi-level parking garage, I called Zoey. She answered on the first ring.

"Hey, I'm here," I announced excitedly.

"Great. I'm standing near the entrance. I've got tickets, and you're not going to believe this, but Brian, a friend of dads, gave us backstage passes. However, Dad doesn't know, so we've got to keep a low profile. He can't find us backstage. Got it?"

"Got it. That's awesome. I'll be right there."

Quickly checking my hair and makeup in the mirror, I decided to pull my long blonde curls into a ponytail. Then, applying pink lipstick, I grabbed my leather jacket and locked the car.

"Wow, you're stunning as always," Zoey smiled as I approached the entrance.

Zoe, her preferred nickname, and I were the same age, yet nothing alike in appearance. She was petite, with sunkissed freckles and long auburn curls.

Wearing cut-off jeans with her hair in braids and a black tee-shirt depicting the band's logo, Zoey appeared much younger than her age.

"Geez, Zoe, you look like you stepped out of the *Wizard of Oz.* Braids?" I teased.

"Really, Jade, and who's to say you look appropriately dressed. I'm not the one pursuing Logan James. You are. Are you excited to see him?"

"Oh, I don't think exciting even covers it."

"Does he have any idea you're here?"

"No. I want to surprise him."

"Jade, seriously, I know we haven't talked, but what if things don't work out? It's been two years since you've last seen him. What if he isn't exactly thrilled to see you?"

"You worry too much. I can't wait to see him."

"Dad got us on the floor, row twelve. I'm sorry, it was as close as we could get last minute."

"It's fine. I'll see Logan after the concert."

Without mentioning a word, I knew Zoey worried about me. She knew the world of rock and roll and everything it involved. The chances of Logan having remained unattached for two years in that environment weren't exactly stacked in my favor. Two of the band members had already been replaced due to drugs. However, knowing how much this opportunity meant to me, I knew she would stand by me regardless of tonight's outcome. Zoe knew my life at home wasn't great. I was living proof that having all the money in the world doesn't guarantee happiness.

"Okay, if you're ready, let's go in and get something to drink before we find our seats," Zoey suggested handing me a ticket.

After our bags were checked at the gate, we were finally allowed inside the arena. Fighting our way through the crowd, we walked over to one of the many beverage stands. Ordering two sodas, we were at last ready to find our seats.

Entering the main floor, the opening band had just finished and exited the stage. Looking around the arena, it held over twenty thousand people. It was completely sold-out. Our timing was perfect. The stage lights began to flash, signaling the arrival of Riot Storm, as we found row twelve and our seats. The anticipation gave me goosebumps. The noise from the fans was off the Richter scale as the entire arena quickly erupted with screams, excitedly calling out the name of the band and its members. Jarrod, the drummer, walked on stage first. My heart raced, noting his buffed, muscular profile, tattooed body, and long, blonde curls falling below his shoulders. Next on stage was Noah, the bass guitarist. He was tall, slender, dark brown hair with no hint of tattoos. Ethan, the lead guitarist, appeared next. He was also tall, sporting ink from head to toe, long brown hair, ripped jeans, and sneakers. However, his looks and personality made him a favorite with the girls as screams resonated throughout the arena. Finally, I held my breath as Logan made his grand entrance causing the girls to go wild.

"Good evening Los Angeles. I'm Logan James, and we're Riot Storm. It's great to be home. Thanks for coming out to party with us." The sound system loudly reverberated his strong voice.

The fans went crazy as the band opened with their hit single, *Twisted Hearts.*

"What do you think? Has he changed?" Zoey asked loudly, trying to be heard above the crowd's roar.

"Oh my God, Zoe, just look at him!" I gasped, entirely mesmerized.

"Breathe, Jade. Breathe," Zoey laughed.

Nothing about his new appearance was familiar. Every inch of his muscular physique was covered in tattoos. Wearing a black tee-shirt and ripped jeans, his long blond curls were pulled back in a ponytail.

Logan was every girl's dream. He was tall, thin, and his chiseled facial features were the only recognizable aspect I remembered. His new look was sexier than hell. He literally took my breath away. Unbelievably, Logan effortlessly embodied the features of a rock god. His unorthodox stage presence gave him total control over his fans. The girls sitting nearby screamed. It reflected their tremendous love for Logan and the band. He had me at, *hello,* the famous line spoken by Bridget Jones.

"Wow, Jade, he's covered in tattoos, and he's wearing his hair pulled back in a ponytail," Zoey laughed.

I was captivated by his new appearance and instantly transported back when we were together. Nothing at the moment mattered to me, only the fact I was here and totally lost in him once again. Even sitting among a crowd of over twenty thousand screaming fans, it felt the arena held only us. Nothing could come between Logan and me.

As the guys performed their next set, I knew all the words by heart. I couldn't wait to be with him, touch him, and let him know how much I had missed him. Looking over at Zoey, she was dancing. Everyone was out of their seats. It appeared every young girl in the arena was entirely awe-struck by the guys. It seemed I wasn't the only one who knew the lyrics to each song. Did he possibly know how much his fans loved him? Undoubtedly, it gave him a feeling of euphoria to have such endearing admirers. However, I had been a fan of Logan's long before the world ever knew his name.

Taking a break, he reached for a water bottle and introduced each band member. His blonde hair and tanned physique made my heart melt. I only wished he knew that I was in the audience. However, it didn't matter, I would be seeing him as soon as the concert was over, and I couldn't wait. Just thinking about it made me feel as giddy as a young teenager.

I was in another place and time as the concert went on for over an hour. A place that only included us. Finally, as Logan announced their last song, my heart stopped. This was it. After two long years, I would finally have the chance to tell him how much I had missed him. Thinking back, how could I have ever let him walk out of my life so easily? Why hadn't I tried to keep in touch with him? Why did I so easily break off our relationship? Why had it seemed the right thing to do? So many regrets. Would he understand that it was my way of letting him go, freeing him to chase his dreams?

"Good night Los Angeles," Logan screamed. "We've had a blast."

"See you in Denver," Ethan yelled as the guys left the stage.

As Zoey gently elbowed me, I jumped. "Jade, are you alright? You seem spaced out. Are you sure you want to follow through with this?"

"Yes. Are you crazy? I was lost, remembering what our lives were like before Logan left. All the fun times we had. I have to see him. Let's go."

"Okay, follow me, and if we see my dad, hide," Zoe laughed.

Grabbing my hand, she began pulling me through the crowd and toward the back of the stage. We hadn't gone very far when a burly security guard instantly stopped us.

"Family," Zoey quickly announced, showing her backstage pass. Evidently, he wasn't bothered by needing to see any further identification.

"Do you have any idea where you're going?"

"No, but I think the dressing rooms are down this corridor. At least, I hope so," Zoey laughed.

Hurriedly, I followed Zoey through a labyrinth of narrow concrete corridors with exposed overhead pipes and wiring. I kept my eyes peeled for any sight of her dad. I was sure he wouldn't be amused that we were looking for Logan.

"Jade, down this way. I just caught a glimpse of Ethan. I think Logan might be in one of the rooms near the end of this corridor," Zoey whispered as we made our way past roadies and reporters.

Just at that moment, a guy suddenly appeared out of nowhere, grabbing Zoey's braid. "Where do you think you're going?" Brian, Dad's assistant, scolded. "I know I gave you backstage passes, but that doesn't mean you can have access to the band members."

"Oh, we're lost. We're trying to find the exit, but it's a concrete jungle back here," Zoe answered nervously, offering no further explanation.

"Well, you're going in the wrong direction. The exits are behind you," Brian fumed. "I hope you don't run into your dad. He'll kill me if he finds out I let you backstage."

"No worries, we're leaving," Zoey mentioned as he walked out of sight. "Geez, just my luck we would run into Brian."

Stopping in front of a door that Zoe suspected was Logan's dressing room, she smiled. "I'll stand outside and keep a close watch for my dad while you go in and talk to Logan?"

"Thanks."

"If you need me, call my cell. Good luck."

Knocking on the door, I held my breath. After the second knock, a voice yelled. "Busy, try Ethan's room. He's entertaining groupies two doors down." I cringed. It was distinctly Logan's voice.

"Logan, it's Jade," I whispered.

"Who?"

"Jade," I repeated.

"Whatever you want, it better be important."

Opening the door, he was wearing a black tee-shirt and boxer shorts. His long blonde hair appeared tousled as it hung loosely past his shoulders.

"Hey, I said I'm busy," Logan quickly snapped without looking up to see who was at the door.

"I'm sorry. This has been a huge mistake," I gasped in horror, turning to leave.

Finally, as Logan's eyes met mine, he was in total shock. "Jade, wait. What the hell? What are you doing here?"

"I came to the concert and was hoping to see you, but obviously, you're busy." Crying as tears streamed down my face, I was mortified. It was apparent Logan was shocked to see me.

"Wow, Jade, this is quite a surprise. What brings you to Los Angeles?"

"It's a long story. I should go," I mumbled softly, wiping my eyes.

"No. You're here, and you're not leaving. Come inside."

"It's okay. I know you're busy."

"It's not a problem. She was on her way out. Grab your clothes and get out," he motioned to the half-dressed, blonde groupie who was sitting on his couch. "Now, I said," he urgently demanded.

Quickly closing the door behind her, he took my hand, pulling me inside.

"Really, I should leave."

"No. Something is wrong. I can feel it."

We were always intuitively connected, and maybe there was still something between us. However, this wasn't going as I had planned.

"Jade, what's wrong? Why are you here?" Logan questioned, leading me over to the couch. Reaching for a box of Kleenex, he handed me a tissue. "I'm sorry that you had to see me with someone. Honestly, she means nothing. Trust me, groupies follow us everywhere." Taking another tissue, he gently wiped the myriad of tears trickling down my face. "You know I had a hard time getting over us after I left. You meant the world to me. Seriously, I thought I would never see you again."

"I felt the same, but I would never have stood in your way when you were offered the chance to join Riot Storm. Letting you go seemed like the right thing to do."

"For who, you or me? Jade, you have no idea how hard it was leaving you."

"We were not at the right time of our life to continue a long-distance relationship. You had just graduated, and I still had two years of high school left."

"What's going on?"

"I've left home. Mom and dad have become unbearable to live with. Mom's drinking again, and dad is always working. Seriously, I think they should get a divorce. They fight constantly. I feel bad that I had to leave Charlie. However, he's younger. Hopefully, it doesn't bother him as much."

"Geez, Jade, I'm sorry. Really, I am. What are your plans?"

"Well, I haven't thought that far ahead. I just left this morning. When Zoey mentioned you were performing in Los Angeles, I knew I had to see you. You're not going to believe it, but I drained my entire college fund and transferred the money into a private account so that my parents couldn't get their hands on it. So I'm not going back to Marin."

"Wow, Babe, do your parents know about the money? Geez, this sounds serious. Well, that settles it. You're staying with me. No questions asked. We have reservations at the Westin Hotel in Beverly Hills. However, I'm afraid we leave in two days. Our next venue is in Denver. I remembered you joked about becoming a groupie before I left Marin. Does that still appeal to you?" Logan laughed.

"I'm not sure whether they know I closed the account. I don't care. Second question, a groupie, that's funny."

"Oh, I almost forgot. I thought I saw Zoey standing in the corridor when I opened the door. Does Alan know you guys came backstage?"

"Not exactly," Brian, a friend of Zoey's dad, gave us a backstage pass.

"Is she still waiting for you? By the way, we all know Brian. He works for Alan."

"Yes. I think so."

"Why don't you call her and let her know that you'll be staying at the Westin tonight."

"I can't stay. My car is parked in the garage across the street from the arena."

"Not a problem, give me your keys. I'll get Ethan to drive it over to the hotel."

"Thanks, but I'm not sure about staying at the Westin tonight."

"If things are as serious as you just said, I think staying with me is the least of your problems. We all have individual suites at the Westin, or if you'd prefer, I can bunk with Ethan, and you can take my room for the night," Logan smiled. "Call Zoey before Alan discovers she's backstage loitering outside my dressing room," he laughed.

"Okay, if you insist. It's a new silver Mercedes convertible," I reluctantly agreed, handing over my keys. It's parked on level three near the exit.

I reached into my purse for my cell phone. I couldn't believe I was about to spend the night in Logan's hotel room, despite an indication of anything further happening between us. Quickly, I called Zoe.

"Zoey, I'm going to stay the night at the Westin Hotel with Logan. I wanted to let you know. Hopefully, you can sneak out of the arena without your dad seeing you."

"Jade, seriously, he had a girl in his dressing room. Are you insane? I hope you know what you're doing?"

"Trust me. I know what I'm doing. Ethan is going to drive my car over to the hotel. I'll call you in the morning."

"Okay, if you're sure. I don't want to see you get hurt again. I'll talk to you in the morning," Zoey replied, completely worried her best friend was about to make a colossal mistake.

"Thanks. We'll talk tomorrow."

Jade, wait one second. I need to make a quick call before we leave the arena," Logan smiled, quickly disappearing into the next room.

"Are you ready," Logan questioned upon his return. A limo is waiting outside the back entrance to drive us over to the hotel. Oh, take this. It'll provide a quick disguise just in case we run into Alan," Logan smiled, handing me a baseball cap. "Also, keep your head down. You never know who might walk past on our way out. I don't want to explain this to Alan, Brian, or anyone else for that matter. At least, not this evening."

Tucking my hair under the cap, I was nervous but ready to take the risk, hoping Alan wouldn't see me with Logan. Taking his hand when he returned, I followed him through the long, narrow concrete jungle. Luck was on our side as we reached the outside entrance without being noticed.

Once inside the limo, we both took a deep breath and laughed.

"Wow, that was easier than I expected," Logan winked.

My feelings for Logan were returning with a vengeance as I snuggled inside his strong, muscular arms.

Staring into his gorgeous, sapphire eyes, I could feel myself literally melting into his sexy body. Things were happening at warp speed. The fact I had just left home earlier that morning, drove to Los Angeles, and now I was cuddled inside his arms was truly unbelievable.

"Would you like a drink?" Logan offered as he lit a cigarette and poured himself a shot of bourbon. "Perhaps a soda or sparkling water?"

I smiled. I knew Logan wasn't going to offer me anything more substantial. At least not until he knew where this was going, and right now, everything was still up in the air.

"A coke sounds great."

He filled a glass with ice and popped the top on a soda can.

"Wow, you're drinking bourbon these days?" I teased.

Logan laughed, looking down at his drink as he lounged back in his seat with his cigarette. "I have Alan to thank for introducing me to the finest bourbons while we were in Europe. I must say he knows the best."

Reaching for his cell phone, Logan called Ethan.

"Hey man, I need a favor. I left car keys in my dressing room. They belong to a friend of mine. I need you to drive her car over to the Westin. It's a silver Mercedes convertible, and it's parked in the garage next to the arena. Third floor. Thanks, man."

"That's taken care of," Logan smiled, taking a sip of his drink. "What are your plans?" he winked with a concerned stare.

"Well, I'm not exactly sure. I'm just taking things one day at a time. I've always been kind of spontaneous. You should know that."

"How could I forget? It's one of the reasons I fell in love with you," Logan smiled, setting his drink on the console.

Had my ears deceived me? Did he just use the word love? Was there a slim chance he still had feelings for me after two years? I could only pray. However, I didn't have to wait long for an answer. He gently reached over and untied my hair, allowing my long, blonde curls to fall loosely around my shoulders.

"That's much better," Logan winked, giving me a quick kiss. "I've always loved your hair down."

Even though it was only a beginning, his kiss sent shivers throughout my entire body. I was still very much in love with the new Logan James.

I slowly began to trace the outline of his tattoos up his arm with my fingers. As I reached his upper forearm, I froze. Instantly, he grabbed my hand, stopping me as he quickly pulled his black tee-shirt down to cover what I'd just exposed. Logan had a heart tattoo with my initials 'JD' scrolled inside it.

The limo suddenly felt too quiet as he stared into my eyes. The silence was overwhelming.

"Guess you've discovered my first tattoo. You know what everyone says about tattoos. Once you get one, you get another," Logan smiled, breaking the awkward silence.

Not knowing whether I should acknowledge what I'd seen or not, I decided to address the elephant in the limo. I had to know.

"Logan," I paused. "Are those my initials?" I asked hesitantly.

Time stood still, waiting for his reply. If those were my initials, I felt like my heart would burst. If not, I would never be able to look at him the same way. But did I even want to know? What were the chances that I would have seen it so soon? Was it possibly a sign that he'd never stopped loving me?" My heart was racing wildly out of control.

"Yes."

Oh, my God, maybe he wasn't over us after all. His simple answer gave me hope.

"Jade, you have to know that when I left, I had serious doubts that I had made the right decision. Leaving you was one of the hardest things I've ever done. But being offered your dream of lead singer in a rock band, especially Riot Storm, was compelling. The fact you still had two years to graduate made it an easier decision."

Was there any truth to his confession? I so wanted to believe every word. However, finding a girl in his dressing room was shocking. The fact he'd spent the past two years traveling the world with a rock band, especially Riot Storm with their notorious reputation, gave me reasons to doubt his sincerity. Could I get over his bad-boy image?

On the other hand, he definitely wasn't a monk, nor was I a nun. Didn't the world of rock and roll come with vices such as girls, drugs, and unbelievable parties? So, perhaps, I should cut him some slack.

Suddenly pulling me into his arms, Logan kissed me with such passion it literally took my breath away, erasing every doubt. None of it mattered, only the fact that we were together again, and I was still hopelessly in love with him.

"God, I've missed you," he whispered.

"I've missed you too."

Arriving at the luxurious Westin Hotel, it was quickly beginning to appear the idea of two separate rooms was laughable.

As the chauffeur opened our door, we walked towards the entrance of the grand hotel with our arms draped around each other.

Unexpectedly, the paparazzi had been waiting for Logan's arrival. Instantly lights from numerous cameras began flashing all around us. I was caught on camera with my arms locked around Logan James entering the Westin Hotel in Beverly Hills. It would no doubt be in all the newspapers tomorrow, as well as all the rag tabloids. I guess the ruse was up as far as my parents knowing my whereabouts.

"Jade, I'm so sorry. I should have expected this. I hope this doesn't cause problems for you?" Logan explained, rushing us inside the safety of the lobby.

"I don't blame you, and it's too late for worries," I laughed. "Guess I'll be receiving some rather nasty phone calls and texts from home tomorrow."

"Jade, I'm really sorry."

"Don't be. It's okay."

"The paparazzi was bound to find me sooner or later, and in this age of technology, it's almost inevitable," Logan apologized.

"Good evening, Mr. James. I hope you'll find everything to your liking. If there is anything more we can do, please let us know," the concierge stated.

"What was that all about?" I inquired as we walked towards the elevator.

"Nothing."

Continuing to Logan's suite, he swiped the room key and opened the door.

A huge smile crossed my face. Sitting on the credenza was a large bouquet of red roses, and an entire dinner was beautifully prepared and waiting for our arrival.

"Geez, Logan, isn't this a little extravagant?" I blushed. However, I couldn't have been more pleased. "How did you manage this so quickly?"

"I believe it's called a cell phone," Logan teased. "I'm starved. You have to eat, and I remembered how much you love roses. Trust me. You can work up quite an appetite when you come off stage."

Hearing his explanation, my mind raced back to earlier that evening when I discovered the blonde in his room. Guess that would depend upon what kind of appetite he was referring to, I thought—quickly dismissing the ugly thoughts from my mind. I had to learn to live in the moment and avoid any feelings regarding where this was going. I couldn't expect to be back in his life after only one night.

Watching as he lifted the silver tops from the chafing dishes, the aroma was heavenly. Then, walking over to smell the roses, the fragrance of the bouquet was exquisite.

"Have you eaten dinner this evening?" he questioned, exposing a delicious main course of filet mignon, wild rice, broccoli, and rolls.

"No, not unless you consider dinner a bag of chips and soda I had earlier at a gas station."

"Geez, you must be starved. Have a seat," Logan smiled, pulling out my chair.

Putting a large portion of everything on a plate, he grinned. "Bon appetite," he added, handing me silverware.

"That's a lot for one person."

"You don't have to finish your entire meal. Trust me. It isn't mandatory," Logan laughed.

"Wow, thank God you still have your sense of humor."

"Jade, I'm still me. The same guy you've always known," he winked, caressing my face with the soft touch of his hands.

Wow, I almost had to pinch myself. Was this really happening? Getting a second chance with Logan James, the rock star was more than I could have ever hoped for.

"I saved the best for last," Logan announced. "Chocolate brownies drizzled in extra chocolate sauce. I know you love brownies."

Immediately taking a huge bite, they were delicious. "Wow, amazing," I smiled, wiping chocolate from the crevices of my mouth. Logan remembered everything, including my favorite dessert.

After dinner, he pushed the cart holding the silver chafing dishes outside into the hallway. Grabbing my hand, he pulled me over to the sofa.

"Take off your shoes. Let's get comfortable. Oh, I almost forgot we have champagne."

Walking over to the bar, Logan popped the cork on a bottle of Moet & Chandon. Filling two fluted glasses, he walked back to the sofa.

"I think we should celebrate," he laughed, handing me a glass of the sparkling beverage.

"Thanks."

"So," he paused, taking a quick sip. "What have you been up to these past two years?"

"Well, truthfully, not much. Nothing as exciting as your being a famous rock star," I smiled, taking a small sip. "I finally graduated."

"Awesome. However, that was a given," Logan smiled.

"What was your favorite country on tour?"

"Well, I'm not sure that I had a favorite. I loved the whole damn tour. In fact, Alan is talking about a Pacific Rim tour next year."

"Geez, that sounds exciting."

"Yeah, the guys and I would love to see that part of the world."

Hearing a soft knock on the door, Logan walked over.

"Hey man, I just wanted to let you know the Mercedes is here. Great car," Ethan mentioned. "Oh, I gave the keys to the valet. I'm going down to the bar with the guys. What's the plan regarding our rooms for tonight?"

"I'm not sure, but if you happen to see the *Do Not Disturb* sign on the door later, you've got your room all to yourself. If not, I'll be bunking with you."

"Okay, but you're going to owe me for this. By the way, who's the girl?"

"We'll talk later," Logan quietly mentioned closing the door.

"Ethan just came by to let you know your car is safely parked in the valet lot."

"Thanks. It was my graduation present."

Refilling our glasses with champagne, Logan handed me another drink as he sat back lazily on the sofa beside me. Pulling me into his arms, I felt warm and giddy. Perhaps it was the champagne, but I prefer to think it was being snuggled against his warm, sexy body. I'm sure there were a lot of young girls who would have easily given anything to be where I was tonight, cuddled inside the warmth of his embrace. However, once again, my mind tortured me with doubts. Logan James, the famous lead singer for Riot Storm, was not necessarily the Logan James I fell in love with. Regardless of what he said, it was hard to imagine them being the same. Only time would tell which Logan I was about to spend the night with. Downing my drink, I didn't want to know. Not tonight.

Walking toward the door, he placed the *Do not disturb* sign on the door. Taking my empty glass, he set it on the coffee table along with his. Then, pulling me into his arms, he slowly swept my hair behind my ear, tenderly kissing the nape of my neck.

"Wow, Jade, you smell phenomenal. It's been a long time, a really long time since we've been together."

Logan's passionate kisses rendered me breathless and dazed as his caresses invaded my body with tingles of excitement. Intense heat radiated from the top of my head to the tips of my toes, and I was instantly transported back to the time of us.

Scooping me up in his arms, he carried me into the bedroom. Pulling back the duvet, he sat me on the edge of the bed as he slowly removed his tee-shirt, exposing his muscular, tattooed chest. His physique effortlessly portrayed the image of a rock god. Tousled strands of long blonde hair fell loosely around his shoulders. Staring into his smoldering blue eyes, I locked his bad-boy image out of my mind. I was hopelessly lost.

"Babe, I've missed you. I've missed us," he whispered, slowly removing my outer garments.

Dimming the lights in the room, Logan pulled me into his arms. Feeling the warmth of his skin against mine was sheer ecstasy. It was easy loving Logan. The entire night was spent making up for the past two years. As the early rays of the morning sun slowly crept into the room, it found us still wrapped in each other's arms, not having slept at all.

"Wow, Babe, last night was incredible," Logan winked.

"Unbelievable," I whispered, smothering his face with kisses.

Staring into his eyes, I was already beginning to psychoanalyze our romantic evening. Did it mean we were together again, or did he see it as a one-night stand? Perhaps Zoey was right. Maybe I had allowed my feelings for Logan to override common sense and forced my way back into his life without getting to know more about the guy sleeping next to me. I could only hope the consequences of last night didn't come back to haunt me. However, I knew that I was more than ever in love with the new Logan James.

"Why don't you shower and dress. I'll order room service," Logan smiled, sitting up in bed as he lit a cigarette.

"Oh my God, my suitcase," I gasped. "It's still in the trunk of the Mercedes."

"Sweetheart, don't panic. I'll have Ethan or the concierge bring it in for you. I believe you'll find a robe in the bathroom."

As the warm water washed over my body, it felt cathartic. It represented a new start and a new direction for my life. Then, lathering shampoo through my hair, I suddenly felt Logan's hands gently massaging my back.

"Conserving water," he whispered.

Turning to face him, once again, I found myself melting at the mere sight of him as the water gently flowed over his ribbed muscular body.

"Shampoo?" I smiled, handing him the bottle.

"Later," he grinned wickedly, pulling me into his arms.

Stepping out of the shower, we put on bathrobes and leisurely enjoyed breakfast. It was delicious. Logan had remembered everything, including the fact that I loved blueberry pancakes.

"What are your plans?" Logan asked with an intense stare sipping his coffee.

"Well, I'm not really sure."

"Our next gig is tomorrow night in Denver. We leave this evening. I want you to come with me. I'm not leaving you behind."

Evidently, he was used to getting his way, as there hadn't been the slightest hint of inquiring whether I wanted to join him.

Before I could even respond, my cell phone began blowing up.

"Wow, I guess my parents have seen the photos from last night. I'm afraid I better take the call."

"I'll give you some privacy," Logan frowned. "I'm sorry," he mouthed inaudibly as he grabbed his cigarettes and walked outside to the patio.

"Jade, what the hell are you doing? You do know everyone has seen the photos. What were you thinking? You're with Logan." mom exploded.

"Stop bombarding me with questions. The photos were an accident. Logan had no idea the paparazzi were waiting for him outside the Westin last night."

"Jade, for heaven's sake, he's the lead singer for Riot Storm. What did you expect? When are you coming home? I've been worried sick about you?"

"That's just it. I'm not. Didn't you read the note I left on the island in the kitchen? No more questions, I've got to go."

Before mom could get in another word, I ended the call.

"So, how did that go?" Logan questioned moments later as he walked inside.

"As Mom expected. I'm not going home. But, sooner or later, mom will have to accept the fact I'm eighteen and can make my own decisions."

"Speaking of decisions, I hope you don't mind, but I just made arrangements for your Mercedes to be stored. So it will be safe until you return."

"Geez, Logan, I don't remember agreeing to go with you to Denver, and now you've had my car stored without asking. Don't I have a say? Please don't become my mother," I fumed.

There was never a doubt I would follow him to Denver or wherever, for that matter. However, what wasn't okay was the fact he didn't ask. It was evident the rock star Logan James got his way without thoughts or consequences of those around him.

"Jade, I want you with me at the Coliseum in Denver when we go on stage tomorrow night. So you're not getting away so easy this time. The band has a Lear jet at LAX, the Los Angeles International Airport, so I really don't foresee any problems."

"Okay, but next time," I paused, staring at him with the faint hint of a smile. "Ask."

"Got it."

Did he really? It was cause for worry. However, it was probably a moot point. I was totally in love with him.

"Hey, I'm going to work out for a couple of hours and swim a few laps. Care to join me?" Logan smiled quickly, tying his long blonde hair into a ponytail.

"Thanks for asking, but I have a few phone calls to make before leaving for Denver this evening."

"Okay, if you're sure. Tell Zoe I said, "Hi."

Picking up my cell, I called Zoey.

"Hey, I was beginning to think you forgot about me."

"Never. I've been a little preoccupied."

"I'll say. The photos were cute."

"Oh, you saw those?"

"Are you kidding? Who didn't? Dad was pissed that Logan was caught off guard."

"It was an accident."

"Okay, give me the details. Did you sleep with him?"

"Geez, Zoe."

"Well, I'm waiting."

"Okay. I slept with him."

"Wow, guess I should have expected that. However, I was hoping you might take things a little slower. I worry about you."

"Zoe, that's ridiculous."

"What are your plans for today? Want to grab lunch?"

"Well, I'm still at the Westin, and I'm flying to Denver this evening with Logan and the guys."

"Oh my God, Jade. Really? Does my dad know?"

"I'm not sure, but I guess he will when I board the plane this evening."

"Jade, you're putting me in a weird situation with my dad. You're my best friend, and you've become a groupie, and I hate to tell you, but he hates groupies."

"Zoey, I know your dad manages Riot Storm, but I was in love with Logan long before he joined the band. I guess we'll deal with Alan this evening. Logan wants me at the coliseum when he goes on stage tomorrow night, and I'm going. End of discussion."

"Well, I would certainly love to be aboard the jet tonight when dad and Brian see you walk on with Logan."

"Zoe, no worries. I'll call you tomorrow.

"Okay, enjoy the flight. I'm sure it'll be interesting."

Later that evening, as Logan and I boarded the jet, all eyes were on us. However, my presence never became an issue. Logan James, the rock star, held enough power to silence Alan and Brian. So, I was on my way to Denver with the guy I loved.

Chapter Three

Colorado

As the plane touched down in Denver later that evening, the flight had been uneventful. It hadn't turned into the heated argument between Alan, Brian, and Logan that Zoey had warned might happen. If there were repercussions, Alan was apparently keeping things to himself for the moment. Perhaps the fact I was Zoey's best friend had something to do with it. Regardless, it was the second small hurdle after the paparazzi event, which could have caused significant problems between Logan and Alan. However, I was becoming a permanent fixture in Logan's life, and Alan would have to come to terms with the fact that I wasn't your ordinary groupie.

Entering the limo, Logan pulled me into the back seat putting his arms around me.

"Here's the deal," Alan paused, finally breaking his silence. "Logan, I'm your manager, not your father, and what you or any of you do for that matter is your private business. However, if it becomes a problem for the band, it becomes my problem. So I don't think you want to go there," Alan added with a serious demeanor.

At that point, Ethan tried to hide his laughter as the entire limo erupted into a hilarious roar. The guys felt as if they were being scolded like naughty children.

"Lighten up, Alan," Jarrod interjected, trying to change the atmosphere inside the car.

"Jarrod's right. Where would you be without us?" Logan agreed as he reached for a bottle of bourbon. Then, pouring each of the guys a shot, "Here's to one hell of a concert," he toasted, quickly changing the subject.

As the limo parked under the brightly lit entrance of the Ritz Carlton, Brian gave the guys last-minute instructions.

"Sound check is at 4:00 p.m. The limo will pick you up at 3:00 p.m. Don't be late, and you've each got your own suite. I'm sure you'll appreciate having separate rooms," Brian stated, glancing at Logan. "You can pick up your room keys at the front desk. Alan, I don't know about you, but I'm going to the lounge for a drink. Want to join me?" Brian added.

"Definitely."

Exiting the limo, the guys quickly made their way inside.

"Wow, I feel like a third wheel. Do you think Alan will ever warm up to the idea that we're together?" I whispered.

"Give him time, but honestly, I don't give a damn what he thinks. You're with me, and the discussion ends there," Logan snapped, cupping his hands against the wind to light a cigarette.

"So, what are our plans once we check in?"

"Really, Jade, that's cute," Logan winked wickedly.

"Geez, Logan, don't you ever think of anything besides sex?"

"Not where you're concerned."

Walking into the spacious lobby, Logan picked up our room key.

"Hey, man, want to grab a drink before we turn in for the night? The guys and I are going to the lounge," Ethan inquired.

"Thanks. Not tonight. We're busy."

"Right," Ethan grinned, following the guys towards the Loft Lounge. "See you in the morning."

Unlocking the door to our suite, it was sheer luxury as always. Once again, hanging the *Do Not Disturb* sign on our door, Logan took my hand, quickly pulling me inside.

"Honestly, Logan, do you think that's necessary. I mean the sign?"

"Definitely. There's no such thing as privacy, staying on the same floor with these guys."

Walking over to the bar, he poured himself a shot of bourbon. "Want a nightcap?"

"I'm good, but thanks for asking."

Tossing back his shot of bourbon, he playfully grabbed me from behind, pulling me toward the bedroom. A wicked smile slowly crept over his face.

"Geez, Logan, you certainly don't waste any time," I whispered, lightly kissing his cheeks.

"Why should we? Waste time, that is," he teased.

Dimming the lights, his steamy passionate kisses sent shivers down my spine. He was right. Two years had been an eternity to be apart. Slowly lifting his shirt over his head, I kissed his muscular, tattooed chest. I was once again entirely lost in us.

Spending another sleepless night wrapped in Logan's arms, I knew I had made the right decision to follow him to Denver. As the sun bathed the room in a soft glow the following day, I found myself staring at the new Logan James, the rock star. His body at rest was a perfect dichotomy. His gentle demeanor was entirely foreign to his presence on stage. Deciding to let him sleep, I quietly slipped out of bed to order room service.

Hearing a soft knock at the door indicated the arrival of breakfast. The aroma of freshly brewed coffee, omelets, hash browns, and bacon quickly infused the air. Pouring a cup of the steaming brew, I quietly walked into the bedroom.

To my surprise, Logan was awake.

Sitting up in bed with his exposed, tattooed chest, piercing blue eyes, and messy bed hair, he took my breath away. He was every girl's dream. However, he belonged to me, or so I thought.

"Wow, my kind of girl. You've made breakfast," he teased, putting out his cigarette.

"Do you want to eat in the living room?"

"No. Nothing is better than eating breakfast in bed," Logan winked. "Especially with you."

Taking two plates filled with the mouth-watering omelets, hash browns, and bacon into the bedroom, I sat down on the bed next to Logan.

"We should start every day like this," I suggested cutting into my omelet. "Do all rock stars live this extravagantly? Is this a reflection of how the past two years have been for you on tour?"

"Babe, slow down. What's with all the questions?"

I had only been with Logan for two days, and suddenly my mind was obsessed with thoughts of what his life must have been like over the past twenty-four months. Did he have a new girl in his bed every night? Surely, there were hundreds of girls who would have taken every chance to be with him. Was I merely a new diversion for him when he was off-stage? Did I dare press him for answers to questions that might haunt me if I knew? Deciding it best not to know, I tried not to focus on his previous life with the band. However, it wasn't easy. What I failed to see was that living in the moment and having unanswered questions could sometimes be a dangerous place to exist.

After breakfast, Logan kept to his routine by going downstairs to work out in the gym. It left me alone in the room to ponder all the questions now swirling through my mind. Then, unexpectedly hearing a knock at the door, I jumped up from the sofa.

"Hey, Jade, is Logan here?" Ethan questioned as I opened the door.

"No. Sorry, you just missed him. He's working out at the gym."

"Okay. Thanks."

"Anything important?"

"No. I'll catch him later."

"Why don't you come in for a few minutes? There's plenty of hot coffee."

He was just the person I needed to speak with. No one could paint a more accurate description of Logan's past better than Ethan.

"Okay," Ethan smiled hesitantly as he slowly sauntered into the room.

I'm sure he was curious why I invited him in, considering that Logan was at the gym.

"Have a seat. I'll get our coffee. Cream or sugar?"

"Neither."

"Ethan, I'm sure you know that Logan and I have a past. We were together up until he signed on with the band. I'm interested in learning more about his past two years. Were there a lot of girls in his life?"

"Really, Jade? Don't you think that would be best discussed with Logan?" Ethan questioned, taking a sip of coffee.

"Ethan, I know you are friends with Logan. I can understand why you might be reluctant to talk about this, but I'm in love with him if you haven't guessed. He's changed, and I need to know if Logan is still capable of committing to a serious relationship?"

"Okay, but what I say stays in this room. Do you understand?"

"Yes. Of course. I'm not trying to put you in the middle or cause problems between the two of you. I just need answers."

"What do you want to know?" Ethan asked, walking over to refill his coffee.

"Well," I paused. "We had broken up before Logan joined Riot Storm. So there wasn't any reason for him to stay committed to our relationship, but has he had any serious connections with anyone?"

"Honestly, Jade, I really don't know how to answer that. But, frankly, I'm not sure I should."

"Be honest with me. I'm a big girl. I can take it."

"Jade, Logan's past as well as his reputation is literally tattooed all over his body. Do you really want to know more? Doesn't his new appearance or behavior give you an indication? Seriously, he's the lead singer of Riot Storm. He's never had girl problems. So what do you want me to say? That girls are in and out of his life like a revolving door. I'm sorry. I don't want to hurt you, but Jade, a guy like Logan, can have anything he wants, especially girls. I think I've said too much," Ethan scowled, downing his entire cup of coffee.

"Thanks for being honest. I didn't expect Logan to be a monk," I teased.

"A monk?" Ethan roared as coffee spewed from his mouth. "Oh my God, that's hilarious," he laughed, reaching for a napkin. "Listen, Jade, the words Logan James and monk used in the same sentence are an oxymoron if I've ever heard one. I don't mean to burst your bubble, but members of famous rock bands such as Riot Storm are not monks by any stretch of the imagination."

"I know. Don't be silly."

"I've got to go. The last thing I need is for Logan to walk in and find me here. Thanks for the coffee."

"Oh, you're welcome. Thanks for talking with me. See you later tonight."

"Remember, you're not to say a word about our little discussion or that I was here. The last thing I need is to go on stage tonight with Logan pissed at me."

"No problem," I assured him, closing the door.

Lounging back on the sofa, I finally had my answers. Ethan had confirmed what I already suspected. I would pack what few things I had and leave immediately. The timing was perfect with Logan at the gym. I would simply leave a note. I would never be content being the flavor of the week. I had to leave before, once again, my heart was broken.

"Logan, the past two days have been incredible. However, I was naïve to think I could simply walk back into your life. Trying to recreate what we once had isn't going to work. I'm sorry. I love you." Jade

Placing the note where it would easily be found, I grabbed my few things and closed the door. Entering the elevator, it felt like my heart was being ripped out of my chest. Reaching the lobby, I decided to get a taxi to the airport. Leaving before Logan returned was my only option. I couldn't bear to face him.

Wiping tears from my eyes, I waited anxiously near the curb for a cab. Leaving seemed to be my only recourse. Finally, as the taxi arrived,

I held my breath, opening the car door. Suddenly, I froze, feeling strong hands grabbing me from behind. Logan's arms encircled my waist as he shut the door, preventing my entry.

"What the hell Jade? What's going on? Why are you doing this?" Logan vented angrily, pinning me against the cab. Still, in his gym shorts, he smelled of sweat, yet it was awkwardly masculine and sexy. Pulling me into his arms, it was evident he'd just discovered the note.

Without total conviction, I hesitated for a moment bracing myself against the cab. Then, finally, I managed to say what was needed. "I'm leaving."

"Leaving. You're not going anywhere until you tell me what's going on," Logan demanded. "We need to talk. We're going back up to the room."

Quickly handing the cabbie a tip, Logan picked up my one small tote and grabbed my hand, pulling me away from the curb. Leading me towards the lobby, it was clear he had read the note.

"Damn, Babe, I simply left to work out for an hour, and I come back to an empty room and a note. What the hell! What's going on? I think I deserve an answer?"

"Logan, I think we should call this off and go our separate ways before one of us gets hurt. Trust me. It's for the best."

"First, am I missing something, or do I get a say in this? You've decided it's best. Jade, the past two days have been amazing."

"You're right. They have been incredible, but how long can this honestly last?" I asked, wiping tears from my eyes as I followed him into the elevator.

"Jade, I've never felt this way about anyone. But, honestly, sweetheart, I thought you knew, especially after the past two days."

Unlocking the door, Logan walked over to the bar. Pouring a double shot of bourbon, he tossed it back in one long, continuous gulp. Pulling me over to the sofa, I knew he wanted answers. But, reluctantly, I didn't know where to start without referencing my recent discussion with Ethan.

"Logan, when I left home, the thought of seeing you was the only thing that kept me sane. When you left Marin to join the band, you took my heart with you. I never stopped loving you, not even for a second. I've always loved you."

Grabbing some tissues from the coffee table, Logan lovingly wiped the tears from my eyes. He looked devastated and perplexed.

"Logan, you're not the same person. I'm not sure what I expected. However, I know it was wrong to assume that you would be anyone other than who you are, the lead singer of a famous rock band. I thought leaving would make it easier on both of us."

"Damn, Jade, what I do for a living or these damn tattoos doesn't change me. I love you. Can't you see that? I don't understand how you could get things so wrong in the space of only an hour. What happened?" Logan paused. "Or should I ask who got to you? Did one of the guys stop by the room?" Logan knew the rivalry between the guys was intense, especially when it came to girls. Reaching for his cigarettes, he only needed to know which of the guys had betrayed his trust.

"Jade, did one of the guys stop by while I was at the gym?" Logan reiterated, taking a drag on his smoke.

Knowing there was no reason to deny the fact, the ruse was up. Logan could easily tell if I lied. However, I felt like I was throwing Ethan under a bus, and unfortunately, I couldn't be sure how Logan would react.

"Ethan stopped by for a few minutes," I confessed.

"Damn, I knew it. I suppose I was the topic of conversation. What did he say?"

"Please don't be upset with him. It's all my fault. I was curious about a few things, that's all."

"Oh, is that right."

Putting out his cigarette, he could only imagine what Ethan might have said. Their friendship had been on dubious terms, primarily where girls and groupies were concerned.

"Really, Babe, I don't give a damn what Ethan might have told you. I thought you knew the real me, not the famous rock star image of whom I appear to be. Jade, I love you. I've always loved you, but I'm not going to lie to you. There have always been girls. What's happened over the past two years with anyone else stays in the past. Honestly, I thought I would never see you again. Do you understand? I'm not perfect. However, with you in my life, trust me, I'm no longer looking. You are my forever. I love you. You have to believe me."

Pulling me into his arms, I once again melted into his warm embrace. Kissing him passionately, I was hopelessly lost. Starring into the intensity of his captivating blue eyes, I was more than ever in love with Logan regardless of his rock star bad boy image.

Taking my hand, Logan pulled me up from the sofa. "I need a shower," he winked wickedly. Then, playfully, he pulled me into the bathroom.

This was the energetic guy I had fallen in love with. He was right. How could I possibly judge him by anything as superficial as his tattoos, his new appearance, or even the number of girls which might have conceivably slept in his bed? He was with me now, and that's all that mattered.

Running my hands through his long hair, I massaged his scalp with shampoo. I knew I would follow him anywhere. There wasn't a doubt that I loved him with every ounce of my being. The shower suddenly became steamy as the feel of the warm water cascading over our bodies became sexually invigorating. Any remaining thoughts of Logan's past easily washed down the drain, at least for the moment.

After getting dressed, Logan ordered dinner. Suddenly realizing he had left the room, I had no thoughts as to where he might have gone until later that evening. Then, I discovered Ethan's swollen eye. Apparently, Logan had slipped from the room long enough to pay Ethan a visit.

Arriving at the concert, the ride over in the limo was somewhat subdued. It appeared Ethan's eye was not open for discussion. However, the fans would never know, thanks to a great make-up artist.

Later that night, Riot Storm performed to over eighteen thousand screaming fans in a sold-out arena. The following day, we were on our way to St. Louis, Missouri.

Chapter Four

Missouri

*A*s the jet began its approach into Lambert International, the air inside the cabin was infused with the smell of pot. The guys anxiously started storing their stash as they prepared for their arrival in St. Louis. Even though the duration of the flight was less than two hours, the animosity between Ethan and Logan was still tangible. It appeared even the calming effect of marijuana wasn't enough to diffuse the tension. However, I was focused entirely on the landscape below as I watched the soaring Gateway Arch come into view. It was spectacular.

"I'm beginning to feel like a father of rambunctious children," Alan frowned. "We're in St. Louis for three days. I expect you to put your tiffs aside. We have a concert to perform, but more importantly, we're family," Alan stated.

I knew traveling with Logan would change the dynamics of the band, but it was a price we were willing to pay to be together. However, I discovered early on as a groupie, you didn't come between bandmates. I felt responsible for the problems between Ethan and Logan. I needed to do whatever I could to make things right between them.

Arriving at the prestigious Four Seasons Hotel, the band's protocol never seemed to change. Picking up room keys in the lobby, Logan and I took the elevator to our suite. Opening the door, the incredible view of the Gateway Arch was clearly visible. A well-designed living area offered every possible amenity for an enjoyable stay, including a fully stocked bar and large-screen television. Tossing our one travel bag onto a mahogany credenza, Logan pulled me over to the leather sofa taking in the incredible view.

"We have the entire day to ourselves. So why don't we check out the city?"

"And how do you expect to pull that off without getting recognized?" I teased.

"Geez, Jade, you are a newbie to my world. A baseball cap and sunglasses can disguise almost anyone. It'll be fun. Trust me. You can't spend the entire tour locked away in a hotel room," Logan smirked, reaching for his cigarettes.

"Okay. I've always wanted to check out the arch. I've also heard the St. Louis Zoo is a must-see."

"Really, Babe, the zoo. I think I'm surrounded by enough animals," Logan laughed, walking over to the bar. Then, pouring a shot of bourbon, he returned to the sofa, lounging further back against the soft cushions.

Hearing the distinct sound of my cell phone, I reached for my purse. Taking a glance, it was Zoey

"Hey, I heard you're in St. Louis for a few days." Zoey excitedly exclaimed as I answered the call.

"Hey, Zoe. How are things?

"Boring."

"Why don't you come to St. Louis? It would be fun. I need time with my favorite girlfriend. I've got a small situation going on between Logan and Ethan, and I could use your help," I whispered.

"Say no more. I'm on my way. I was looking for an excuse to get out of Los Angeles for a few days. Oh, don't say a word to dad. I want to surprise him."

"Great. We're staying at the Four Seasons. Call me when you arrive."

"Will do. See you later this evening. Love you."

Laying my phone on the coffee table, I snuggled inside the warmth of Logan's arms.

"That was Zoe. She's flying to St. Louis this evening, but she doesn't want Alan to know."

"Great. I've always liked Zoey. Thank God she's nothing like Alan," Logan smirked, changing the subject. "Why don't we get out of here? The concert is tomorrow night, and there are no sound checks this evening, we're wasting time. So let's get out of here."

Hurriedly, Logan grabbed a pair of sneakers and pulled his long hair into a ponytail. Finally, putting on a baseball cap and sunglasses, he was right. At first glance, he was unrecognizable as a member of Riot Storm. Quickly I changed into a stylish pair of designer jeans, a tee-shirt depicting the band's logo, my tennis shoes, and sunglasses. I was finally dressed for a day of fun.

"Wow, Babe, really, you're wearing that?" Logan laughed. "I'm not sure it's a good idea. But, you do know I'm the lead singer for the band," he teased.

"Hey, it's an advertisement for your concert."

Calling for a taxi, we ran out the door. Logan and I were on our own for the next few hours. Trying to keep everything inconspicuous, other than the fact I was wearing the band's logo, made our little escapade fun.

Arriving at the Gateway Arch, Logan paid the cab driver to wait. If God forbid he was recognized, we would need a quick escape.

Purchasing our ticket, we held our breath as three other people entered the tiny, crowded capsule for the four-minute ride to the top. Trying not to laugh, as a young girl stared at my tee-shirt, I couldn't help myself.

"Are you a fan of Riot Storm?" I questioned.

"Who isn't?" she eagerly answered.

At that point, I felt Logan's hand inconspicuously slip under my tee-shirt, giving me a hard pinch. His reaction only made me more determined to play with him.

"Are you going to the concert tomorrow night?"

"Definitely. Who isn't in love with Logan James?" she smiled.

"Well, that makes two of us."

I knew Logan was about to become unglued at that point, so I didn't say another word about the band. However, I loved watching him squirm. The young girl would never know that Logan James was sitting across from her.

Reaching the top of the 630-foot arch, Logan put his arm around me as we took in the panoramic views of the Mississippi River and surrounding vistas.

"Jade, you do realize what you said could have created a huge incident. Are you crazy?" he whispered.

"Crazy in love with you. Lighten up. We're out to have fun. I'm starving. Let's get down from here and grab something to eat," I smiled, giving him a quick kiss.

Suddenly returning my kiss with passion, he pulled me to his chest.

"Logan, let me go. We're not alone. For heaven's sake, we're in a public place, and everyone is watching," I whispered as a blush spread across my face.

"Okay. Stop dropping hints about my identity while we're in public, or I'll make you pay for it later," Logan winked wickedly.

"Really, is that a promise?"

"Oh, it's on. Trust me," he winked mischievously.

As the morning sun brightly streamed in through the tiny window, we took in our last views from the arch before taking the shorter three-minute ride back down. It was uneventful, as I dared not mention the band.

Jumping into the waiting taxi, our driver suggested the Shaved Duck for drinks and food. Later he recommended the Planter's House for cocktails. Dropping us near the quaint corner entrance of the Shaved Duck, Logan once again tipped the cabby to wait for our return.

A delicious aroma infused the air as we were seated in a booth near the back of the cozy restaurant. Deciding to order the smothered fries and pulled pork with buttermilk cornbread, we gorged ourselves on the southern delicacies. I ordered an iced tea and enjoyed taking quick sips of Logan's Modern Man Pale Lager. Before long, I was beginning to feel a bit tipsy. However, Logan insisted we continue our day out with a visit to the zoo.

"Babe, I feel dizzy. I'm not sure I can walk through the zoo this afternoon. So maybe we should save it for another time. Zoey should be arriving in about an hour, and I would like to go back to the hotel," I suggested guiltily as Logan reluctantly agreed.

"Geez, Jade, you only had a few sips of my drink. But, okay, we'll go back to the hotel if you insist."

"Thanks. Perhaps later tonight, we can take Zoey to the Planter's House for dinner and drinks."

Finally, helping me inside the taxi, Logan pulled me close, kissing my forehead. "I shouldn't have shared my drink with you. You're an underage lush," he winked with a laugh.

Logan had no idea that my plan for later that evening would include Ethan. It was my attempt at trying to get them over their recent tiff. I was entirely to blame for Ethan's black eye, and I felt I should try to resolve their issues.

Arriving back at the Four Seasons, Logan unlocked the door to our elegant suite. It appeared we hadn't been missed as there were no messages from Alan or the guys. Removing his baseball cap, Logan tossed it on the nearby sofa table along with his sunglasses as he let his hair down. Then, he removed his shoes and gave me a wicked, seductive stare.

"I believe you owe me," he grinned, pulling me towards the bedroom.

How lucky could one girl get? Tingles of excitement instantly raced through my entire body as I followed him to the bedroom. I was about to jump into bed once again with Logan James, the rock star. Even though we had been in a relationship years ago, I much preferred the new and improved Logan James.

The curtains closed magically as Logan picked up the remote control on the nightstand. For the remaining hours of the afternoon, we made love as all young lovers would do, barely coming up for air. That is until my cell phone rang.

"Zoey," I smiled hesitantly, checking my phone.

"Really, Babe, do you have to take the call?" Logan insisted.

"Yes, I do. She's probably downstairs in the lobby." Glancing at the clock on the nightstand, it was 5:30 p.m.

"Hey Jade, I'm downstairs. I'm coming up."

"Okay. We're in suite 411."

"Babe, get dressed. Zoe is on her way up."

"Really, Jade."

"Yes. Really. Get Dressed."

Hurriedly grabbing my jeans and tee-shirt, I managed to tie my unruly bed hair back into a ponytail as I walked into the living room. Then, hearing a soft knock at the door, I walked over.

"Hey, Zoe, come in. How was your flight?"

"Well, it definitely wasn't a private jet, that's for sure. I hate flying commercial. Does Dad know that I'm here?"

"No. Remember you asked us not to tell Alan. Would you like a drink?"

"Definitely."

Pouring us each a glass of white zinfandel, Logan finally walked out of the bedroom.

"Hey Zoe," Logan smiled, only half-dressed as he buttoned his shirt.

"Sorry. Bad timing?" Zoey questioned with a laugh taking a quick sip of her drink.

"Well, we can always make it a threesome," Logan smiled, naughtily reaching for his cigarettes.

"In your wildest dreams," I quickly interjected. "Why don't we all go down to the Planter's House for drinks and dinner? It's been highly recommended. How does that sound?"

"Great. I'm game," Zoey answered.

"Whatever, it's my one day off," Logan reluctantly agreed. "It feels like I'm just along for the ride at this point," he added, pouring himself a drink.

"Awesome, I'm going to change. I'll be right out," I mentioned disappearing into the bedroom. Then, closing the door, I quickly called

Ethan. Hopefully, he would agree to tag along if he knew Zoey was in town. It was common knowledge among the guys that Ethan liked Zoe. They had met two years earlier when he joined the band.

Fortunately, Ethan answered on the first ring.

"Hey Ethan, do you have plans for tonight?"

"Jade," Ethan immediately interjected. "I need to talk to Logan. It's important. Alan just called. We have an impromptu cocktail party tonight at 7:00 p.m. downtown at the Broadway Oyster Bar. The entire establishment has been reserved for us on behalf of the local radio stations," he continued. "It appears we are popular in St. Louis and Brian said it's mandatory. Please let Logan know. The limo will pick us up at 6:30 p.m. I've got to run, but I'll talk to you later. See you soon."

Walking into the living room, I hadn't even had the chance to let Ethan know that Zoey had arrived.

"Logan, the band has a commitment tonight. Guess we'll have to forget about going to Planter's."

"What the hell? How do you possibly know? Neither Alan nor Brian has called," Logan vented. Then, before I could explain the phone call to Ethan, his cell phone rang.

Looking down at his phone, it was Alan.

"Logan, I've just been informed the local radio stations have reserved the Broadway Oyster Bar for us tonight at 7:00 p.m. It's a great photo opportunity for the band with the local DJs. Sorry, it's mandatory. The limo will pick you up at 6:30 p.m. We're also going to be featured on the local television stations tomorrow. I know the concert is already sold-out, but it's a golden opportunity to promote the band. Dress casual. It's not a black-tie event. See you tonight."

"Hell, can't a guy even get a night off," Logan fumed, pouring another shot of bourbon.

"Babe, isn't that the price of being famous," I countered, trying to make light of the situation. "Well, Zoey, guess you'll be seeing Alan sooner than expected."

"Oh my God, I agree with Logan. But, geez, I just got into town, and my dad is already dictating my schedule."

"Well, I guess you could stay in for the night. That is if you don't want to go."

"And do what? Stare at the walls. No thanks. I'll go," Zoey frowned, downing her entire glass of wine. "I was going to ask dad if I could tag along with the band for the duration of the summer tour. Perhaps, I'll get a chance to discuss it with him."

"Just what we need, another groupie," Logan grimaced.

"Hey, watch your mouth. You have Jade with you, and you love it," Zoey retorted. "Where would you be without my dad?"

"Yeah, and where would your dad be without me?"

"Calm down. You're both acting like spoiled children. So, our plans got changed for one night. But, it's not the end of the world. I'm sure you'll both live. I need another drink," I reprimanded, pouring myself another glass of wine. Perhaps it was a good idea for Zoey to tag along on tour. I could use another female on the road, and I needed Ethan and Logan on good terms again.

Later that evening, as we all piled into the limo, it was evident none of the guys were happy about the spur-of-the-moment event.

Reaching for a bottle of Blanton's Bourbon, Ethan poured each of the guys a shot, forgetting to include Zoe and me. "Here's to another promotional event," he toasted.

Grabbing the bottle of bourbon from Ethan, Zoey poured us each a shot.

"Geez, Ethan, thanks for including us."

"Sorry, wasn't sure you girls preferred bourbon."

"Well, you could have at least offered," Zoey fumed.

"Hey guys, calm down. You need to be on your best behavior tonight," Jarrod laughed.

His statement was comical. There was no such thing as a textbook, well-behaved rock band.

Noah, along with Logan, kept quiet. They knew too well how fast things could escalate, and tonight wasn't the night. Alan and Brian would expect the guys to portray the perfect image of a rock band. Quickly dismissing the thought, I smiled.

Arriving downtown at the Broadway Oyster Bar, Noah and Ethan exited the limo first. Instantly hit with flashes of bright lights from the camera crazy paparazzi, they tried to keep their temper under control, presenting a wholesome image. Next, Jarrod exited along with Logan. Their appearances easily reflected the tattooed members of a rock band, long hair, and tall, muscular frames. Even their cocky attitude towards the invading paparazzi seemed befitting of a bad boy rock star image. Finally, Zoey and I exited the limo as a sudden flash of light almost blinded us.

Walking inside, we were immediately met by Alan and Brian, along with local dignitaries of WKXV news and a few well-known radio disk jockeys.

Noticing Zoey walking in, Alan immediately rushed over.

"Oh my God, sweetheart, what a surprise," Alan grinned, giving her a giant hug and kiss. "Why didn't you let me know you were coming to St. Louis? Baby, it's so good to see you. I had no idea you would be here."

"Well, it wasn't planned. I got in this afternoon. I needed a break, and I wanted to see Jade."

"Whatever the reason, you know I'm always happy to see you. How's mom and the kids?"

"Fine, but missing you as always."

"Zoe, sweetheart, it's business as usual. Sorry, but I have a photo op with the band. We'll talk later tonight at the hotel. I love you. Enjoy yourself and stay out of trouble."

"Thanks, Dad. Talk to you later. I love you."

Pulling Zoey off to the side of the room, we watched as the guys gave interviews and posed for photos. They knew the routine, and the boys were good at it even though we knew they were merely acting.

Finally getting a slight reprieve, Logan walked over.

"Damn, I hate these events," he whispered.

"Well, they help pay the bills," Zoey added.

"Wow, Zoey, you're are Alan's daughter."

"Okay, you two keep it civil," I demanded.

"As soon as we're finished, the guys and I are going down to a little bar near the river. One of the DJs suggested it would be a great place to hang out and have a few drinks. Do you want to tag along?"

"Yes. You're not getting away from us that easy. Are you crazy?" I insisted.

"All right, I think we have one more session of photos and an interview with a prominent television news anchor. Then, hopefully, within the hour, we can slip away with Alan's help. Brian can tie up all the loose ends as far as I'm concerned. He owes us. Watch the door in case you see us making our escape. The limo is waiting."

"Logan, don't you dare leave without us," I vented.

"Yeah. I'm not going to be stuck with daddy all evening. Do you understand?"

"Zoey, chill out. I get it. I've got to get back to the guys before they think I skipped out on them."

"Relax, Logan, it's almost over," I inaudibly mouthed in his direction. "I love you."

"Wow, what a bunch of wimps. With the money those guys are making, you would think they could handle a few unexpected press events," Zoey fumed.

Later in the limo, the guys appeared more relaxed as we were driven to a small quaint bar located on the banks of the Mississippi River. We were looking forward to a night of fun. It seemed Ethan and Logan were finally on good terms once again. Thank God.

"Damn it, guys, we're Riot Storm, and this is how we party," Jarrod suddenly stammered, opening another bottle of bourbon. Taking a huge gulp, he passed the bottle over to Ethan. Jarrod was already feeling three sheets to the wind, and things were about to get out of control. Looking around the limo, I smirked. The guys were hardcore drinkers and not your average church pew fillers, as Alan tried to make them appear.

"Hell, yeah," Ethan added, taking another long continuous sip from the bottle of liquor before he passed it on to Noah and Logan.

"Geez, Zoey, I think we may have our hands full. Getting these guys back to the hotel later tonight won't be easy," I remarked, taking note of Logan as he took one long continuous gulp from the bottle.

"Hell, yeah, we're the best," Logan roared.

"Damn, I think the guys are already plastered," Zoey laughed.

"Yeah, and we're headed to another bar. I think a little publicity went to their heads," I giggled.

"Oh, I don't think it was the publicity," Zoey laughed. "Well, you know what they say. If you can't beat them, join them." Grabbing the bottle away from Logan, Zoey took a huge sip. Passing it over to me, I hesitated for a moment. Then without thought, as I looked around the limo, I brought the bottle up to my lips and tossed back a giant gulp. If everyone was getting hammered, I certainly didn't want to be the only one sober. There definitely wasn't anyone checking for underage drinkers in the back seat of a limo, I laughed, taking another long, continuous sip.

Arriving at the WaterShed Bar, the limo parked out front as the driver came around to open our door. I was sure he'd seen this scenario played out before. After all, wasn't this the reason for having a limo driver? One by one, the guys managed to stagger out of the car. I held onto Logan as we entered the bar. Zoey grabbed Ethan's arm to steady herself.

"Babe, are you okay?" Logan questioned.

"I think so, but ask me again in a few minutes," I giggled.

Walking into the dimly lit bar, it was evident we had brought the party. Hopefully, no one would recognize the guys. Walking in, Logan quickly spotted Harry, one of the local DJs, who was at the Broadway Oyster Bar. He ushered everyone to the back of the bar and finally into a small candlelit room enclosed with dark wood paneling. Tables centered with glowing candles were scattered evenly around the room. Within a few minutes, the waiter walked in. Harry ordered drinks for everyone. As soon as we all had a glass in our hands, Harry made a toast. "Welcome to St. Louis, my watering hole, and one hell of a concert," he toasted loudly to be heard over the music which was blaring from the other room. "Everything is on the house tonight compliments of WKXV."

The aroma smelled heavenly as the waitresses brought out enormous platters of boiled crawfish and hushpuppies. Watching as the guys filled their plates to overflowing with the southern delicacy, they washed the crayfish down with pitchers of the local brew. It looked appetizing. Finally, Zoey and I decided to taste the local fanfare.

"It's not bad," Zoe laughed, tasting her first crawfish. "The hushpuppies are phenomenal."

Watching as I cringed, popping one of the shrimp-like creatures into my mouth, Logan laughed hysterically. "Babe, chase it with beer," he added, handing me his mug.

"Not bad," I smiled. Hurriedly washing it down with gulps of beer, I wasn't about to admit defeat as I followed it with a golden-brown hushpuppy. "Delicious."

For the next hour and a half, we ate tons of freshwater crustaceans followed by pitchers of beer. I couldn't remember a time when I'd had more fun. However, I would later pay for my epicurean adventure.

Suddenly hearing a loud commotion, Harry came running in. It sounded like the bar was coming apart at the seams. You could distinctly hear chairs hitting the walls.

"Sorry, guys, I'm afraid things have gotten out of control in the other room. I've got to get everyone out of here ASAP. Unfortunately, a brawl involving some locals has erupted inside the main entrance, and the police have been called. Trust me. This isn't the publicity the band needs. Follow me. I'll get you out through the back entrance. Hurry, we don't have much time. I want you all out of here before the police arrive," Harry panicked.

"Wow," Zoey laughed. "Is this a joke?"

"I only wish it were. Neither Riot Storm nor WKXV needs this kind of exposure in the headline of tomorrow's newspapers. Especially since we've got the press releases from earlier tonight hitting all the news channels in the morning." Harry added, entirely shocked by the sudden skirmish.

As Logan quickly pulled back my chair, the room began to spin as I got up. Instantly, I felt extremely dizzy.

"Oh my God, I think I'm going to pass out. I feel faint." I freaked, grasping Logan's arm to steady myself.

"Damn, Babe, this isn't a good time to faint. I'll carry you."

Looking at Zoey, she was laughing hysterically as she held onto Ethan. Logan swiftly scooped me into his arms. My recollection of the events became foggy as we rushed out of the quaint bar.

Hurriedly, Logan carried me as we followed behind Harry. Zoey held tightly to Ethan as we quickly descended a dilapidated staircase outside to a back alley. Finally, everyone was safely inside the waiting limo. Swiftly, making our escape only moments before the police arrived, we'd just dodged a proverbial bullet with the local cops and press. Alan would be livid, not to mention the fact that Zoey was with us. It was a close call, but a small price to pay for the hours of fun and the tasty cuisine paid for by the local radio station.

Finally, as the limo drove away down the dark narrow alley, the guys roared with laughter at the mere thought of the band becoming entangled in a local bar brawl.

"Damn, man, that was a close call," Jarrod laughed.

"Hell, too close," Ethan remarked as Zoey fell asleep in his arms.

Reaching for a bottle of Dom Perignon, Logan poured each of the guys a tall drink of the costly brew. The members of Riot Storm were die-hard drinkers. It appeared they could almost drink themselves sober if that were even possible.

Arriving back at the Four Seasons, the limo drove around to the back. The hotel had a private entrance for celebrities.

"Can you walk?" Logan asked, giving me a quizzical stare as he tried to revive me.

"I can try."

However, as I tried to stand, everyone and everything around me became a dizzy blur. Noting my unsteadiness, Logan took no chances as he once again carried me into the hotel. The last I saw of Zoey, she was holding tightly to Ethan. It was apparent she was staying the night in his room.

Suddenly opening the door to our suite, I was hit with the worst case of nausea I've ever felt.

"Logan, I feel sick."

Hurriedly carrying me into the bathroom, he raised the seat on the toilet as I began vomiting violently. It seemed everything I had previously eaten that evening was making a reappearance and not in a good way.

Warming a wet washcloth, Logan gently pulled back long strands of my hair from my face as he lovingly wiped the refuse from my mouth.

"What a guy?" I thought. Logan never once left my side. We sat on the cold marble floor of the bathroom as I retched fiercely. Afterward, he once again warmed the towel to wipe my face, removed my clothes, and carried me to bed. Logan was a true gentleman in every sense of the word. My knight in shining armor. However, the following day I had little memory of the previous evening or his acts of kindness.

Slowly opening my eyes as the bright rays of the morning sun streamed in through the curtains, my head was pounding. I had the worst headache of my life. Trying to sit up only made it worse. Looking over, I noticed a glass of orange juice on the nightstand and two aspirin.

Logan strolled out of the bathroom toward the bed, wearing only a towel tied around his waist. His appearance easily personified the word sexy.

"How's my girl this morning? I brought you some orange juice and aspirin. Thought you might need them," he smiled lovingly, kissing my forehead.

"Thanks, Babe. I've got the worst headache."

"Take these," Logan suggested handing me the aspirin. "I'll order coffee. Do you feel like breakfast? Perhaps some toast?"

"Toast smothered in butter and jam sounds great with coffee. Lots of coffee."

"So, what do you remember from last night?" Logan smirked.

"Not much. I remember going to a bar and then getting violently sick. Did you put me to bed?"

"Of course, I couldn't let you sleep in your clothes. They were covered in vomit."

"Where's Zoey?"

"Oh, don't worry about Zoe. I believe she crashed in Ethan's room."

"I'm going to order breakfast and then run down to the gym for a few minutes. Would you mind? I'll stay until the toast and coffee arrive. Oh, I almost forgot, Alan just called to remind me the band has an interview with the local news stations this morning. So I'm sorry, it shouldn't take long. Hope you don't mind hanging out in the hotel room."

"Not at all. I know your routine. Go work out. I'll be fine. I'll probably give Zoey a call."

"Thanks. I won't take long," Logan stated, quickly changing into his gym attire.

Walking out of the bedroom just as breakfast arrived, he was ready for the gym. He was determined to get in his usual exercise routine before the band's interview.

Later that morning, I sat in bed and downed several cups of coffee, watching the televised news coverage of Riot Storm. Surprisingly, it included a glimpse of Zoey and me as we exited the limo the previous evening with the guys at the Broadway Oyster Bar. It felt surreal, almost unbelievable. I was now part of their entourage and news coverage as well.

Reaching for my cell phone, I called Zoey. She answered on the first ring.

"Hey, did you catch the news coverage of the band this morning?"

"No. I slept in. So, how did it go?"

"Well, we made the news along with the band. Our photos were captured with the boys."

"So, our three minutes of fame," Zoey laughed. Did Dad see the coverage? He doesn't want me seen in any publicity photos of the band.

"I'm not sure, but I guess you'll find out soon enough."

"Thanks for the warning. See you later."

That evening as the guys went on stage, Zoey and I, along with Alan and Brian, watched from the side of the stage as the guys gave another spectacular performance.

"Good evening St. Louis. It's great to be here," Logan yelled.

"We love you," Ethan loudly exclaimed, waving his guitar high in the air.

For the next two hours, the guys held the sold-out crowd captive as the fans thundered back their love for the band. Finally, the following morning, we were on our way to Chicago. Alan's parents lived just north of the city in Waukegan. Reluctantly, Zoey would be spending the night with her grandparents.

As the jet lifted into the air, the Gateway Arch once again came into view. Memories of our time together at the arch flooded my mind. And I was where I always wanted to be, sitting next to Logan James.

Chapter Five

Illinois

$\mathcal{A}$s the jet began its approach into O'Hare, the view below was breathtaking. The shimmering water of Lake Michigan appeared to hug the city's landscape, giving the immense skyscrapers an impressive appearance. Snuggled close to Logan, I was sure this venue would be exciting. I couldn't wait to see the city with Logan by my side. Taking a final look around the cabin, Ethan had fallen asleep with his arm wrapped around Zoey. It was apparent Alan had finally come to terms with the fact Zoey and Ethan were an item.

As the jet slowly taxied across the tarmac, I noticed the limo waiting for our arrival. Standing up to stretch his long legs, Logan grabbed our carry-on bag. Exiting the plane, a light mist of rain began to fall as we entered the limo for the ride downtown.

"A quick scenario for Chicago," Alan announced. "Brian will give you the details. I have a few phone calls to return."

"We're here for only two days. The concert is tomorrow evening at the United Center. It's completely sold with a capacity of 23,500. Sound check will be at 4:00 p.m. We're staying at the Peninsula. It's only a three-minute walk to the Museum of Contemporary Art and four minutes to the Chicago Avenue Bart. We're conveniently located.

I don't have to remind you that I need to know if you leave the hotel. Discretion is key. You narrowly avoided an incident in St. Louis, and it will not be repeated in Chicago. Do I make myself clear?" Brian stated. "One more thing, Alan will be staying in Waukegan tonight. It's Alan's hometown for those of you who don't know. His parents still reside in Waukegan, so Alan and Zoey will be staying at their home tonight. Ethan, you're welcome to join them. They'll be leaving later this afternoon and arriving back early tomorrow morning, and for the rest of you, don't give me any reason to call Alan. Understood," Brian continued.

"Got it, boss," Jarrod smiled.

"Keys are waiting at the front desk as usual, and before you ask, yes, each of you have your own room," Brian explained as the limo approached the entrance of the luxury hotel. As the car came to a stop, the guys, along with Zoey and I, eagerly jumped out and quickly disappeared inside the hotel.

As Logan opened the door to our room, it was spectacular with phenomenal views of the Chicago skyline. Walking over to the immensely tall floor-to-ceiling window, I was totally mesmerized.

"Do you ever get tired of this lifestyle?"

"No. Babe, are you crazy? Bring that sexy body over here," Logan teased, pulling me towards the bedroom.

"Geez, Logan, is sex the only thing you think about?"

"Only when I'm with you."

Passionately kissing the nape of my neck, I was instantly putty in his hands. I was a willing victim. Totally in love with the famous bad boy, Logan James. I didn't have the strength or desire to push him away. Following him into the bedroom, he slowly began unbuttoning my blouse as I pulled his black tee-shirt over his head.

Suddenly, there was a light knock at the door.

"Babe, did you hear that?" I whispered.

"They'll go away. Forget about it."

Pulling me down to the bed, he slowly continued to undress me as the knock at the door intensified.

"You should see who it is. It might be important."

"Damn it. Somebody is going to die," Logan vented, running to the door wearing only his black boxers.

Opening the door, it was Ethan.

Overhearing their conversation, I giggled.

"Geez, Logan, boxer shorts," Ethan laughed.

"Yeah, and why are you here?" Logan fumed.

"Zoey and I thought you and Jade might want to have a few drinks and dinner before we leave to visit her grandparents later this afternoon."

"Hell, Ethan, does it honestly look like I'm interested in drinks or dinner? Damn, man, can't a guy have a little privacy?"

"Sorry," Ethan roared hilariously. "I'll let Zoe know you were," he paused. "Should I say a little tied up? Oh, the next time, you might want to rethink your choice of clothing before you answer the door."

"Damn. Ethan, haven't you ever heard of a cell phone? Get the hell out of here before you wind up with another black eye."

"I'm leaving," Ethan chuckled. "Carry on. I'll call you later."

Slamming the door, Logan was furious.

Walking back into the bedroom, Logan grabbed his cigarettes.

"Oh, hell, I need a drink," he fumed.

Walking out to the bar, Logan poured us each a shot of bourbon. Then, returning with the drinks, he handed me a small glass.

"Was it important?" I questioned without a hint I had overheard their entire conversation.

"What?"

"The person at the door?"

"Hell no. It was Ethan. I swear with modern technology, he's a moron forgetting to use a cell phone. He wanted to know if we were interested in drinks and dinner before they left for Waukegan."

"Babe, calm down. It's not the end of the world," I laughed. "Come over here," I demanded, patting the edge of the bed. Then, gently messaging the tense muscles in his shoulders, I lovingly ran my fingers through his hair.

"Why don't we take in a movie? It's still early," I suggested.

"Okay. What do you want to see?"

"I don't care as long as it's with you. Why don't you call Brian and let him know?"

"To hell with Brian, nobody tells me what to do."

Something was apparently wrong with Logan, and I needed to find out what had him so agitated. Maybe the movie wasn't the best idea. Perhaps, we just needed to talk.

"Why don't we order dinner, or would you rather we go out?" I suggested.

"Let's eat in tonight. I'm not sure I want to go out?"

"So, what sounds appetizing to you?"

"Pizza."

"Wow, that was a quick decision, but a great choice. Chicago is known for pizza."

I reached for my cell phone, quickly checked out the best pizza delivery, and placed an order. I ordered two deep dish pizzas loaded with extra cheese, pepperoni, mushrooms, onions, and green pepper from Lou Malnati's. Logan was right. I couldn't wait to taste a yummy slice of pizza from the well-known establishment.

Within a short time, a knock at the door indicated the arrival of their famous deep-dish delicacy. Grabbing a couple of beers from the small fridge next to the bar, we were all set to have an indoor picnic.

"Why don't we eat in bed? Then, afterward, we can order a movie."

Hopefully, getting Logan relaxed would be conducive to him letting his hair down, so to speak, and telling me what was bothering him.

"Sounds good to me."

Taking the pizza and beer into the bedroom, we lounged back on the bed. Stuffing ourselves with the famous delicacy, we acted like silly kids having a sleepover. Maybe now was a good time to ask a few questions.

"Babe, you've seemed a bit moody today. I love you. Is something bothering you?"

"No. Why are you asking?"

"Logan, it doesn't take a rocket scientist to know something is wrong. Trust me, I love you, and I only want to help."

"It's nothing. Really," Logan snapped back, twisting the top from another bottle of beer.

"Please, I can't help you if you won't let me. But, whatever it is, you can trust me. Logan, you know how much I love you," I pleaded as tears slowly filled my eyes.

"Damn. Babe, you're crying." he frowned, wiping my eyes with the back of his hand.

"Here's the deal," he hesitated. "I might be facing surgery, and I'm worried that Alan is going to replace me with Ethan. And on the other hand, Zoey is already involved with Ethan, and it would make perfect sense as far as Alan is concerned."

"Surgery? What do you mean? Are you sick? What's wrong?" I was more than nervous at this point.

"Jade, stop with all the questions. It's not that serious. It's simply a knee replacement surgery. Remember in high school back in Marin when I hurt my knee playing football. I had a motorbike accident last year while we were on tour in Germany, and it complicated my old injury. Trust me. It's not that serious. They perform knee replacements all the time. It's simply the fact I'm having a lot of pain in my left knee, and I'm honestly worried that Alan is going to replace me."

"My God, Logan, I wouldn't have suspected anything if you hadn't told me. I'm sorry. Is there anything I can do?"

"No. It's simply something I've got to take care of without losing my position with the band. You have no idea how much being the lead singer with Riot Storm means to me. No idea," he reiterated, reaching for his cigarettes.

"So, you simply take a six-week absence from the band. That is roughly the recovery time, right?"

"Jade, we're booked solid for the next four months with an upcoming Pacific Rim tour afterward. You have no idea the stress I'm under."

All at once, things made perfect sense. The fact that Logan worked out every morning. The fact that he hit Ethan. There was no way I could have possibly known what was worrying him.

"Is this the reason you work out every morning?"

"Yes. I have an exercise routine that is supposed to strengthen my knee, and then I usually spend a few minutes in the hot tub. Unfortunately, it doesn't appear to be working. The pain seems to be intensifying."

"And," I slowly hesitated. "Did the possibilities of Ethan replacing you have anything to do with the reason you hit him."

"Oh, hell, no, he had that one coming."

Now that I knew what was bothering him, maybe I could do something. However, I could never let him know. Zoey loved Logan like a brother, and I honestly didn't think the fact she was involved with Ethan was important. Logan was irreplaceable as the lead singer. Ethan's voice wasn't nearly as strong as Logan's. I couldn't imagine Alan replacing Logan with Ethan.

"Geez, Babe, I know you're worried, but just take things one day at a time. Do you want to watch a movie?" I asked, removing the pizza boxes from the bed.

Snuggling inside the warmth of his muscular arms, I loved him more than I'd ever loved anyone. Kissing him lightly on the nape of his neck, he was every girl's dream. Suddenly, he pulled me against his body, kissing me vigorously. It was safe to say we weren't going to watch a movie. Loving Logan felt entirely natural. Everything about him felt right. We never left the bedroom.

Opening my eyes the following morning as the sun slowly washed over our room, bathing it in a soft glow, I could feel Logan's intense stare.

"Wow, I hope you haven't spent the entire night staring at me," I smiled.

"Jade, lying next to you, I couldn't take my eyes off you. Just the two of us, you in my arms waiting for the morning sun, makes my entire world perfect. Nothing else matters, not even an impending surgery," he winked, giving me a quick, passionate kiss. "However, we can't live off love. I'm starved," Logan smirked, getting out of bed.

Hurriedly getting dressed as Logan ordered breakfast, we only had a few hours to check out the city. Hopefully, it would ease his worries. Unfortunately, there wasn't anything I could do to help until I talked with Zoey, and she wasn't due back until sound check at 4:00 p.m. However, when she returned, I had to ask questions. I couldn't wait to find out if she knew anything about the possibility of Logan's knee surgery or the fact, he was so desperately worried that Ethan would replace him.

After finishing breakfast, we decided to stroll along the Navy Pier. It would be a relaxing way to spend a few hours before the concert. Grabbing his disguise, we were ready for a couple of hours of fun.

Like two kids at play, Logan put his arm around me as we left the Peninsula Hotel. Pulling me close, we decided to walk the short distance to the Navy Pier. I found myself staring at his gorgeous profile hidden behind sunglasses and a baseball cap. Making our way down the busy streets, I treasured every moment we had together as there wasn't a lot of downtime between venues.

The closer we got to the pier, the aromas from the numerous food vendors which lined the dock and the fresh air blowing in from the lake were hypnotic. Finally, approaching the Navy Pier's Centennial Wheel, we decided to take our chances at not getting recognized as we purchased tickets for the seven-minute ride. Each gondola held six passengers and offered incredible views of the pier and city skyline. It appeared Logan's disguise gave no hint to his identity, as a young family asked him to snap a photo as the giant wheel crested the top. Afterward, pulling me into his arms, he gave me a quick, passionate kiss as we took in the incredible views. I felt like I was on top of the world as he held me against his muscular chest.

"What's next?" I smiled as the giant wheel slowly came to a stop.

"How do hot dogs smothered in sauerkraut sound?"

"Delicious."

Walking over to the nearest vendor, we passed a couple with kids. They were desperately attempting to herd their rambunctious, young children through the immense sea of people. It easily appeared everyone was out to enjoy a fun-filled day taking advantage of activities available at the Navy Pier.

"Have you ever thought about having children?"

"Where did that come from?" Logan stopped giving me a rather curious stare.

"Oh, I don't know. I suppose seeing the cute smiles on the faces of those energetic kids in our gondola."

"Well, I've never given it a lot of thought. Babies and touring don't exactly seem like the right fit. But, maybe one day when my life settles down a bit," Logan smiled, giving me a quick kiss on my forehead. "What about you?"

"Oh, I'd love an entire house full of boisterous children. I'd like to think I could do a better job than my parents."

"Enough talk about babies. I'm starved," Logan smirked, quickly changing the subject as he pulled me towards a hot dog vendor.

Ordering hot dogs and soda, we were surprised to discover an open bench. Hurriedly walking over, we sat in the warm sun. The breeze gently wafting in from the lake felt refreshing and invigorating as we ravenously devoured our hot dogs covered in extra sauerkraut and mustard. Our afternoon was perfect.

"Wow, Babe, you're covered in mustard," Logan laughed, wiping my face.

"Thanks."

Watching as he gently wiped the condiment from my face, I knew Logan would make a great father. I also knew that I never wanted to be without him. He was the complete package. I had known that since the first day we met in high school.

"Geez, it's getting late. We better hurry if we want to check out the Fun House Maze," Logan mentioned glancing down at his watch.

"Wow, that's what I love about you. You're just a big kid at heart. So I'm not leaving until I challenge you to a game of miniature golf."

"Really, you better bring your A-game. No one beats me in carpet golf," Logan laughed, pulling me up from the bench.

The next few hours flew by as I challenged Logan to a quick game of golf. Of course, he won. Trying to keep up with him as we made our way through the Fun House Maze was hilarious. Finally, as a cool breeze drifted past us, we spent our last few minutes eating cotton candy, strolling towards the end of the boardwalk. Enjoying the sights and sounds of the Navy Pier had been the ideal place to alleviate Logan's worries. It was cathartic.

"Wow, we have to go," Logan panicked, suddenly noting the time on his watch. "I can't be late for sound check."

Grasping my hand, we raced back toward the entrance of the pier. Speedily making our way through the crowds, no one knew the prominence of the handsome guy holding my hand as we dodged our way through groups of people both young and old. Only I knew he was the famous rock star soon to be on stage in front of thousands at the sold-out United Center.

We arrived back at the hotel with just enough time to shower and dress before meeting the guys downstairs.

"Hey, Babe, can you bring my razor from the overnight bag," Logan yelled from the shower.

Walking into the steamy bathroom, I had no idea that Logan was up to his usual antics as I handed him the razor.

Caught off guard, Logan laughed wickedly, quickly pulling me inside the shower, fully clothed. As he slowly removed my wet tee-shirt, I once again became his willing victim as we lathered each other with body wash. What girl's dream wouldn't include a romantic rendezvous in a hot steamy shower with Logan James? I smiled, massaging his solid, muscular chest covered in ink. Then, melting into his arms, how lucky could one girl get, I mused.

Stepping out of the shower, Logan wrapped me inside a warm towel as I pulled back my wet hair with a clip.

"We better hurry. The limo will be arriving soon," Logan suggested, playfully kissing my cheek.

"Well, you shouldn't have pulled me into the shower," I teased, swatting him on the butt with a towel.

"Oh, are we complaining?" Logan laughed mischievously as he drew me to him for another quick, passionate kiss.

"Babe, we're never getting out of here if you continue," I snickered, pulling away from him.

Watching as Logan dressed in a trendy pair of torn jeans, his usual black tee-shirt, and his favorite sneakers, he took my breath away. He'd never looked sexier as he lit up a cigarette and downed a quick shot of bourbon.

Reaching for my hairdryer, I hurriedly styled my hair. Choosing to wear a short black halter dress with heels, I was finally dressed and ready to watch my favorite rock star go through sound check at the venue.

Locking the door, we walked towards the elevator, meeting up Ethan and Zoey.

"How was Waukegan?" I asked.

"Same as ever," Zoey complained.

"Don't get me wrong, I enjoyed the visit with my grandparents, but we missed the only chance we had to see the city."

"What did you guys do?"

"Oh, we spent the morning at the Navy Pier."

"Exactly, that's my point," Zoey scowled.

"Zoey, do you have a few minutes while the guys run through their sound check?" I whispered, exiting the elevator.

"Sure. What's up?"

"We'll talk later."

"Okay," Zoey questioned, giving me a quizzical stare.

Entering the limo, the guys began their usual ritual, passing around a bottle of their favorite bourbon and smokes. Alan and Brian had left earlier for the venue leaving the guys up to their usual antics. Becoming more obnoxious than ever, Jarrod lit a joint.

"Hey, man, hand it over," Logan demanded, grabbing the marijuana.

Watching in silence as Logan grabbed the joint, everyone in the car waited to see his reaction, thinking he would forbid their use of pot. However, noting their response, Logan lounged back, putting the joint in his mouth. Then, taking a long draw, he looked at Jarrod.

"What?" he laughed, looking around the car. "You guys didn't think I would waste a good joint, did you?" Logan roared.

"Don't panic. There's more where that came from," Jarrod laughed, reaching into the pocket of his distressed blue jeans.

"Geez, you guys are behaving like a group of crazy teenagers," Zoey giggled.

Arriving at the United Center, its enormous capacity seated 23,500. As the limo drove around to the back entrance, the guys quickly extinguished their pot. Then, exiting the limo, they promptly hurried inside, leaving Zoey and me behind.

Watching as the boys soon disappeared, Zoey grabbed my hand before I stepped out of the limo.

"What was it you wanted to talk about?" she questioned.

"Why don't we go inside and find seats. We can talk while the guys go through sound checks."

"Okay."

Walking inside through a labyrinth of connecting corridors, it was enormous. Entering the vast arena, it appeared to have its own ecosystem as a dense layer of fog hovered near the upper levels.

"Wow, where do you want to sit?" Zoey laughed, looking at thousands of vacant seats.

"It doesn't matter. It's empty. However, we can watch the guys from the front rows," I suggested as Zoe followed me into the fourth row.

"Okay. What's on your mind? Is something wrong?"

"No. It's nothing like that. Last night I learned Logan might be facing a knee replacement. Were you aware of that?"

"Yes. I thought everyone knew about Logan's bum knee."

"Well," I paused. "It honestly caught me by surprise. I had no idea. Is your dad considering replacing Logan if he has surgery?"

"What?" Zoey reacted in total shock.

"Not even. Where did you hear that?"

"From Logan," I hesitated.

"Wow, really, is that what Logan told you? Does he think Ethan might replace him?"

"Yes."

"That's utter nonsense. Trust me on this, I like Ethan a lot, but he's not Logan James. Dad would never replace Logan. You have to believe me. Is Logan worried?"

"Yes. I'm not sure why Logan is so upset. Maybe the fact you and Ethan are together, and Alan invited Ethan up to Waukegan. I really don't know."

"Well, that's just crazy. However, that probably accounts for Ethan's black eye. Do you want me to talk to him?"

"No. Definitely not. I simply wanted to hear your input and find out if Alan had any thoughts of replacing him."

"Listen, Jade, I know you're new to the band, and believe me, a lot of crazy talk goes on around here, but for the most part, there's usually nothing to any of it. If you ever have any questions, please come and talk to me. Trust me, being Alan's daughter, I'm privy to a lot of things the guys wouldn't know. However, keep that one quiet. Dad is aware of Logan's possible knee replacement. If it happens, his position with the band will never be in jeopardy. I will let you know that dad and Brian have discussed the idea of taking a hiatus if it does become necessary at the end of the summer tour. Also, Dad mentioned that our vacation complex in Hawaii would be the perfect location for Logan to recuperate if surgery becomes necessary. Geez, I can't believe that Logan is so insecure."

"Zoey, I appreciate everything you've told me. Please don't let anyone know that we discussed this, especially Ethan. I don't want to create any further friction between them. I was hoping to give Logan some reassurance after talking with you."

"Well, you might want to give that some thought. It would be all too easy for Logan to figure out that we talked, and I'm sure it would kill his ego even further if he thought you were stepping in to save his position. Not that he needs to worry about that, but you know how guys are, right?"

"Got it. I understand. Logan would be livid if he knew we had this discussion. There's no way I want him to know. However, on the other hand, by knowing, hopefully, I can find subtle ways to ease his worries."

Suddenly, Ethan yelled from the stage. "Hey, Zoe, why don't you come up and let's sing one of the songs we've just written?"

"What? You sing and compose? Maybe you're the one Logan should be worried about?" I laughed.

"Ethan, you're crazy. It's not finished. Don't embarrass me," Zoey yelled.

"If you've written something, let's hear it," Logan insisted with a laugh.

"Damn it, Logan, don't tease me," Zoey yelled. "Later."

"I had no idea you were writing?"

"Yes. I've always kept a journal of songs that I've composed. So you never know, one day the band might use one of them in their sets. At least Dad keeps encouraging me."

"Wow, Zoey, that's amazing. I knew you were a great pianist, but I had no idea that you were composing as well."

"It's nothing, just a hobby. Let's walk down to the guy's dressing room. There's probably tons of food."

Following Zoey, Logan hurriedly caught up with us as we entered the long narrow corridor.

"What were you two chatting about?"

"Oh nothing, just the fact we must be out of our freaking minds to hang around with you guys," Zoey smirked.

"Speak for yourself. I'm totally in love with this dude," I smiled, standing on my toes to give Logan a quick kiss.

"Ditto," Logan winked, pulling me close.

"Get a room, you two," Ethan laughed, quickly catching up with Zoey. "Noah said our dressing room is filled with a smorgasbord of fresh seafood, including lobster and sushi."

"What? No local favorites, pizza, bratwurst with sauerkraut, or hot dogs?" Logan frowned.

"Geez, Babe, we just had hot dogs covered in sauerkraut."

"Seriously, Jade, you can never have too many hot dogs or bratwurst."

Later that evening, Zoey and I watched as thousands of excited screaming fans filled the United Center. The guy's performance was spectacular, and their fans never left disappointed. Logan and the band had a great relationship with their audience. They were determined to make each concert their best, leaving nothing on the stage. It ensured their fans would excitedly return, craving more each time. Our next venue was New York, Maidson Square Garden to be exact.

Boarding the plane the following day, I was shocked to see Noah with his arms wrapped around a petite young girl. She was gorgeous. At first glance, she appeared affluent, not Noah's type. Sporting a pair of designer sunglasses, along with an expensive leather jacket and matching Gucci purse, her long blonde curls were swept back with a silver comb. She appeared oddly out of place with Noah. However, as we walked past towards the back of the plane, the young girl's intense stare at Logan gave me an uneasy feeling. Logan seemed to be surprised and unusually tense at the mere sight of her. His sudden knee-jerk reaction gave me a reason to believe they had met before. I had to know more about her.

Continuing towards the back of the aircraft, I couldn't wait to question Zoey about her sudden appearance.

"Hey Zoe," I quietly whispered, easing into my seat. "Who's the girl with Noah?"

"Oh, that's Kelsey Kensington. I don't know a lot about her except that her father, Edward Kensington, is an icon in the music industry. I hate to tell you, but I don't think she's here because of Noah. I think she has her eye on Logan, if you catch my drift. She's from Chicago, and I saw her last night before the concert outside the guy's dressing room. My father and Edward Kensington have worked together in the past. However, as I said, I don't know a lot about her, only that she's wealthy, arrogant, and not someone I would want as a friend. Don't worry. I'm sure Logan isn't stupid enough to get involved with her. He's with you now. However, that doesn't say a lot for Noah. I'm surprised that Dad let her travel with us to New York."

A perfect storm was brewing, and it had nothing to do with the weather. We were on our way to New York with an unexpected passenger. It hadn't taken Zoey to inform me that Logan was her target. Just the mere sight of her and the way she stared at Logan as we passed was more than enough to let me know that Noah was simply being used. Poor guy. There was no way that I was going to let Logan out of my sight once we arrived in New York.

Chapter Six

New York

The sprawling skyline of New York City came into view as we approached John F. Kennedy International Airport. It was breathtaking. Glimmers of the afternoon sun glistened brightly, reflecting from the immense tall glass-enclosed structures. As the plane landed and taxied across the tarmac, I quickly turned my attention to the handsome rock star who was sleeping peacefully next to me. It was time to wake Logan from his slumber. I gently kissed him, running my fingers softly through his long curls.

"Babe, we've landed. You've been asleep since we left Chicago," I whispered, gently nudging him.

"Sorry. I must have been extra tired."

Watching as he wiped the sleep from his eyes, I couldn't have loved him more than at this very moment.

Entering the limo, I ensured that we were seated as far from Kelsey as possible. I wasn't taking any chances. I knew her type all too well, and she wasn't about to get her hands on Logan. Not on my watch.

Unexpectedly, the traffic into the city was light. The ride downtown to the hotel didn't take long. However, it seemed Kelsey never once took her eyes off Logan. The fact she was only with us due to Noah's poor judgment and invitation made me cringe. She had managed to accompany Noah to New York, and we were left to deal with the consequences. Noah was oblivious to her real intentions. He was a great guy but too naïve where girls were concerned.

Arriving at the Plaza Hotel on Fifth Avenue, the limo parked under the shimmering lights at the entrance. Briskly walking inside the magnificent lobby, I held tightly to Logan.

"Once again, everyone has a suite," Alan smiled, passing out room keys. "You can thank me later by giving the good people of New York a concert to remember. Don't disappoint me."

Zoey and Ethan managed to catch up with us before the door to the elevator closed.

"What are your plans for the evening?" Zoe questioned.

"Anything which doesn't include Noah or Kelsey," I quickly smirked.

"Geez, Jade, do I sense a little jealousy?" Ethan laughed.

"I hardly know her," Logan reluctantly reiterated.

I distinctly remember his answer being vague and unassuming.

"You don't have to worry where she's concerned. But, of course, I can't say the same for Noah," Ethan roared with laughter. "We've warned him about her, but he refuses to listen."

"Yes. Alan doesn't like Kelsey. I'm surprised he let her board the jet. However, I'm sure it's because of his connection to her father. Edward Kensington is well known in the music industry," Logan interjected, trying to offer up a plausible explanation why she was allowed to travel with Noah.

"So I've heard," I replied, avoiding any true feelings I had regarding the fact she was on the flight.

"Yes, with the last name of Kensington in this business, she can do whatever she wants," Ethan chimed in.

"Oh yeah, well, she can't have you," I blurted out unexpectedly without filter control. Staring at Logan, he flashed me one of his silly grins, amused by my sudden outburst.

"Wow, Babe, that's sweet," he laughed. "Honestly, do you think that's why she's here?"

Zoey and I instantly snapped back in unison as the guys exited the elevator. "Yes!"

The guy's reactions and answers seemed honest enough. However, I wasn't buying into their fantasy. Logan's reaction to seeing her was a dead giveaway.

"Give a guy a little credit. You're my one and only," Logan smiled wickedly as he unlocked the door to our suite, quickly pulling me inside.

"Zoe, I'll call you," I reacted as the door closed.

Logan playfully pulled me into the bedroom. Obviously, he was attempting to take away my concerns regarding Kelsey. We weren't going anywhere for the moment. Gently pushing me down to the bed, he slowly removed my clothes, kissing me passionately. I was putty in his hands as he gently caressed every inch of my body with tender kisses. His distraction was working. Maybe, I should give him the benefit of the doubt. How could I even question what we had together?

"Sweetheart, if you don't remember how much I love you, let me remind you," he whispered.

Returning the excitement of his kisses, I loved Logan James with every ounce of my being. There was only one person in the world for me, and I was in his arms. Feeling the warmth of his firm, muscular body against mine, there was no place on earth I would rather be. Every heated kiss melted away my worries, or so I thought. We simply loved each other like two love-starved teenage kids for the rest of the night. Thank goodness the band wasn't scheduled for a sound check until the following afternoon.

Finally, coming up for air the next morning, we were famished.

Reaching for his cigarettes and lighter, Logan rested his head against the headboard of the bed.

"Does that satisfy any doubts you had earlier?" he winked playfully.

"I suppose," I coyly responded. Logan's sexual prowess was never in question. However, I couldn't resist the temptation to play along with his silliness.

"You suppose. What kind of answer is that?"

"Logan, I love you. I'm teasing." Rock stars were notorious for needing their egos stroked. "I'm hungry. Why don't you order room service while I jump in the shower."

Putting out his cigarette, Logan reached for the phone sitting on the nightstand. After ordering my favorites, blueberry pancakes with lots of bacon, Logan came into the bathroom. It was only moments before he stepped inside the shower, still wearing his black boxer shorts. Pinning me against the shower wall, warm water washed over us. His hands trembled as he lovingly caressed my body.

"Jade, I love you. Please never doubt what we have together," he whispered.

It was then I realized something was troubling Logan, and there was no doubt it was connected to Kelsey.

Watching my handsome, muscular guy slowly put his arms around me, burying his head against my chest, it was apparent he was worried. Logan was never one to show emotions, and it melted my heart. As the warm water trickled over us, I desperately wanted to question his past relationships. Still, instead, I felt compelled to hold him in my arms. Seeing Logan this distraught was foreign to me. What he didn't know was the fact that I would most likely forgive him. The guys were famous rock stars, and girls like Kelsey were part of the world they lived in. Also, the fact that we had been apart for several years made me painfully aware that I couldn't possibly hold him accountable. However, I still had numerous questions swirling around in my head, and I knew just the person who had the answers.

Stepping out of the shower, Logan lovingly covered me in a luxurious cotton towel as he handed me an elegant bathrobe provided by the hotel. Suddenly hearing a soft knock at the door, it denoted the arrival of breakfast.

Quickly tossing him a robe, I hurriedly pushed him towards the bathroom door.

"I'm starving. I suggest you answer that."

"Babe, there's no hurry. I specifically asked them to leave breakfast outside in the hallway."

"Yes. There is. I'm craving pancakes," I snickered, trying to lighten the moment.

"Well, I suppose you'll be happy to know I remembered how much you love blueberry pancakes and bacon."

"Why are you waiting? Open the door," I laughed, swatting him with my towel."

Covering a tall stack of pancakes with maple syrup, we sat in the living room devouring breakfast. Then, reaching for the coffee, Logan refilled our cups.

"Sound check begins at 4:00 p.m. We have a few hours, and we're in New York. Is there anything special you would like to do?"

"No. I could care less about the city. I just want you all to myself. Does that sound crazy?" I asked, tentatively unsure of his response.

"Really, Jade, that's cute, but there's so much to see and do in New York. So you can't be serious?"

"Oh, but I am. I don't want to share you with anyone, at least not this afternoon."

"Geez, Sweetheart, I'm flattered," Logan winked wickedly. "You're giving up the best shopping, restaurants, and an opportunity to see the skyline from the Empire State Building. Are you sure?"

"Yes. I have the best of everything sitting right next to me."

"Oh my God, Jade, what an unbelievable thing to say. You definitely know how to melt a guy's heart," Logan smiled, pulling me into his arms.

Lifting me from the sofa, his intense kisses sent tingles of excitement rushing from the top of my head to the tips of my toes. It was sheer ecstasy until his phone rang and there was an unexpected knock at the door. Suddenly, it was Grand Central Station. It was quickly beginning to appear that today's chance of being alone was diminishing with each passing second.

Walking towards the door, Logan answered his cell phone. I couldn't imagine what urgency would bring someone to our room.

"Hey Jade, Ethan and I are going to do the tourist thing today. Want to join us?" Zoey inquired. "We brought disguises," Zoe laughed, pulling out black wigs and baseball caps.

"I'm not sure. Logan and I had just discussed staying in for the afternoon."

"Are you crazy? We're in New York. For heaven's sake, Jade, don't be a party pooper," Zoey insisted.

"I'm afraid something just came up," Logan interjected, putting down his phone. "Jade, why don't you go with Zoe and Ethan. I'm sure you'll have fun. After all, it is New York like Zoe said."

"What and leave you behind? Really Logan."

I was more than a bit frustrated, not to mention perplexed by his suggestion. What possibly could be so important? Perhaps the better question was who could be so important? Logan appeared too willing to give up our time together, and I was pissed. But, whatever his reason, he seemed committed to keeping his appointment, and I wasn't about to hang around and be consumed with worry. At least, if I got the chance, I could corner Ethan with all my questions.

"Okay," I reluctantly agreed. "The tourist thing is on for the afternoon. Let me get dressed. It won't take long."

"You're going to need something warm," Zoey suggested following me into the bedroom. "Autumn can be quite chilly in New York."

Walking into the bedroom, the door was left ajar. The guy's conversation in the other room was quiet, and I couldn't hear the topic of their discussion. However, I worried it centered around Kelsey without knowing the details.

"Geez, I thought the girls would never go in the other room," Ethan quietly ranted. "Logan, what's going on? We don't have any scheduled meetings this afternoon, and I hope to God I don't hear the name, Kelsey Kensington coming out of your mouth. I thought you were through with her after we toured Germany?"

"Damn, Ethan, give me a break. Yes. It was Kelsey. For heaven's sake, keep your voice down."

"I knew it. What the hell does she want? Are you willing to risk what you have with Jade? Logan, I love you like a brother, but this girl is nothing but trouble. Do I have to remind you?"

"Ethan, trust me, I would never jeopardize my relationship with Jade. I love her. Love her. Do you even understand the meaning of the word?"

"Oh my God, I can't believe this. I really can't. I've just overheard every word, every single word," Zoey whispered furiously as she walked out of the bedroom. "You better thank your lucky stars that Jade walked into the bathroom, and the door was closed. Hopefully, she didn't hear you. Logan, Ethan is right. What the hell are you doing? What are you possibly thinking? Kelsey Kensington is trouble, and unfortunately, she has the connections to make your life miserable."

"Trust me, you both have this all wrong. I despise Kelsey for the hurt and anger she caused me while we were on tour in Germany, but she swears we must talk. I get the feeling it's important, and I need to find out why she's here. I think we can all agree it isn't because of Noah."

"Poor Noah, he's so naive," Zoey sighed.

"Alright, meet with her if you think it's so freaking important. I'll try to keep Jade from suspecting that your meeting has anything to do with Kelsey, but she isn't stupid, you know," Ethan warned.

Suddenly, the room fell silent as I walked out of the bedroom.

"Wow, Babe, you look stunning," Logan winked. "Maybe, I should tag along as your bodyguard."

Wearing my long, blonde curls pulled back in a ponytail, designer jeans with a black tunic sweater, and matching boots, I ensured that I was eloquently dressed for the streets of New York.

"What were you guys discussing? Things got awfully quiet when I walked out of the bedroom."

"Oh, nothing, trust me, just the upcoming concert," Logan added. "We're excited. It's Madison Square Garden, and we're sold out."

Without knowing the details of their conversation, Zoey, as

promised, recounted every word to me, leaving nothing out. The guys had no way to know that I would be privy to their entire discussion.

As Logan dressed for his meeting, I left with Zoey and Ethan for a day of sightseeing. We visited Lady Liberty, the Empire State Building, and later we ate at the distinguished restaurant, Keens Steakhouse. Its rich history dates back to 1885. The mutton chops were delicious, and of course, their scotch selection was superb. Ethan managed to get us in without a reservation by dropping Alan's name and, of course, that of the band. I never had the chance to corner Ethan alone for answers, but it was still at the forefront of my mind. I was more determined than ever to press him for answers

Finally after, several hours, we had just enough time to return to the hotel and dress before the concert. However, when I unlocked the door to our suite, Logan wasn't there. Even though I was somewhat bothered by the fact he hadn't returned, I knew as the lead singer of Riot Storm, he would be walking in any minute to shower and dress for sound check. The limo always arrived at 3:00 p.m., and the guys were never late. Noticing the time, it was 2:30 p.m. I began to panic until I heard the door open. Then I really panicked. Logan was completely inebriated. I had never seen Logan so wasted before. His condition was more than troubling. There wasn't enough coffee in the entire world to get him sober in the time remaining. However, I had to try. Calling Ethan's room was the only recourse. He was on his way as soon as the call ended.

"Oh, hey Babe, what brings you here?" Logan grinned, slurring his words as he slowly staggered into the living room.

"Logan, what the hell is wrong with you?" I ranted. "You've got sound checks at 4:00 p.m., and the limo arrives at 3:00 p.m. Are you crazy?"

"No, Doll, I don't think so, but let me check," Logan laughed. "Where's the bathroom? I feel sick."

Continuing his slow, unsteady wobble towards the sofa, Logan tripped over the coffee table. Rushing over, I managed to catch him just as his head was about to hit the corner.

"Damn, Logan, I'm not your doll," I exclaimed. "What happened?"

Luck was on my side. Somehow I managed to get him to the sofa just before he passed out. Then, hearing a loud knock at the door, I ran over to let Ethan and Zoey in.

"What the hell? What happened to him? We leave in less than a half-hour for the venue," Ethan raged, running over to his best friend, who was passed out on the sofa. "Zoey, order coffee, lots of coffee."

"This isn't good. If my dad finds out about Logan, the shit will hit the fan. Tonight is Madison Square Garden, for God's sake," Zoey yelled. "I'm freaking out right now. Dad will kill Logan. Well, maybe not kill him, but trust me, he'll wish he was dead."

"Geez, Zoey, calm down. Your outbursts aren't helping. Do something. Call for coffee to be brought up immediately. Don't just stand there, wet some hot towels," Ethan ordered. "Damn, she did a number on him."

"Ethan, you just use the word, she? Did you mean Kelsey?" I questioned angrily.

"Oh, shit, maybe?"

"Ethan, yes or no?" I angrily demanded.

"Okay," Ethan hesitantly responded, knowing that telling the truth meant he was betraying his best friend's trust. Okay. Yes, he went to see Kelsey."

"Geez, Ethan, you couldn't keep your mouth shut," Zoey exclaimed.

"Oh my God, Zoe, are you in on this too. I don't believe it. Everyone knows but me. Zoey, we're supposed to be friends, best friends. What's going on?"

"For Pete's sake, can't we fight about this later. We have our hands full with Logan," Ethan ranted, running over to answer the door. Jade, get some ice from the fridge. We'll never get this down him. The coffee is too hot."

Continually wiping Logan's face with the warm towels, it somehow miraculously began to revive him. "Wow, I think it's working. Do you think he could sit up?" Zoey asked, running to the bathroom to reheat the towels.

"Where am I?" Logan slowly questioned somewhat incoherently as Ethan and I managed to get him upright into a sitting position.

"Man. What happened to you? Oh, hell, it doesn't matter. Don't answer. Drink this," Ethan scolded, trying to get a cup of coffee down Logan.

"Where's Jade? I need Jade."

"Logan, I'm here. I'm so sorry. What did she do to you? I had a bad feeling about her. I knew she was trouble from the moment I saw her."

"Oh, Jade, I love you. But, can you ever forgive me?" Logan pleaded with a glazed drunken stare.

"Logan, forgive you for what? I have no idea what you're talking about. I love you."

"Can we stop the idle chit-chat for a moment and get him into a warm shower. Unfortunately, we don't have much time," Ethan demanded.

"Jade, find something for Logan to wear, preferably jeans and a black tee-shirt. Wait, do you think you can help me get him up?"

"Yes."

"After we get him upright, I'll help him into the bathroom while you turn on the warm water in the shower. After that, I think we can get him sober enough to get downstairs and into the limo."

"I hate that girl. Hate her!" I yelled from the bathroom.

"Save that for later. Our focus is Logan. He has to go on stage tonight."

Helping Logan inside the shower, the warm water appeared to revive him as he slowly began to come around. Finally, our efforts were working.

"Wow, I think we've dodged a bullet this afternoon." Ethan grinned, somewhat relieved. "Calling the limo driver, Ethan informed him they were running a few minutes late.

It was 3:15 p.m. Everyone was finally dressed, including Logan, and we headed downstairs to the lobby. Meeting Jarrod and Noah outside by the curb, we all entered the limo for the short drive to Madison Square Garden.

"Man. What happened to you? You look like crap like you've been hit by a truck?" Jarrod questioned, sitting next to Logan.

"Dude, let's just say I've been better and leave it at that," Logan mumbled.

"Whatever. You look like hell."

"Thanks, bro," Logan frowned with a look that implored Jarrod to stop any further interrogation.

"You better pray that I don't see Kelsey at the concert," I whispered to Zoey.

"Jade, tonight is not the time or place to confront a girl like Kelsey. Please, the last thing we need is more drama."

"Oh, I'll give her drama if she comes near Logan."

"Jade, her last name is Kensington, lest you forget. Her name carries a lot of weight in this industry. You can't start something you might not be able to finish. She could destroy Logan's career. Plus, none of us truly know the details of their meeting today."

"Well, whatever she did, it sent Logan over the edge. Trust me. I will find out what happened."

"Okay, but not at this venue and not tonight," Zoey demanded.

Sitting in the limo next to Logan, I was mesmerized as Madison Square Garden came into view. The brightly lit marquee headlined Riot Storm featuring Logan James, also the words, sold-out.

Arriving at the back entrance, Logan still appeared slightly intoxicated. Alan and Brian were accustomed to the guys showing up somewhat under the influence of either alcohol or drugs. This scenario had played out many times before. However, what did matter was their ability to perform. Zoey was right about her dad. Alan had zero tolerance for any band member who showed up for sound checks, either totally inebriated or entirely under the influence of drugs and couldn't go on stage. Thankfully, this wouldn't be cause for worry with Logan. Even though he was evidently intoxicated, he was still capable of performing.

Hurriedly exiting the limo, everyone rushed into the arena. Zoey and I decided to watch from the sidelines as we quickly followed the guys through the long labyrinth of concrete corridors and to the stage.

We both kept our eyes peeled for any signs of Kelsey. Finally, Logan picked up his guitar and, without hesitation, belted out the lyrics to their most popular hits. Ethan felt an enormous rush of relief, giving me a thumbs up. The evening appeared to be getting off to a great start. Standing in the wings, I admired my handsome guy.

"Good evening, New York," Logan yelled, sending the girls into a frenzy. "It's good to be back." "Are you ready to party?" Ethan screamed, holding his guitar high in the air. Logan grabbed the mic and belted out the lyrics to their most famous songs as he ran to the edge of the stage. Logan was good at entertaining his fans, and tonight was no different despite the fact he was still under the influence of alcohol. Logan was every girl's dream, tall, thin, with gorgeous, long blonde curls. His tattooed muscular physique effortlessly portrayed the image of a rock god. I knew there was no way that I would ever allow anyone to steal him from me, especially Kelsey Kensington. First, however, I needed to learn more about his inner turmoil and the demons he appeared to fight. Whatever had transpired between Logan and Kelsey earlier in the day had instantly sent him into a tailspin, and I would get my answers.

The concert went off without a hitch. The fans in New York loved Riot Storm. Their roaring reaction for an encore evidenced it. The guys always graciously returned to the stage, sending their fans into a state of euphoria. Unfortunately, there was no sighting of Kelsey during or after the concert. However, I knew she was there, somewhere, lurking in the shadows. I could feel her presence. Finally, leaving the venue, we were on our way back to the hotel.

Snuggled warmly inside Logan's embrace during the short ride to the hotel, I contemplated my strategy. There was no way I wanted to jeopardize the fact we were together. After years of being apart, I was finally where I always wanted to be, snuggled safely inside his arms. First, however, I had to know what transpired between Logan and Kelsey.

Reaching the hotel, everyone opted to turn in early instead of having drinks at the hotel bar, typically their ritual. I grasped Logan's hand as we exited the limo, taking advantage of the situation. Hurriedly pulling him inside the hotel and over to the elevator, I was anxious to be alone with the one person who had the answers I so desperately needed. Leaving Zoey and Ethan behind, I knew they would easily understand.

"Geez, what's the rush?" Logan winked, pushing the button to the top floor.

"I've missed you. You were gone all afternoon, and after watching your performance, I want you all to myself."

"Wow, Babe, that's sweet," Logan teased. He pulled me into his arms, lightly pressing me against the elevator wall, kissing me passionately. Then, utterly oblivious that the elevator door suddenly opened, he continued our long zealous kiss giving no thought to the young couple who entered. Reaching our stop, I felt awkward. However, my embarrassment only grew worse as the couple instantly recognized Logan.

"Great concert. Could we possibly get a photo?" the guy asked, reaching for his cell phone.

Without hesitation, Logan eagerly agreed as I volunteered to take the snapshot.

"Thanks."

"No problem," Logan smiled, putting his arms around the young couple as they posed for the photo.

After taking their photo, we stepped out of the elevator. Unlocking the door to our suite, Logan pulled me inside.

"Wow, what you did in the elevator was sweet and thoughtful," I smiled.

"Oh, you mean the unexpected kiss?" he grinned.

"No, silly, allowing the couple to have their photo made with you."

"We have the best fans in the entire world. I wouldn't be where I am today without them," Logan explained, walking over to the bar. Popping the cork on a bottle of Moet & Chandon Champagne, he poured us each a tall glass. "I always try to be accommodating to fans when it's possible."

Handing me a glass filled with the sparkling beverage, Logan led me over to the sofa.

"Jade," he hesitated briefly. "We need to talk."

To my surprise, it appeared Logan might finally be ready to explain why he'd returned to the room entirely wasted. Taking his drink, Logan lounged back on the sofa, pulling me into his arms.

"Babe, I did meet with Kelsey this afternoon. I didn't want to alarm or worry you, so I thought it best not to mention her name," Logan paused, taking a sip of his drink. "I'm sorry. I haven't seen her in over a year, and she made it sound important. She can be very demanding."

"Why would you even agree to meet with her? Are you still in love with her?" I waited pensively for his answer. I knew if his reply was anything other than, no, my heart wouldn't be able to take it.

"No. Jade, you have to know that I'm in love with you. I've always been in love with you."

"Oh, thank God. Logan, I couldn't live knowing that I had lost you once again." Snuggling closer, I was overwhelmed with relief. Tears slowly trickled down my face.

"Sweetheart, I love you. I'm not trying to hurt you. I just want to keep things open and honest between us." Sitting his glass down, he reached for a box of Kleenex. Taking a tissue, he gently wiped my eyes. "Jade, when I left, it was so hard getting over what we had together. I missed you more than you could know. But after months of touring overseas, I realized that we might never see each other again. Finally, I allowed myself to entertain thoughts of moving on, and that's when I met Kelsey. I had no idea of her prominence or the fact her dad was Edward Kensington," Logan paused, taking another long slow sip of his drink. "We met in Frankfurt. She came backstage after one of our concerts. After that, we started dating. At first, it felt nice to have someone in my life. However, trust me when I tell you, it didn't take long for me to realize how selfish she was. We were together for about six months when I realized I had made a huge mistake. At that point, she began using her father's status in the music industry as a form of blackmail to keep me from leaving. She threatened to ruin my career if I left. I knew Alan and Edward were close friends, and I didn't want to bother Alan with my personal problems. After a short time of being held hostage to her threats, I was willing to risk my entire career to be free of her. Thank God it never came to that." Reaching for his cigarettes, Logan continued.

"Jade, I knew when I saw her on board the jet, she wasn't there because of Noah. I knew it was her way of either trying to see me or rekindle what she thought we had together. Babe, you have to believe I had no idea she would be on that flight. I was just as shocked as you when I saw her. When she called this afternoon, I knew I had to meet with her, even if it was only to get her out of my hair. You have no idea how persistent she can be when getting things she wants. I had no choice. I had to see her and let her know for sure there wasn't a snowball's chance in hell that we were ever getting back together. However, I'm sure she hoped to rekindle our past relationship," Logan paused, extinguishing his cigarette.

"Unbelievable as it might sound, Kelsey claims she was pregnant when I left. I swear I had no idea. Not that it would have made a difference in my decision to leave, but I would have taken on the child's responsibility without question. Unfortunately, Kelsey lost the baby five months after I left. Jade, I had no idea Kelsey was even pregnant. She wanted me to know that our son was laid to rest in their family mausoleum in Chicago. I suppose the guilt of never telling me about our son, whom she named Jordan Kensington, finally got to her. I was devastated. You can only imagine the hurt I felt knowing I had a son. Someone that I would never see, never hold, or watch grow up. Babe, I hate the fact she never told me. Trust me. It changes nothing between us. I love you more than ever. God willing, one day, we will have kids of our own," Logan hinted with a faint smile. "I hate Kelsey for what she did. She never told me until today, and I will never forgive her. Never."

"Logan, I'm so sorry. No wonder you felt the need to get wasted. I can't even begin to imagine the horrors of being told you had a son and the fact you lost him before he was born." I empathized, kissing him.

If Kelsey's guilty conscience was her plan to bring Logan back into her life, it had failed. Instead, he hated her more now than ever, and rightfully so.

"Jade, I really don't want anyone to know, especially the guys. I'm not up to discussing it at this time. Maybe one day I'll tell Ethan, but not now. Can you please keep this just between the two of us?"

"Yes. I completely understand."

My heart ached for Logan. He appeared utterly distraught. I couldn't comprehend how he could go on stage and give such a brilliant performance after receiving such devastating news.

Setting our glasses down on the coffee table, I grasped Logan's hand, pulling him toward the bedroom. Lovingly, I gently pulled his black tee-shirt over his head. Kissing every inch of his sculpted chest, I knew that I could never take away his hurt. I could only spend every second of the night loving him with every ounce of my being. We were fortunate to find each other for the second time, and I wanted him to know our love was strong enough to sustain us for a lifetime, no matter the circumstances. Turning out the light, I pulled him down beside me.

As the early morning sun peeped in through the curtains, it found us still wrapped in each other's arms. Rolling over to face Logan, I was mesmerized at the mere sight of him. My handsome rock star had finally fallen asleep. Staring at his striking profile, I could only hope that sleep would provide him a much-needed escape.

Deciding to let Logan get some rest, I quietly walked into the bathroom. Stepping inside the shower, the warm water felt invigorating yet cathartic as it gently washed over my body. Reaching for a towel as I stepped out of the shower, I prepared to dress for the day. Suddenly, I felt the grasp of Logan's strong, masculine hands encircle my waist. Turning to face him, I smiled.

"Geez, babe, I thought you were asleep."

"Jade, I knew the very instant your warm, sexy body left my side," Logan winked with a wicked smile. "You can't get away from me that easily."

The towel wrapped with a loose knot around my slender frame fell softly to the floor as Logan scooped me into his arms, carrying me back to the bedroom.

"Logan, my hair is wet, we have a flight this morning to Washington, and I haven't packed," I reminded him. "I think we need to stay focused."

"Who says I'm not focused?"

"Logan James, you're a bad boy."

"Oh, really," he laughed. "So, you're not attracted to bad boys? I think I can change your mind," he teased, gently laying me on the bed.

Before I could even respond to his silly question, I found myself powerless against his advances. Helplessly, I melted into his arms like molten wax. I couldn't resist his sexual magnetism. It was alluring, and I had never felt this way with anyone. He'd stolen my heart from the moment we first met in high school. With tears in my eyes, I held Logan in my arms, hoping the love we shared would magically erase the hurt and anguish that haunted him. Fortunately, the morning passed in a state of bliss as we spent the next two hours in bed.

Glancing at the clock, I panicked.

"Logan, we have less than an hour to pack. The limo is picking everyone up at noon."

"Don't worry. All we have to do is throw a few things into a suitcase."

"Easy for you to say. I have curling irons to pack and tons of accessories."

"What can I do? I'll help you pack."

"No. You order coffee and breakfast. I'm starved."

Later that morning, as we departed Kennedy International, the skyline looked even more vivid than when we arrived. We were on our way to Washington DC, the nation's capital, and our next venue. Staring at the handsome rock star sitting next to me, he consumed my every thought.

I felt New York was a turning point in our relationship. I now wanted to marry the handsome guy sitting next to me more than ever. It didn't matter that he was Logan James, the famous rock star. I knew the real Logan James long before the world was ever aware of his existence. Leaving New York, with the knowledge that he'd recently lost his son, I desperately wanted to marry him. I wanted nothing more out of life than giving him a family of our own. I didn't want an enormous, elaborate wedding. However, I knew my parents were more than capable of making that happen. I merely wanted a ring on my left hand that would signify to the entire world that we loved each other.

Furthermore, I wanted a chance to show the world I had better parenting skills than my parents. It was unfathomable the degree to which my parents lacked empathy for their children. I knew I could do a better job. Now, I just had to make Logan aware of my feelings.

Arriving in Washington, unexpectedly, the evidence of change was already set into motion. One which neither of us saw coming.

Chapter Seven

Washington DC

$\mathscr{A}$s the Lear jet circled the capital on our approach into Dulles International, I was fixated on the scenic landscape below. Hopefully, if time permitted, I wanted to visit the numerous landmarks. On the other hand, Logan appeared totally oblivious to the scenery and its history. With earbuds in his ears, he was completely immersed in his music. Looking across the aisle, Zoey was snuggled in Ethan's arms, sleeping peacefully. Amazingly, things inside the cabin were subdued, considering it held the larger-than-life members of the famous rock band, Riot Storm.

As the jet taxied across the tarmac, it slowly came to a stop next to a stretch limo. We were on our way downtown to the Hyatt Regency. However, today we were traveling without Alan and Brian, a fact which I'm sure made Zoey happy. They had flown down the previous night to set up a promotional appearance. Once again, as we were settled comfortably inside the car, the guys opened a bottle of Jameson. It had long been another tradition of theirs when arriving at a new venue. Immediately, it began making its rounds inside the car.

The limo parked under the well-lit entrance of the luxurious hotel.

The guys stumbled out of the car, making their way inside the elegant lobby where Brian was waiting.

"Hey guys, welcome to Washington. I'm glad you're here. I've got great news," Brian smiled as he methodically detailed their agenda. "We've got a promo spot tomorrow at 8:00 a.m. It's being televised on a popular morning show, Today in Washington. The car will be here promptly at 7:00 a.m. Don't be late," Brian warned. "I know that's early for most of you, so I highly suggest you don't stay out late tonight. Enjoy the city, but as always, keep a low profile. You're on your own for this afternoon. Sound check is tomorrow at 4:00 p.m. Oh, the Capital One is completely sold-out, and you're all set to pick up room keys at the front desk. See you early tomorrow morning," Brian grinned, walking towards Zoey. "Hey, Zoe, I almost forgot, your mom came in last night. She's with your dad right now, but she wanted you to know they'll be seeing you later this evening."

"Great, just what I need both parents hovering over me," Zoey fumed.

"Geez, Zoe, you should be happy to see her. I bet my parents still have no idea that I've even left home or where I'm at," I teased jokingly.

"Well, Jade, since you brought it up, I have to tell you, your parents call daily, trying to get in touch with either Alan or me. Trust me. They're totally informed. However, you didn't hear it from me," Brian grinned.

"Wow, really, I never expected to hear that? But, Brian, you're under no obligation to tell my parents anything. It's my life, and honestly, I wish you wouldn't," I hastily snapped back in anger.

"Whatever you want. As you said, it's your life," Brian scoffed hurriedly, making his way to the lounge inside the lobby.

"Wow, I think we better get these girls upstairs before they become entirely unglued," Ethan roared.

"Geez, who knew? You both have parent issues," Logan laughed.

"Seriously, Logan, I've overheard Jarrod and Noah on their cell phones arguing with their parents," I harshly reminded him.

"Wow, Jade. What's that supposed to mean? That I don't love my parents," Jarrod harshly interrupted.

"Okay, let's take this upstairs. I don't think we want to air the band's dirty laundry in the lobby," Logan added.

Walking towards the elevator, I felt light-headed. Undoubtedly, it was the mere mention of my parents.

"Jarrod and I are making reservations for dinner later this evening at Tortino's if anyone wants to join us," Noah cautiously mentioned stepping inside the elevator.

"Thanks. We'll let you know," Logan replied. Then, as the elevator came to a stop on our floor, he reached for my hand.

"Call me later," Zoey added. "We're in room 1012."

"Got it," I smiled, stepping out of the elevator with Logan.

Suddenly, my knees buckled from beneath me as Logan unlocked the door to our room. Completely unexpected, and without warning, I felt light-headed.

"Wow, babe, are you alright?" Logan questioned, catching me before I hit the floor. "Do you want me to carry you?" Logan's face reflected worry as he put his arms firmly around my waist, keeping me steady.

"No. Don't be crazy. I can walk."

"Okay. If you insist."

Putting our carry-on bags on the credenza, I could tell that Logan was somewhat concerned. However, I felt fine.

"Let's order room service. I'm hungry," I suggested trying to change the subject.

"Good idea. You probably need something to eat. What sounds appetizing?"

"It might sound crazy, but I'm actually craving a burger with tons of fries and lots of ketchup. How does that sound?"

"Easy enough," Logan teased. "Two burgers with fries coming up," he repeated, reaching for the phone to order room service. "Why don't you relax on the sofa? I'm worried about you."

"Don't be silly. I'm fine."

I removed my shoes and curled up on the sofa at Logan's insistence.

He walked over to draw back the stylish silk drapes, instantly bathing the room in the warm glow of the afternoon sun. The décor of our suite was sophisticated and well designed with modern French Colonial furniture.

"I know you wanted to visit the Lincoln Memorial and other landmarks, but do you feel up to it?"

"I think so, but why don't we wait until I've had something to eat. Then, I'll see how I feel afterward."

"Sounds like a plan," Logan smiled, kissing me on the forehead.

A short while later, a light knock at the door indicated the arrival of our burgers and fries—a simple meal for such a grand hotel and elegant surroundings.

"Sweetheart, I think your burger and fries have arrived," Logan announced, walking towards the door.

Immediately the room filled with the aroma of a burger bar. The smell of hot french fries and hamburgers cooked to perfection with caramelized onions and all the trimmings infused the air.

"Wow, it looks amazing," Logan smiled, sitting the tray of food on the coffee table. Then, ravenously taking a giant bite of his burger, he winked. "Phenomenal."

"Totally," I agreed, biting into my juicy burger. Afterward, smothering my fries with ketchup, they tasted delicious. "I'm not exactly an epicurean, but this is by far the best burger and fries I've ever eaten."

"I'll say. You're even wearing it," Logan laughed. Then, taking his napkin, he wiped the remains of ketchup from my mouth.

"I don't think I've ever seen two people devour burgers and fries this fast. I feel stuffed," Logan grinned, lounging back on the sofa.

"I know. You're right. We ate too fast," I agreed, leaning against Logan's chest.

"Babe, I love you and your crazy addiction to the simple things in life," Logan whispered, gently pulling my hair away from my face. He pushed my long curls behind my ears, softly kissing the nape of my neck. Closing my eyes, I felt drowsy. The last thing I remembered before falling asleep was Logan carrying me into the bedroom and placing me under the warm covers. I must have slept for a couple of hours. When I finally opened my eyes, I was surprised to discover Logan sleeping next to me.

I stared at the love of my life. His appearance while sleeping was a dichotomy. He appeared childlike and innocent compared to the hardcore rock star, who could energize an entire audience with his crazy antics on stage. Suddenly, the sound of my cell phone woke him from his slumber. Looking down at my phone, it was Zoey.

"Hey, my parents want to see you. You're both invited to dinner later this evening. They've made reservations for everyone at the Article One American Grill downstairs. It's casual. Can you make it?"

"Hold for a moment while I ask Logan."

"Babe, Zoey's parents have invited us to join them for dinner this evening. Do you want to accept their invitation?"

"Of course."

"Okay. What time?"

"Seven. We'll meet you in the lobby."

"Thanks. Sounds wonderful. See you at seven."

Glancing at the clock, it was 4:30 p.m.

"Wow, that was a snap decision regarding dinner."

"Jade, Alan is my manager. You never turn down a dinner invitation with someone of his significance."

"Now that we've slept the afternoon away, what do we do for the next two and a half hours?" I questioned. "There's not enough time to visit any of the memorials and get back in time to shower and dress for dinner."

"Um, let me think about that. Come over here, and I'll show you," Logan teased mischievously.

"Logan, you're definitely a bad boy. However, that's not going to work in your favor this time," I laughed. "Why don't we watch a movie?"

Sitting up in bed, he frowned. I knew watching movies wasn't his favorite activity. Still, I knew he would cave, allowing me to pick the movie we watched.

"Really, and what movie do you suggest? I should be spending time in the gym. My knee is giving me trouble again."

"Oh, you poor baby. Let me make it better," I grinned, leaning over to give him a quick kiss.

Playfully, Logan pulled me down next to him. Wrapping me tight in his arms, he didn't let go. Instead, like a fly caught in a spider's web," he laughed playfully, holding me against my will.

"Logan James, you release me right now. This isn't going to work. I'll force you to watch the entire three hours of *Doctor Zhivago* if you don't let me go."

"Oh, really, well, I hate to disappoint you, Babe, but I love that movie."

"You're lying," I giggled, quickly freeing myself from his grasp. Then, grabbing a pillow, I tossed it at him. "We're watching an old movie, *You've Got Mail*. It's one of my favorites. I love Meg Ryan and Tom Hanks.

Standing at the bedroom door, I motioned for him to join me in the living room.

Reluctantly, he followed.

Later, as the movie credits slowly scrolled upward on the screen, we had just enough time to shower and dress before meeting Zoey's parents for dinner.

Finally, after a frantic rush, we were both ready. Hurriedly locking the door, we were on our way downstairs.

Walking into the lobby, I instantly recognized Zoey's mom, Joyce Zimmerman. She always stood out in a crowd with her flaming red hair and flamboyant personality. Personally, even though Zoey and I were best friends, I'd never liked her mom. Immediately, she began her insufferable assault.

"Jade, it's so good to see you. I spoke with your mom this week, and she's worried sick about you. But, Logan, I must say you look handsome as ever."

Wow, did she just interject my mom into the conversation before we even sat down to eat? I refused to respond to such a statement.

Apparently, I was the recent topic of conversation between mom and Joyce. After college, they had remained friends, and my dad, Charles, had introduced Joyce to Alan. It was clearly evident that mom had arranged this entire dinner. She had most likely sent Joyce to spy on me.

"Well, you can let her know that I'm just fine," I silently seethed.

Noticing my level of discomfort, Logan squeezed my hand.

"Easy, Babe, you don't have to kill the messenger," he whispered.

The entire dinner seemed like a never-ending interrogation. I could hardly take a bite of the prime rib, which tasted delicious without feeling nauseous. I couldn't wait for the meal to be over. I felt for Zoe. She had no idea her mom had ulterior motives for inviting us. After everyone finished eating, Logan and I quickly thanked the Zimmermans and made a hasty retreat.

"Oh my God, Logan, I'm so pissed. You do realize my mom set that whole thing up," I quietly fumed as we walked towards the elevator.

"Jade, I'm sure your mom is just worried about you. Give her a little credit. After all, you did leave without saying goodbye.

"Yes, well, there was a good reason for that, and besides, I left her a note. Logan, you more than anyone can remember what my life was like at home. I hated the fact my parents were constantly fighting and arguing. I'll always feel guilty for leaving Charlie behind."

"Well, you're with me now, so you can relax. No more talk about your parents," Logan smiled empathetically, giving me a quick kiss.

Reaching our floor, my phone rang just as we stepped out of the elevator.

"Jade, I'm so sorry. I had no idea. Really, I never saw that coming," Zoey apologized.

"Zoe, it's not your fault. I don't blame you. I knew mom would go to desperate lengths sooner or later, trying to find out everything she could about me. I'm sorry that she involved your mom. But, as I said, I don't blame you."

"Would you and Logan like to join us later for a nightcap?"

"Thanks, but I'm not exactly feeling my best right now. I'll call you in the morning."

"Okay, feel better. We'll talk tomorrow."

Waiting for Logan to unlock the door, I felt nauseous. I just managed to make it inside. Running to the bathroom, I closed the door. Kneeling on the cold marble floor in front of the toilet, I wretchedly threw up every morsel I had eaten. Quickly grabbing a washcloth, I warmed it and washed my face. What was going on? For a brief second, I had my suspicions, but I wasn't ready to let my mind go there. Checking my appearance in the mirror, I didn't want Logan to be overly alarmed.

"Babe, are you okay?"

"Yes, it's just stress. I'm fine."

"Well, the way you bolted for the bathroom, you didn't seem fine."

"Logan, I let Joyce get to me, and I shouldn't have. I blame myself."

"Maybe we should call it a night. I have to get up early in the morning. Remember, Alan has the band booked for a promo at a local television station tomorrow."

"Yes, I remember. I'm feeling a little tired."

Grasping my hand, Logan led me towards the bedroom. Quickly changing clothes, Logan drew back the lofty blue toile duvet. Finally, despite the early hour, we were in bed for the night. Snuggling inside the warmth of Logan's muscular arms, he gently kissed me goodnight. Within minutes we were both sound asleep, not waking until early the following day.

Turning off the alarm, Logan gently kissed me on the forehead.

"Good morning, gorgeous, don't get up. I think you could use the rest," Logan whispered. "I shouldn't be gone too long. I'll see you when I get back. I Love you," he smiled, racing towards the bathroom to shower and dress.

Fluffing my pillow, I rolled over in bed, feeling the empty spot where he'd slept. I already missed the warmth of his body next to mine. It didn't take Logan long to shower and dress. Then, stopping to give me another kiss, he was out the door. Apparently, I was more tired than usual as I slept the entire time Logan was away.

Arriving back at the hotel, Logan quietly walked into the bedroom.

Taking off his shoes, he slid under the covers pulling me against his warm muscular body.

"Hey sleepyhead, I'm back," he lovingly whispered, brushing back my long curls.

Softly kissing me awake, I rolled over.

"How did it go this morning?" I asked drowsily.

"Oh, great. We were given the VIP treatment, but I'm not sure why Alan arranged for the band to do the morning show because the concert was already sold-out before our arrival."

"Alan loves publicity, that's why."

"Are you hungry? Why don't I have breakfast sent up, and we can eat in bed."

"The best idea I've heard all morning. I'm starving. I want pancakes, lots of pancakes covered in maple syrup and bacon. Can I get a side order of scrambled eggs and hash browns too?"

"Geez, sweetheart, of course, you can have eggs and hash browns. I'm pretty sure I can cover the cost of breakfast," Logan laughed, pulling me into his arms. "Ethan and Zoe are up to their usual antics, playing the role of tourists later this morning. Ethan asked if we'd like to tag along. I believe he mentioned the Lincoln Memorial. Do you feel up to it? I know you weren't feeling your best last night."

"Yes. Please let them know. Can you call for a car? I think it would be better than taking a taxi or public transportation. We don't have much time, and there are so many landmarks I want to see."

"Sounds like a plan. But, first, I'll order breakfast and give Ethan a call."

It wasn't long before breakfast arrived, and I hurriedly consumed every morsel.

"Wow, sweetheart, you must have been starving. If I didn't know better, I'd swear you were eating for two," Logan teased.

Hearing Logan's profound, unexpected statement, I choked. Milk spewed from my mouth. What an utterly bizarre thing for him to say after last night and my surprising episode of sickness.

"Are you okay?"

"Yes," I gasped finally, catching my breath. Then, wiping my mouth, I cleared my throat.

Running into the bathroom to brush my teeth and get ready, I casually glanced into the mirror. I definitely didn't exude any signs which might make Logan come to that conclusion. Even the mere thought and speculation of pregnancy seemed foreign to me. Clearly, my being sick and nauseous were not in any way remotely connected to the possibilities, and Logan's comment was just uttered nonsense. However, we had been on tour for several months. Even though birth control was an essential aspect of our relationship, unplanned pregnancies were known to happen. Dressed in my favorite denim jeans and a white fitted cotton shirt, once again, I pulled my long blonde curls into a ponytail. Grabbing my oversized bag as my last accessory, I was ready. Walking out of the bathroom, I tried to push the thoughts of the unexpected possibilities out of my mind.

"Jade, you look stunning. We should hurry. The car is waiting. Ethan and Zoe are meeting us in the lobby." Logan closed the door, grabbing his leather jacket, his usual baseball cap, and sunglasses, which he routinely used as a disguise.

Arriving at the National Mall, Logan and I strolled along the walkway with our arms locked around each other. Taking in the incredible views, it was like history came alive in the form of spectacular monuments. The Lincoln Memorial was a majestic work of art, and its scale was impressive. However, it had to be seen in person to appreciate the craftsmanship required to erect the sculpture. Afterward, we spent time at the Vietnam Veterans Memorial. Logan's grandfather had served in the armed forces during Vietnam. It meant a lot to him that he took the time to honor him and the other courageous men who lost their lives during the war. Lastly, visiting the Jefferson Memorial, our time was becoming limited. Sound check, as usual, began at 4:00 p.m.

"Sorry, we don't have time to see everything this afternoon," Logan apologized as we walked back towards the waiting car.

"Yes. We would need a few days to take in all the monuments and museums," Zoey agreed.

"If we hurry, I think we might have just enough time to grab a pizza," Ethan suggested.

"Pizza sounds amazing," I interjected.

Asking the driver for his preference of pizza establishments, he quickly recommended the Pizzeria Paradiso and, more specifically, their Calzone. It came with ricotta, spinach, red onion, prosciutto with herbs, and their special birreria tomato sauce on the side.

He was definitely spot on with his recommendation. Leaving the establishment, we were entirely stuffed and vowed to return the next time we were in Washington.

Leaning against Logan's broad shoulders, I napped during the short ride back to the hotel.

"Wow, Jade's asleep. She's out like a light bulb," Zoey remarked, watching as Logan lovingly caressed my face. "Is she feeling okay?"

"Zoe, I'm not sleeping, just closing my eyes for a while, and yes, I'm fine," I reminded them as I opened my eyes.

"Babe, you need to rest. Remember you were sick last night. I think dinner was a little unsettling," Logan mentioned kissing my forehead. He knew I hated being put on the spot with all the questions.

"Jade, I'm truly sorry. If I had only known my mom would interrogate you, I would never have suggested you accept their dinner invitation. I'm sure your mom set the whole thing into motion," Zoey mentioned changing the subject.

"Yes. I'm sure Amanda had something to do with it," Logan mentioned. "But, I can't say I blame you for leaving home. Your parents are the most egotistical couple I've ever met," he added.

"You've got that right," Zoey agreed.

Rubbing my eyes, I sat up as the car arrived back at the hotel. We had just enough time to change and freshen up before we once again met the guys downstairs.

Later that evening, as the guys performed in front of a sold-out crowd at the Capital One Arena, Zoey and I watched their performance from our usual spot. We were hidden from the view of the fans, yet within close proximity to the guys. I never tired of the band's interaction with their fans. You could feel the electricity and excitement as Logan took control of the stage. He exhibited a fiery passion for entertaining his devoted fans as he ran back and forth to each end of the stage, holding the audience entirely captive. Even the sweat smoldering from his muscular, tattooed body along with his long, blonde curls, which shimmered under the hot lights, gave him a formidable presence. He was every girl's dream, and the fact he belonged to me gave me goosebumps. He effortlessly portrayed the essence of a rock god.

"Good night, Washington. Thanks for coming out to party with us. We love you," Logan yelled as their last song ended.

"We love you, Washington!" Ethan screamed, holding his guitar high in the air.

As the guys walked off stage, the fans, as usual, made their desire for an encore known by loudly screaming the band's name. However, the guys always came prepared to give their fans what they wanted, returning to the stage to perform another set of songs.

Finally walking off stage for the last time, Logan grabbed my hand, leading me down the long narrow concrete corridors to the band's dressing room. Once we were all inside, Alan locked the door keeping the photographers and reporters outside to give the guys some much-needed privacy.

"Guys, that was one hell of a performance," Brian yelled.

"Yes, great show," Alan added, walking over to Logan.

"Congratulations, Logan, the fans loved you. I'm sure your performance will be covered tomorrow on the local news channels. You're becoming a huge celebrity. It's great publicity for the band."

"Where's Joyce? She didn't stay for the concert?" I inquired out of politeness.

"No. She came down with a terrible headache. I'm afraid the noise level was too loud, so she went back to the hotel."

"I'm sorry. I hope she feels better," I added.

Logan gave me a slight pinch as Alan walked away.

"Geez, Babe, really, you're suddenly concerned about Joyce. That's cute," Logan whispered.

"Logan, I was only trying to be gracious. Alan came over to congratulate you on your performance. You should be appreciative. Let's get something to eat. I'm starved." Immediately, I pulled Logan towards a delicious buffet prepared for the band and their crew. It offered a variety of hot and cold meats, along with hors-d'oeuvres and salads.

"Jade, Brian has reserved a gym for the guys tonight. We're going to play racquetball to relax. Do you want to tag along, or would you prefer the limo drop you back at the hotel?" Logan inquired, filling his plate with cold cuts.

"Let me ask Zoey if she's going? I'll be right back."

Spotting Zoey and Ethan, I walked over.

"Hey Zoe, Logan mentioned the guys are going to play racquetball later. Are you going?"

"Not a chance. I'm going back to the hotel. After all the walking we did today, I have a date with a comfortable bed. Why? Are you going?"

"I wanted to find out if you were before I committed to tagging along. However, going back to the hotel sounds great to me. I'm rather tired myself. I'll let Logan know, and he can arrange for the limo to drop us back at the hotel. Thanks, we'll meet up later."

Cutting back in line, I grabbed my plate from Logan. He'd filled it with everything imaginable.

"Geez, Logan, isn't that a bit much," I grimaced.

"Well, you've been eating a lot lately, and you just mentioned the fact you were starving."

"Thanks, but that's ridiculous. Honestly, it makes me somewhat nauseous just looking at it."

"What? Are you sick? One minute you're starving, and the next, you're nauseous. Oh my God, are you pregnant?" Logan replied rather loud, making a quick assumption."

"Logan, for heaven's sake, don't talk so loud. Do you really want everyone to overhear our personal issues?"

"We need to talk. Is there something you haven't told me?" Logan whispered with the hint of a gleam in his eyes.

"Logan, this isn't the time or place to discuss our personal life," I reiterated softly. "I don't know. I'm not sure. I mean, this is all happening way too fast."

"Jade, I'm not going to the gym with the guys. We have to talk."

"Yes. You are," I demanded, becoming emotional. "We'll talk later when you get back," I whispered, trying to hold back unexpected tears. What was wrong with me? Inconspicuously, I wiped my eyes.

Noticing my dilemma, Logan sat the plate down. Then, forgetting about food, he gently put his arm around me, leading me over to the sofa.

"Jade, are you alright?" he questioned discreetly, wiping my eyes. "Do you want to go?"

"No. I'm fine. You're going to the gym with the guys, and I'm going back to the hotel with Zoey. We'll talk about this later tonight. Now would you please get me something to drink before everyone notices, and maybe a few hor devours. I'm hungry."

"Geez, sweetheart, you've got me going in circles. First, you're starving, then suddenly you're nauseous, and now you're hungry," Logan looked perplexed. Then, staring at each other in a state of utter confusion and shock, unexpectedly, we burst out with laughter as people often do when baffled by something unexpected and unexplainable. However, we couldn't control our laughter, and it suddenly appeared we'd become the center of attention.

"What's so funny?" Ethan inquired loudly from across the room.

"Oh, nothing, just a private joke," Logan smiled, walking over to retrieve our food.

Later that evening, Logan left with the guys to play racquetball. Zoey, and I returned to the hotel.

Feeling rather tired as we entered the elevator, Zoey and I decided to part ways for the evening.

Unlocking the door to our suite, I quickly undressed and jumped into bed. Fortunately, it was only moments before I had fallen asleep. Waking several hours later with an urgent need to use the bathroom, I noticed it was 4:00 a.m., and Logan had not returned to the hotel. Panicking, I called Zoey.

"Hello," Zoe answered on the first ring.

"Zoe, I hate to bother you. Did Ethan get back from the gym?"

"Didn't Logan or one of the guys call you?"

"No. What's going on?"

"Well, it appears Logan injured his knee again. The guys are in the emergency room. Jade, he's okay, don't panic. He's probably facing a knee replacement soon, but we all knew that. Ethan said they should be back at the hotel within the next hour. Try to get some sleep. We'll talk in the morning."

"Okay. Thanks.

There was categorically no way I could go back to sleep until Logan came in, and I knew that he was alright. But, thank God, hearing the door open, I didn't have to wait long. Grabbing my robe, I walked out to the living room.

"Jade, why aren't you asleep?" Logan questioned as he limped inside on crutches wearing a knee brace.

"Because I was worried about you. Oh my God, what happened?"

"Well, to make a long story short, I was playing racquetball, and I guess I wasn't paying attention, and I fell. I hit the floor hard, and it didn't take much to injure my knee again."

"Are you okay?"

"Yes and no, I suppose. I'm okay for right now. Why don't we go into the bedroom? I want to take this stupid contraption off."

"Can I help you?"

"No. I can walk. Jade, the doctor scheduled me for knee replacement surgery next week," Logan explained, limping into the bedroom.

"That's really soon."

"I know," Logan explained, sitting on the side of the bed, removing his brace.

"I'll help you undress. We can talk once you're in bed."

"Okay. Thanks, Babe."

Finally getting Logan situated in a comfortable position under the warm, cozy comforter, he pulled me into the crevices of his arms. Okay, where do we start?" he mused with a grin. "I think we should finish our discussion from the dressing room before we move on to my injury." Then, pausing for a moment to collect his thoughts, he continued. "Sweetheart, I think the first question would be, are you pregnant?" he smiled, gently laying his hand on my belly.

"Oh, Logan, I don't know. I really don't, and I'm scared," I hesitated as tears flooded down my face. "What would you think if I were? Would you hate me?"

"Jade, it would make me the happiest guy on earth. Seriously, sweetheart, how could you possibly question my reaction. Please don't cry," Logan paused, kissing away my tears. "I'm not going anywhere. We're in this together for the long haul. Sweetheart, trust me, there's no reason to be scared. I'm right here. I'm not going anywhere," he reiterated. "I love you."

"Logan, I never expected this to happen. I'm only eighteen, and most people would say we were completely irresponsible and too young, especially my parents. They would probably disown me. Maybe in the future, I saw us with children, but not now, not while you're on tour," I sobbed uncontrollably.

"Jade, I don't give a damn what anyone thinks, especially your parents. You're the oldest, most responsible eighteen-year-old that I've ever known. I believe things like this happen for a reason when they are supposed to, and to be honest, I believe most babies are never planned. If you are pregnant, I consider it a miracle. It devastated me to know I lost my son, but the fact you're possibly carrying my baby has me ecstatic. The odds of this happening in such a short time are infinitesimal."

"Logan James, how did I ever get lucky enough to fall in love with you, not once, but twice. You're the best thing that ever happened to me. I love you more than you know. But, seriously, Babe, the oldest eighteen-year-old you've ever known. Really? Crying softly, my emotions completely consumed me.

"Jade, Sweetheart, I love you. That statement wasn't meant to be insulting. But, let me rephrase that, I think you're totally amazing and smarter than you realize. You're more than I could ever ask for, and you simply *complete me*, quoting the famous line by Bridget Jones," Logan winked. "You have no idea how lost I felt leaving you behind when I went on tour with the band. I missed you more than you could ever imagine," Logan smiled, continuing to kiss away each tear. "I suggest we purchase a pregnancy test first thing tomorrow," Logan winked.

"Logan, you always manage to keep me sane when I'm emotional and falling apart. Did I tell you how lucky I am that you belong to me?"

"Yes. I believe you did, but no worries. Babe, you can remind me every day for the rest of our lives," Logan beamed, pulling me even closer. "Now, getting back to my knee injury, Alan and Brian have decided to cancel our next concert in Miami. It was the last venue on this tour. Instead, the doctors have scheduled my knee replacement surgery for next week in Hawaii. Alan owns several properties in Hawaii, and he thinks it would be the ideal place for me to recuperate. One of his properties has a large recording studio, and the band and I will record a new album while I recover. So, we leave for Hawaii tomorrow evening. I'm sorry things are unexpectedly moving fast right now. But, you can deal with it, right?" he worried.

"Yes, as long as we're together, that's all that matters to me," I assured him. Then, snuggled securely in the safety of Logan's arms, I fell asleep.

Waking up late the following day to the smell of bacon and eggs, it immediately sent me running in the direction of the bathroom. Evidently, the smell of fried bacon no longer agreed with me. Once again, I found myself kneeling before the porcelain throne, retching violently.

"Oh my God, Jade, what can I do?" Logan inquired, hurriedly limping into the bathroom on his bum knee. Quickly warming a wet washcloth, he gently wiped my face pulling back strands of my long hair. "Wow, Sweetheart, I'm sorry. We're quite the pair, I can't walk, and the smell of food makes you sick," Logan laughed.

"Babe, that's not funny. The smell of bacon is making me extremely nauseous. Please, don't leave me."

"Jade, I'm not leaving, but I thought you loved bacon."

"I do. But not this morning," I smiled, staring at Logan's worried expression. "I'm okay. Did you order orange juice?" I asked frantically, gaining enough strength to stand.

"Yes. I'll get you a glass, but first, let's get you into bed."

"Thanks, but all I want is a warm shower. Aren't we leaving for Hawaii later this evening?"

"Yes. If you feel well enough to travel."

"Just give me an hour or so to rest and get past this episode of feeling queasy." Apparently, I had slept the entire afternoon. Then, it was time to shower and dress.

Standing under the warm water, it felt heavenly. I smiled, knowing Logan was definitely in the game. I knew he would stick regardless of whether I was or wasn't pregnant. However, I was unaware that we would have our answer sooner than I expected.

Stepping out of the shower, Logan handed me a soft luxurious robe. Wrapping my damp hair inside the towel, I walked out to the living area. Sitting down on the sofa, I laughed. There were three pregnancy test kits on the coffee table. Unbelievably, Logan had left to purchase three test kits while I was sleeping.

"Geez, Logan, don't you think three kits are a bit obsessive?" I teased with a huge smile.

"No. We need to know. It's important. Why are you waiting? Aren't you going to take the test?"

"Oh my gosh, Logan, calm down. You're hilarious. Yes. However, it only takes one test kit," I teased. "Okay. Wait here."

Returning to the bathroom, I followed the instructions on the kit and waited for the results. Finally, after what felt like an eternity, I saw the results.

Slowly walking out to the living room with the results in my hand, I curled up in Logan's lap. Then, lovingly, I whispered the results in his ear.

"I'm pregnant."

"Oh my God, Babe, I knew it. I just knew it," Logan beamed with excitement. "Wow, I'm going to be a father," he exclaimed with tears welling in his eyes. "Knowing that I lost my son, this means everything to me. Everything," he added. "You have no idea."

"Logan, I'm relieved to know the baby means so much to you. I'm excited. Let's not tell anyone right now. Let's wait for a couple of weeks. Is that okay?"

"Yes. It's just between the two of us," Logan winked with a huge smile. "What about the other tests? Aren't you going to take those too?"

"Geez, Logan, that's a bit OCD," I laughed.

We had our answer. Despite the fact, Logan had received shocking news from Kelsey and was facing knee surgery, our world couldn't have been more perfect.

Later that evening, as the jet lifted from the runway, the view from my window was extraordinary. Grasping Logan's hand, the National Mall was spectacularly lit and stood out in a vast skyline of city lights. Instantly, memories of our visit the day before invaded my mind. The past twenty-four hours had been life-changing. I knew as a couple we'd grown stronger since arriving in Washington. It had been both cathartic and exuberating. Staring at my handsome rock star, who was seated next to me, tears welled within my eyes. I finally knew my decision to leave home had been the right choice. Now, we were en route to Hawaii with a short stop in Los Angeles.

Chapter Eight

California

Arriving in Los Angeles, Alan had scheduled a short layover in the City of Angeles before our final destination, Oahu. Once again, we had reservations at the prestigious Westin Hotel, where my journey with Logan and the band began. It had only been six short months since our first night together. The band had performed in more than twelve major cities. Unfortunately, for the sake of brevity, I've only covered the most memorable venues.

I was no longer the naive young girl who made life-altering decisions during her previous stay. Instead, I returned as a mature woman whose changing body carried within it a new life.

"Guys, it's only an overnight stop," Brian reminded everyone as he lounged back in the limo. "We leave tomorrow morning. I know a few of you have family in the immediate area. If you plan to stay with them tonight and don't require a suite at the Westin, please let me know," Brian inquired as the limo slowly made its way through heavy traffic.

"Oh, hell, no, I'm not staying with my parents," Jarrod immediately interjected. "Reserve me a suite."

"Yes, me too," Noah added. "I have a date tonight."

"Sorry, dad, I'm not going home either," Zoey smirked, looking at

Alan. "I'm staying at the Westin with Ethan. Please let mom know. I'll call her later."

"Geez, none of you plan to see your family? Just a reminder, we're in the final stages of arranging the Pacific Rim Tour. The probability exists that we may not be stateside after Oahu for a long time. Anyone wanting to change their minds, and stay with family, speak up," Brian added.

Three resounding no's made it quite clear the entire band was once again staying at the Westin Hotel.

After an hour of the worst traffic possible, one of the few disadvantages of being in Los Angeles, the limo parked under the grand entrance of the Westin Hotel. Anxious to stretch our legs, everyone exited the limo in a rush. Hurriedly making our way into the impressive upscale lobby, we picked up room keys and scattered in the direction of our suites.

"We leave tomorrow at 10:00 a.m. sharp. So don't be late," Brian warned loudly as the guys quickly dispersed.

Entering the elevator just before the door closed, Zoey and Ethan crowded inside along with me, Noah and Jarrod. Squeezing in next to me, Zoey smiled.

"Hey guys, it's Friday night. Ethan and I are going to the Avalon. Who wants to go?" Zoey asked. "Jade, you and Logan have to come. It'll be a blast."

"Thanks, but I'm sorta tired. I feel like staying in tonight, and I'm not sure it's a good idea with Logan's bum knee. He's still facing surgery."

"Thanks for asking, but I have a date," Noah smiled.

"Sorry. I've got plans too," Jarrod mentioned. "Maybe next time we're in Los Angeles."

"Geez, guys, you're all a bunch of losers."

"Really, Zoe, you're calling these guys losers. You don't know them," Logan roared.

"Sorry, Zoe, we're only here for one night, and unfortunately, we've all got plans," Jarrod interrupted.

"Seriously? "Zoey questioned. "What kind of plans do you have?"

"Well, let's just say they're not open for discussion," Jarrod laughed, stepping out of the elevator as it reached his floor.

"See ya tomorrow, and stay out of trouble," Logan smirked.

"Right."

"I wonder what he's up to?" Ethan asked curiously as the elevator continued its ascent.

"Who knows?" Logan surmised.

"Well, this is our stop," Ethan announced, grabbing Zoey's hand.

"Mine too," Noah added as they all exited the elevator.

"Wow, Babe looks like we're on our own for the night," Logan smiled as the door closed. "Come over here, little momma, and give daddy a kiss."

"Geez, Logan, I'm sorry. But, honestly, I do feel like a loser."

"Really, well, maybe this will help."

Pulling me into his strong, buffed arms, Logan kissed me with such passion, it easily took my breath away. A sudden intense feeling of euphoria swept over my entire body rendering me helpless. Snuggled against his warm, athletic body, I melted into his arms as he drew me closer.

Reaching our stop, Logan gave no thought regarding his bum knee. Instead, he unexpectedly lifted me into his arms and carried me the short distance to our suite. Unlocking the door, he held me in his arms as he quickly hung the *do not disturb* sign. I'm sure Logan was afraid Ethan would make another impromptu visit or one of the other bandmates. Continuing inside, he carried me to the bedroom, gently laying me on top of the soft duvet.

"Sweetheart, don't ever think you're unimportant," he whispered, slowly unbuttoning my blouse. "I love you. You're carrying our baby. A million nights at the Avalon could never compare to what we have."

Turning out the lights, Logan slipped me beneath the warm covers, pulling me next to him. Feeling the warmth of his touch, suddenly, my mind went blank. Any remaining thoughts of a night at the Avalon vanished with each kiss. I was entirely where I wanted to be. With each caress, I fell further under the spell of Logan James. It was sheer ecstasy. The bond of love shared between us this night would haunt my dreams forever.

Waking the following day, it felt surreal. Turning over in bed to stare at the love of my life, I smiled. As a bad boy, rock star, his appearance on stage was utterly deceiving, and I couldn't resist kissing him awake.

Smothering him with kisses, he slowly opened his smoldering blue eyes.

"Wow, Babe, what a night," he winked wickedly.

"Yes. It was unbelievable. I love you," I replied, with tears welling within my eyes. Suddenly, I became too emotional for words.

"Sweetheart, I love you too, but what's up with the waterworks? Your emotions seem to be all over the place. I hope you're not going to cry for the next nine months," Logan teased, wiping away my tears. "Jade, I love you. How do you feel about breakfast? Are you hungry? I'm starved."

"No bacon. I don't want to take any chances. We have a flight this morning. So maybe a piece of toast with a soft boiled egg and juice would work."

"That sounds good. I'm going to jump in the shower, and then I'll order breakfast. Want to join me?"

"Funny. Thanks for the offer, but I think I might stay in bed for a while."

"Suit yourself," Logan grinned.

Later that morning, after breakfast, I managed to get dressed without getting nauseous. Finally, it was almost time to meet everyone in the lobby.

"Hey, Jade, did you want to call your parents before we leave Los Angeles?" Logan inquired loudly from the other room.

"No. I hope that doesn't sound terrible."

"Not at all. I completely understand."

Taking my time, I put on makeup and curled my hair. Then, dressing in a black pencil skirt, with a white silk blouse and black flats, I walked into the living room.

"Wow, Sweetheart, you look stunning. But, of course, no one would ever suspect you're pregnant," Logan winked, giving me a quick kiss.

"Geez, thanks, I guess."

Truth be known, I wanted the entire world to see that I was pregnant with Logan's baby. However, I knew he was right. His position with the band was important, and the fact we were expecting would eventually affect those around us. Our secret was best kept between the two of us for the moment.

Closing the door, we made our way over to the elevator. We were finally on our way down to the lobby to meet the guys and Zoey. Alan and Brian had arranged to meet us at the airport.

"Did you have fun last night?" I asked, rushing over to catch up with Zoey as I stepped out of the elevator.

"Yes, but it would have been much better if you both had joined us. So," Zoe paused. "Did you guys stay in, as you mentioned? That couldn't have been much fun."

"Oh, I don't know about that. I guess it would depend upon your definition of fun," Logan winked, overhearing our conversation as he walked over.

"Geez, Logan, really," I frowned, giving him a hard inconspicuous pinch. "That's personal," I whispered.

"Damn, Babe, we're all adults here."

"Well, at least some of us were having sex last night?" Noah interjected, joining the conversation. "My date called to cancel at the last minute."

"That's too bad. What happened?" Ethan asked.

"I don't know? She didn't offer an explanation other than something came up."

"Hell, that's pretty rude. I hope you deleted her contact info from your phone."

"Definitely."

"Hey, bro, how was your evening?" Noah inquired as Jarrod joined the group.

"Not bad, but I'm ready to get the hell out of Los Angeles."

"Really, what's that supposed to mean?"

"As I said before, it's not open for discussion."

"Wow, I guess it's safe to say we're ready for a change of scenery. So let's go. The limo is here," Logan announced, taking my hand.

Entering the car, the guys immediately opened a bottle of Jameson and passed it around.

"Here's to leaving Los Angeles," Noah toasted.

"I'll drink to that," Jarrod agreed.

"Damn, Babe, out of our entire group, I think we had the most fun last night, and we didn't leave our room," Logan whispered in my ear.

"That's because I was with you," I smiled.

Traffic was light for a Saturday morning as we reached the airport right on schedule.

"Welcome aboard. Glad everyone made it. Now, let's get this jet in the air," Brian grinned.

"Hey, dad," Zoey smiled, walking past Alan.

"Hey, Sweetheart, your mom and sister missed you last night."

"I'll call them from Hawaii."

Walking toward the back of the plane, Logan and I sat in the last row. I wasn't entirely sure my old friend, nausea, wouldn't return, and I wanted to be close to the bathroom without everyone noticing.

Buckling my seat belt, I leaned my head against Logan's broad shoulders as the Lear Jet taxied down the runway. Suddenly, as the plane lifted skyward, I gently caressed my tummy. We were on our way to Hawaii with an extra passenger on board.

Chapter Nine

Hawaii

Having slept most of the flight, Logan lovingly kissed me awake as the jet began its approach into the international airport in Honolulu.

"Hey, sleepyhead, I hate to wake you, but we're only a few minutes out from the airport. Do you want a warm towel?"

"Yes. I'm sorry. I must have slept the entire flight. I felt extremely exhausted," I answered, wiping the sleep from my eyes.

"Jade, it's okay. I think we both know the reason," Logan whispered, getting up to stretch his long legs, which were cramped from the flight.

Returning with a warm towel, he softly wiped my face. It felt refreshing.

"Thanks, Babe."

"Guys, before we land, I'd like to have your attention for just a moment," Alan stated. "I want to give you a brief explanation regarding your accommodations during our stay in Hawaii. As most of you know, I own several properties on the north shore of Oahu. I've had three of them vacated for your use. Brian and I are going to occupy the main property. It contains my favorite recording studio. There are three bungalows in the immediate vicinity. You'll be happy to know they're all beachfront properties. Logan and Jade will occupy the first unit closer to the main house. It'll be easily accessible to the recording studio while Logan is recuperating. The second bungalow will house Ethan and Zoey, and finally, the third unit is reserved for Jarrod and Noah. I think some of you surf, so you'll be happy to know our location is just south of Sunset Beach on Hoalua Street. I'm sure you'll find the accommodations to your liking. We even have a personal chef available. I'll go over more details regarding our time in Hawaii later. First and foremost, we're all here to get Logan through his knee replacement and record our third album. Oh, I forgot to mention the north shore is holding their annual surfing competitions at the end of the month. So October is the perfect month to be in Oahu. Do any of you have questions?"

Not hearing any response, he took his seat. "Great. We should be on the ground soon," Alan smiled.

"Wow, Logan, Alan is actually vacating his properties for you and the guys. I've been to Hawaii more times than I care to count, and those properties aren't cheap. So the fact he's doing that for you and the band is amazing," I whispered.

"I know. Alan's a great guy. Let's just hope I survive the surgery."

"Damn, Logan, what a thing to say. How's that supposed to make me feel? Really?"

"I'm sorry. I guess the fact that we're here now makes it more real. I'm a little nervous."

"Babe, you've got this. Trust me. You're going to be just fine. I promise."

As the jet touched down on the runway, Logan shifted in his seat. "Our arrival made him nervous. It brought home the realness of his upcoming surgery.

"Don't be worried. I'm here with you. Besides, you have a little girl just waiting to meet her daddy," I whispered. "The surgery will be behind you in no time at all, and you'll be recuperating while recording a new album. That has to be exciting," I mentioned.

"Sweetheart, you just said a little girl," Logan curiously whispered. "Do you know something I don't?"

"No. Don't be silly. It's just a hunch. It's way too early to know if the baby is a girl or boy."

"It doesn't matter. I'm already in love," Logan smiled, gently laying his hand over my tummy.

As the plane taxied across the tarmac, the guys began collecting their carry-on items.

Parking next to the waiting limo, everyone quickly exited the jet.

"Wow, feels good to stretch my legs," Jarrod commented. "I can't wait to pick up a surfboard and get in the water."

"Yeah, me too," Noah agreed. "Geez, sorry, Logan, you won't be getting in much surfing," he frowned, staring at Logan's knee. "That's too bad."

"Don't count me out. Hopefully, the recovery time won't take that long."

After everyone was comfortably seated inside the limo, Brian popped the cork from a bottle of Moet & Chandon Champagne. Filling each of us a glass, I politely passed, trying not to become the focus of attention.

"Here's to a successful surgery and the completion of our third album," Brian toasted. *"May we all live long and prosper,"* Brian grinned, quoting his favorite character, Spock from Star Trek.

"Yes," Alan toasted.

"You're not drinking champagne?" Zoey questioned.

"No. I have a slight headache." But, of course, I should have expected Zoey to be the one person who noticed.

"You guys are going to love the bungalows. They're my favorite units on the property and have the best views of Coconut Beach," Zoey mentioned.

"I'm sure. I can't wait to see them."

The traffic through downtown Honolulu easily rivaled Los Angeles. We were traveling at a snail's pace when suddenly, out of nowhere, I could feel the onset of queasiness.

"Oh my God, Logan, I think I'm going to be sick," I whispered.

"Can you wait until we reach the north shore?" Logan worriedly asked in a faint whisper

"I'm not sure. The traffic is hardly moving. But, Logan, we have to stop. I can't wait," I abruptly insisted. "I'm going to be sick."

"Hey, Brian, Jade is feeling a little under the weather, motion sickness. We need to make a pit stop."

"I'm sorry. Is there anything I can do?" Brian inquired, oblivious to everything around him as the limo continued toward its destination.

I was becoming more nauseous by the second.

"Logan, I'm going to throw up."

"Stop the damn car. Now," Logan demanded somewhat abrasively. "Sorry."

Immediately, Brian instructed the driver to exit the freeway at the nearest gas station. Fortunately, it was only minutes before the limo parked near a Chevron Station, which included a convenience store.

"What's wrong?" Zoey questioned.

"Jade feels a little car sick. That's all," Logan responded, taking control of the situation as I got up from my seat and bolted for the ladies room.

"Not another person leaves this car," I overheard Alan vehemently warn everyone as I exited the limo.

"Oh, hell," Logan remarked, ignoring Alan's threat as he ran after me, sprinting for the ladies room.

Without a word, Zoey opened the car door. Then, also disregarding her dad's warning, she exited the limo and followed us in quick pursuit.

Reaching the bathroom, it was unlocked. Logan didn't hesitate to follow me inside. Quickly locking the door behind us, Logan hurriedly lifted the lid as bouts of vomiting overtook me. Retching profusely for a few minutes, it finally subsided. Turning on the water at the sink, Logan wet a paper towel and wiped my face. It was then I began to hear loud knocks on the door.

"Jade, for heaven's sake, what's going on?" Zoey demanded.

Finally, opening the bathroom door, Zoey was waiting for answers.

But, unfortunately, despite being my best friend and concerned, I was not ready to explain my sudden onset of sickness.

"Geez, can't a girl have a moment?" I frowned.

Noticing the expression on Zoey's face, I knew she was going to press me for details. I desperately needed Logan to play offensive tackle because I wasn't ready to discuss my personal life with Zoey. Pulling me towards him, Logan glanced at Zoey, imploring her not to utter another word. Then, he shielded me inside his arms as we slowly walked back to the limo.

"Jade, we need to talk," Zoey stated, refusing to take Logan's demeanor seriously.

Entering the limo, it appeared the guys barely noticed the entire incident. However, Alan gave Logan the once-over stare as we lounged back in our seats. It was all too easy to read Alan's mind. I instantly felt he didn't believe the car sickness fabrication for one second, precisely as Zoey. Geez, they were both alike. However, they were both civil enough to respect the fact it wasn't the right time or place to interrogate either of us.

"Sweetheart, are you feeling better?" Logan whispered, pulling me closer.

"Yes. I'm sorry we had to make an unexpected stop."

"Jade, you have no reason to apologize. We're in this together, don't ever forget that. I love you," Logan lovingly reminded me with a soft kiss on my forehead.

"Thanks for taking care of the situation with Zoey."

"No thanks needed, but I'm not sure I did you any favors. We both know Zoey, and you know she's just waiting for the perfect moment to corner you."

"Oh, I know, but thanks for buying me some time," I whispered, gently caressing his day's growth of stubble.

As the limo once again entered the freeway, the traffic was moving a lot faster. Falling asleep in Logan's arms, I didn't have long to rest as it took less than an hour to reach the north shore of Oahu.

The limo made a sudden turn off the highway as Logan gently

woke me from my slumber. Sitting up, I hurriedly grabbed my purse reaching inside for a compact to check my hair. Using my fingers, I brushed back my long curls. It was pointless to retouch my makeup in the car as we were almost at our destination.

The resort was paradise at its best. It was exquisite. Knowing Alan, it was nothing less than I expected. Elegant wrought iron gates opened to allow us access to a short drive that curved towards the beach. The grounds were manicured to perfection. It was a landscaper's dream. Tall Queen Palms lined each side of the paved driveway and were stylishly lit to enhance their majestic appearance. The visible glow of Tikki torches could be seen scattered throughout the grounds giving the resort a Polynesian presence. Alan had undoubtedly picked the perfect location for Logan to recuperate from his knee surgery. Even the security was a well-planned execution. Reporters and paparazzi would be contained behind the gated entrance once the news leaked out the band was staying at Alan's posh resort.

The limo parked under a tall, uniquely carved wooden portico that featured oversized wrought-iron lanterns, which glowed brilliantly as they hung from the timbered rafters. Large etched glass doors welcomed you inside the sprawling estate.

"Wow, the execution of the design is to perfection," I whispered to Logan as we stepped out of the limo.

Entering through the double glass doors, the interior of Alan's home beautifully reflected its outer appearance. The sound of trickling water bubbled from large colorful ceramic pots which sat on each side of the entrance giving it a tranquil, relaxing atmosphere. Captivating views of the beach and turquoise waters of the Pacific Ocean were visible through a wall of glass sliding panels that surrounded the back of the living area.

"Welcome," Alan proudly beamed. "I think you'll be quite comfortable here. The bungalows are architecturally built to reflect the main house on a smaller scale. I have golf carts parked out front for your use. I think you'll find them convenient in getting back and forth to the main house. If you need anything, please ask, and if I'm not available, Zoey can help. I have staff available twenty-four hours if you need anything other than what Zoey or I can do for you. Oh, Logan, when you're released from the hospital, I've arranged a full-time nursing staff to be available. Also, as soon as you're mobile and cleared to exercise, I've contacted personal trainers to help with your rehabilitation. We'll talk more about that later. Here are the keys to the bungalows. I'll let Zoey take it from here. I'm sure she'll be delighted to show you your accommodations. I've got a few things to do that require my attention. Please make yourselves at home. Zoey and I are happy to have you staying with us. Oh, one last thing, I think you'll be excited to know we offer on-site, twenty-four-hour food service. Just call the main kitchen, let the staff have your order, and deliveries can either be sent to your unit or picked up. Each of you has my cell number. Use it wisely," Alan laughed.

"Zoey, I would like to freshen up a bit. Do you mind taking Logan and me to our bungalow?" I asked.

"Sure, just a minute. I need to get the keys to the golf carts. Ethan, why don't all of you tag along, and I can show everyone around the complex at the same time."

"Sounds good," Jarrod agreed.

"Why don't each of you drive separate carts? That way, you can park them at your bungalow," Zoey suggested.

Following behind Zoey in our cart, Logan and I were the first stop.

"I hope you'll both be very comfortable. I'll leave you two. Call me later."

Watching as Zoey continued down the paved driveway with the guys, Logan unlocked our door.

"Wow, Alan wasn't kidding when he said the bungalows were well-designed. This place could easily rate five stars in the tourist industry."

"No kidding," I laughed. "And we're so close to the beach."

Walking inside the bungalow, it had high timbered ceilings. Transverse beams were exposed to the rooms below. The large living area was well appointed with Asian-inspired furniture. Off to one end of the room, an ornate credenza held a huge bouquet of fresh flowers.

"Geez, this is gorgeous," Logan exclaimed. "Let's check out the bedroom."

Taking my hand, he led me into the primary bedroom adjacent to the living room. Its décor was completely upscale Polynesian. It contained a dark mahogany king-size four-poster bed and a sliding glass panel. If opened, it would allow in the cool ocean breeze. From the comfort of the massive bed, you could remotely open the blackout curtains to reveal a panoramic view of the Pacific Ocean with its sparkling turquoise water and sandy beach.

"I think we'll be quite comfortable sleeping in here. This room is amazing," I mentioned sitting on the huge bed. Then, grabbing Logan's hand, I pulled him down next to me.

"Babe, I suggest we check out the master bath. If you don't get up right now, you might find yourself stuck in bed for the rest of the night."

"Oh, is that a threat, Mr. James?" I teased.

"No. It's a given."

Following Logan into the main bathroom, it was beyond belief with a steam shower that could easily hold four people.

"Wow, I never expected that," Logan laughed.

Continuing our tour, we checked out the small compact kitchen, which was located next to the living area. Unexpectedly, the fridge was fully stocked.

"Geez, Alan doesn't skimp on his hospitality. We have milk, wine, beer, soda, cold cuts, and dairy items," Logan detailed. "I think you could use a cold glass of milk."

"Yikes, Logan, I hate milk. Is there any juice?"

"No. However, I can call over to the kitchen if you insist."

"Oh, I guess I'll have milk, but just this once."

"Hey, you're carrying our baby. I think you could use a glass of milk," Logan smiled. "Of course, I'm going to enjoy a beer."

"I'm going to freshen up. After the incident at the gas station, I need to get a shower and change clothes." Forgetting about the glass of milk that Logan poured, I walked to the bathroom.

Turning on the warm water, it felt invigorating. Deciding to wash my hair, I reached for the shampoo. Closing my eyes, I worked the shampoo into a rich lather. Suddenly, I heard Logan's voice.

"You forgot your milk."

"Really, Logan, enough with the milk."

Unexpectedly, I felt his hand's caressing my scalp.

"Let me help," he whispered.

"Logan, I think I'm capable of shampooing my hair."

Pulling me into his arms, I was no match against his charm and sexy wit. Taking the initiative, I gently held his face kissing him with every ounce of passion I had within me.

"Damn, Babe, you're my kind of woman," Logan whispered. Needless to say, the shower instantly became hot and steamy, and it had nothing at all to do with the fact it was technically a steam shower.

Dressing in luxurious white bathrobes, Logan walked into the kitchen while I unpacked my toiletries.

"What would you like to do this evening?" Logan asked, taking another beer from the fridge.

"Who says we have to do anything?" I smiled, walking out of the bathroom with my damp hair wrapped in a matching turban. Lounging back on the sofa with his drink, Logan motioned me to join him.

"Why don't we take a walk on the beach after dinner?" I suggested curling up next to him.

Gently pulling me into his buffed tattooed arms," Logan playfully bit my ear. "Are you hungry? We have a kitchen. I can cook."

"Really? What's your specialty?"

"Spaghetti."

"Geez, Logan, that only requires boiling water," I teased.

"Awe, but you haven't tasted the sauce."

"Why don't we just order food tonight? I'm craving burgers and fries."

"Really, Babe, burgers again."

"Would you mind?"

"Sweetheart, if you're craving burgers and french fries, it's fine with me. I would never deny you anything. You're carrying our little girl. I love you," Logan smiled, gently laying his hand over my tummy.

As Alan recommended, calling in our order, it arrived in less than an hour. The burgers were surprisingly delicious. They easily rivaled the best gourmet burgers we had previously eaten on tour. Watching as I once again buried my fries under tons of ketchup, Logan laughed.

"Maybe I should buy stock in Heinz," he teased.

After gorging myself, I began to feel exhausted. Unable to keep my eyes open, Logan noticed my dilemma. Scooping me into his arms, he carried me into the bedroom. He pulled back the warm covers and gently removed the turban, allowing my long blonde curls to fall loosely around my shoulders. Untying my robe, Logan gently slipped me under the covers.

"Sweetheart, I love you," he whispered, kissing me on the cheek. Then, closing the blackout curtains, the room instantly darkened.

The next thing I remembered was waking up hours later. Tying my robe, I walked into the living room. Logan was sitting on the sofa in the dark. He was completely dressed with a lit cigarette in one hand and a glass of wine in the other. Noticing his somber appearance, I knew instantly he was worried about his upcoming surgery.

"Hey, sleepyhead. Did you get some rest?

"Yes," I smiled, walking over to sit on his lap. "I think you promised me a walk on the beach. Remember," I asked, running my fingers through his silky blond locks.

"Yes, but unfortunately, I'm afraid it's dark outside. Do you still want to go?" Logan asked, putting out his smoke.

"Of course. Sorry, I overslept."

"Babe, remember what I said, no apologies," he smiled, finishing his glass of wine. "Well, I think someone needs to get dressed," Logan grinned, untying my robe.

"Logan, stop. We're going for a walk. I'll be right back."

Quickly returning to the bedroom, I put on a pair of trendy gray sweatpants and a matching sweatshirt. Styling my hair into a ponytail, I found a pair of gym shoes. Walking back out to the living room, I retrieved my handsome guy. Pulling him up from the couch, we locked the door and walked down to the beach. The night sky was covered in an abundance of twinkling stars.

"Wow, this is incredibly romantic," I smiled, fixated at the starry brilliance overhead. But, snuggling against Logan as we strolled along the balmy shore, I could sense the dread and worry which radiated from his body.

"Jade, if I were unable to perform on stage again, I'm not sure what I would do. But, unfortunately, it's my life."

"Logan, I know you're worried, and I know it's considered major surgery, but it's a common procedure. Alan is going to ensure that you have the best possible surgeons. This is nonsense. Babe, I love you, but honestly, I think you're over-dramatizing this just a bit," I laughed, stopping to kiss him. "Really, Logan, you surprise me. Do you even know how many fans you have? How many people love you? Remember the young girl at the St. Louis Arch. Sweetheart, you're going to come through this with flying colors. We're all counting on you—no more silliness. Our little girl is just waiting to meet her daddy. She's going to be your biggest fan, and she's going to need both of us in her life. Little girls idolize their daddies. I love you, and I'm going to be right by your side. Now, stop your pity party. It's not going to work. Not with me, I won't allow it."

"Sweetheart, how did I ever get so lucky to find you for the second time."

"Aww, I think I found you the second time, or have you forgotten the concert in Los Angeles? Logan, all that matters is that we're together."

"Jade, did you idolize your dad?"

"Logan, where did that come from?"

"Well, you just said all little girls idolize their dads. Did you?"

"Really? I can't go there. My dad is one of the reasons I left home. It's too raw and emotional for me right now. I can't talk about it. Perhaps one day," I answered as tears welled within my eyes. "I'm getting cold. Can we walk back to the bungalow?"

"Of course. I'm sorry I brought it up. I love you."

Logan kept me warm as we slowly walked back, putting his arms around me. Then, suddenly, he kissed me with such intensity, heat radiated throughout my chilled body.

"Jade, know one thing, we'll be better parents. I promise."

Hearing a knock at the door the following morning, Logan walked over.

"Logan, I need to steal a few minutes of your time," Alan grinned. "Why don't you ride with me over to the main house. We need to talk."

"Just a moment, I need to let Jade know," Logan replied curiously.

"Hey Babe, it's Alan. I'm going over to the main house. It won't take long, I promise."

"Okay."

-Alan's office-

"Reaching the main house, we walked inside the stunning foyer, and I followed Alan into his private office. After pouring us a shot of Blanton's Bourbon, he proceeded with his lecture.

"Logan, I wanted to speak with you last night, but things came up which required my attention," Alan stated, handing me a drink as he reclined in his high back leather chair. His tempered expression was cause for alarm as he slowly took sips of his drink. "I've been managing Riot Storm for many years. My policy has always been not to involve myself in your personal lives. However, I've always said if your problems affect the band at any time, then your problems become my problems. So, I'm going to be blunt. Is Jade pregnant?" Alan questioned, giving me his famous once-over stare as he took another slow sip of bourbon.

"Yes. I won't lie. I respect you."

"So, Zoey was right," Alan mentioned pouring us another shot. "She suspected Jade was pregnant."

"Wow, Zoey, really, Alan. I know she's your daughter, but hell, when did my personal life become a topic of your conversation. Damn, Alan, I had more respect for you than this."

Becoming too agitated to stay in my seat, I took my drink and began pacing the floor. "You know this is going to cause problems between Jade and Zoey," I fumed, fumbling for my cigarettes.

"Logan, the fact is, it doesn't matter. I had a hunch when Jade suddenly got sick in the limo yesterday. Sit down. You're not the first guy on earth to get a girl pregnant. However, Jade's parents are close personal friends, and she's my Goddaughter, which changes things. You've just totally involved me in your private life. Logan, I've always felt you were my greatest asset in regards to Riot Storm. The band works because of you."

"Goddaughter? Hell Alan, how was I supposed to know? Not that it would have changed anything. Damn, I've been in love with Jade since high school, and furthermore, it's our business. We're excited about the possibilities. I don't know what else to tell you."

"First of all, calm down. Congratulations. Do Charles and Amanda know?" Alan laughed, reaching for the bottle of Blanton's Bourbon. Pouring himself another shot, he once again lounged back. A huge grin slowly crept across his face. My God, Charles is going to be a grandfather," he mused.

"No. I'm leaving that up to Jade. I feel it's her parents, and it should be her decision." Sitting down, I reached for an ashtray putting out my cigarette. Once again, I downed my entire drink in one continuous gulp.

"Care for another?" Alan questioned, reaching for the bottle of Blanton's.

"No. I'm good."

"Here's the band's schedule for the next twelve months. First and foremost, your recovery from knee replacement surgery is paramount. We finish our third album before leaving Hawaii. In December, we open our Pacific Rim tour in Japan immediately afterward. Unfortunately, this tour will require a lot of travel, and it's going to be extremely exhausting. My question would be to know if Jade will accompany you or would she be going home to stay until the baby is born? We've never had a baby on tour. I'm in unchartered waters."

"There's no way in hell I'm leaving Jade behind. She's carrying my baby, and she goes with me. Her staying with her parents until the baby is born is totally out of the question. That will never happen, never," I reiterated, sitting back in my chair as I reached for my cigarettes and lighter. "You know Charles and Amanda, and you honestly think I'm going to let them anywhere near Jade again or our baby. Hell, I'm sure Zoey has filled you in on Jade's life. I'm sorry, I know you're friends with Amanda and Charles. But you can't sit here and tell me you're unaware that Amanda is an alcoholic and Charles is never home," I vented, lighting another cigarette. "So, Alan, let's get to the point. What's the real issue here? Is my position with the band in jeopardy? Are you saying that Jade can't come on tour?" I questioned, lounging back in my chair, waiting for Alan's response.

"Logan, relax. I never said your position with the band was at risk or even the fact that Jade couldn't accompany you," Alan stated, pouring himself another shot of bourbon. "I only referenced the fact this is going to put a new spin on things. As long as you're on stage every night, Brian and I will handle the logistics," Alan explained, suddenly glancing at his watch. "Sorry, I've got to run. I'm late for another meeting. We'll talk later. Everything is going to work out. No worries." With that being said, Alan tossed back his drink. Hurriedly reaching for his briefcase, he headed for the door.

"Well, let's just hope everything is fine between Jade and Zoey," I snapped angrily.

"Gotta run, the girls will figure this out. Congratulations."

Taking one of the golf carts back to the bungalow, I dreaded letting Jade know that Zoey had gone to Alan with her suspicions. The fact that Zoey didn't respect Jade enough to come to her first would be a huge point of contention between them.

Walking in, Jade was in the bathroom drying her hair. Deciding to wait until she finished styling her hair, I grabbed a beer from the fridge and reclined on the sofa. It was only a few minutes before Jade walked into the living room.

"Hey Babe, I didn't know you were back?

"Wow, you look stunning. Sweetheart, come over here. We need to talk."

"Geez, this sounds ominous."

Walking over, I curled up on Logan's lap. Whatever was on his mind, I knew we could soldier through it.

"Jade, I didn't know you were Alan's Goddaughter?"

"Yes. How did you find out?"

"Oh, Alan mentioned it."

"It's no big deal. Alan and Joyce are good friends of my parents. Now, get on with it. What did Alan want to talk about?"

"He point-blank asked if you were pregnant?"

"Oh my God, what did you tell him?"

"The truth, you can't lie to Alan. Trust me, lying to him would only have made things worse."

"Wow, there's no way on earth he could have even suspected. Was it Zoey?"

"Yes. How did you know?"

"Oh, I didn't. However, knowing Zoe, I was afraid she might have suspected and mentioned the fact to her dad. They are close, and I failed to talk to her after following us to the bathroom. I knew she was concerned, but we had just arrived, and I hadn't had time to fill her in on everything. I'm sorry. Did it cause problems for you?"

"Not really. Knowing Alan, I knew this conversation was coming sooner or later. I think he just wanted to give me a hard time. However, learning that Zoey sort of instigated this whole thing, I thought you would be extremely upset with her."

"Logan, Zoe is the sister I never had. Of course, I think she should have come to me first, but I'm not mad. Let's face it. Alan was going to find out eventually. So, perhaps, this worked out for the best."

"Well, I kinda lost it when Alan told me Zoey had come to him without talking to us first. Sorry, I don't know her as well as you, and I felt betrayed."

"Don't worry. I'll call Zoey later this evening. Everything is going to be alright. So, tell me, how did the conversation go with my Godfather?"

"Geez, that's funny. I've never heard anyone refer to Alan as a Godfather. Well, we exchanged a few choice words, but for the most part, Alan knows you're staying with me on tour. He referred to our situation as unchartered waters, but don't worry. Everything is going to be okay."

After Logan recounted every part of their conversation, I was relieved to know my pregnancy wouldn't hopefully become a problem for the band. Weirdly, Alan had always been more of a father figure in my life than my own dad.

Later that evening, I met with Zoe, and of course, we patched things up. Then, unexpectedly, she announced that she would be accompanying Ethan and the band on the upcoming tour. I was excited to know I would have a female partner in crime. Living with six guys wasn't easy.

The following morning, I rode with Logan and Alan to Honolulu for his pre-op appointment. Stepping inside the limo, Alan appeared to be in a cheerful mood.

"Well, I hear that congratulations are in order."

"Thanks. Everyone doesn't know, so please don't say a word to my dad or mom. I'm going to deal with that later. Right now, we're focused on Logan's surgery."

"Jade, you have nothing to worry about. Trust me, I would love to call Charles and tease him about becoming a grandfather, but I'll respect your wishes."

"Thanks."

After spending hours at the medical center, Logan was set to have surgery the following day. So Alan decided to take us to one of his favorite restaurants in Honolulu, Alan Wongs. We enjoyed a delicious meal. It offered the best Hawaiian cuisine, Ginger Crusted Onaga, Long Tail Red Snapper with Miso Sesame Vinaigrette, Mushroom, and Nozawa Corn. The upscale dining experience had us wanting to return as soon as Logan recovered from his surgery.

Finally arriving back at the bungalow after an enjoyable evening with Alan, I felt exhausted. Taking Logan by the hand, I pulled him towards the bedroom. This would be our last night together until he was back from the hospital. Quickly changing clothes, we slipped under the warm covers.

"Are you worried about tomorrow?" I whispered, gently caressing his face.

"No. Should I be?"

"Logan, you have no reason to worry. I'm not leaving you. Suddenly, out of nowhere, I had a light-bulb moment. I've got a question?"

"What's on that pretty little mind of yours?" Logan asked, pulling me closer into his arms. "Sweetheart, whatever it is, you only have to ask? I love you."

"Well," I hesitated.

I knew life didn't come with guarantees, and the fact he was facing surgery, gave me a sense of urgency. Without warning, I was about to ask him point-blank to marry me, shoving the repercussions of a possible no to the furthermost corners of my mind. I prayed his answer would be a resounding yes. Marrying Logan was everything I ever wanted, and being in Hawaii made it the perfect place and time.

"Logan, will you marry me? I want to get married before we leave Hawaii?" My heart raced wildly out of control as I waited pensively for his answer.

"Wow, Babe, I didn't see that one coming. Jade, I would marry you anywhere. What took you so long to ask?" he teased. "I would marry you right now at this very moment if the possibility existed."

For the remaining few hours, we never closed our eyes. Our bodies simply melted into one as if we'd been together forever. Holding me tight against his warm, buffed body, the essence of Logan's cologne was hypnotic. The memories and emotions attached to his favorite after-shave of sandalwood and bergamot transported me back to when we first met. With every gentle touch, I felt breathless, entirely lost in him. Scarcely coming up for air, I pushed every thought of Logan's impending surgery further from my mind. Each heated zealous kiss swept me away as if tomorrow didn't exist until the sound of the alarm clock suddenly brought us back into existence.

The following morning, Logan was admitted to the hospital and settled into a private room. Alan respected our right to privacy for the few remaining minutes we had before he was taken to the operating room. No one was allowed in Logan's room.

"I love you," I whispered as tears softly flowed down my face. "Remember you promised to marry me last night, and I'm holding you to it."

"I wouldn't miss it for the world. I love you."

Watching as Logan was placed on a gurney, wheeled into the hallway, and taken to surgery, Alan put his arm around me. I felt faint.

"Have you eaten breakfast?" Alan inquired with concern.

"No."

"Jade, skipping breakfast isn't a good idea, especially in your condition. The surgery will take about two hours. So you're going with me downstairs to the cafeteria, and I'm buying you breakfast. I think Zoey and the guys are there now getting coffee.

The following two hours were the longest of my life. However, thanks to Alan, Brian, Zoey, and the guys, it appeared they weren't going to allow me to worry. Instead, every one of them, including Alan, accompanied me to the waiting room. Their conversations worked to keep me from worrying, as they entertained me with unbelievable stories of their adventures with Logan on their European tour. Finally, noticing Logan's surgeon enter the room, he walked over to Alan. I held my breath.

"Logan's surgery went great, just as expected. There were no surprises or complications, and I'm sure with rehabilitation over the next six weeks, he'll return to the stage to entertain his fans. He will be in the recovery room for a while, but as soon as he's awake, he'll be brought back to his room. Any questions?" Dr. Marshall asked.

"None that I can think of right now. However, before Logan goes home, I'm sure we'll have questions regarding rehabilitation. Thank you," Alan grinned.

"Thank you," I smiled. At last, I could breathe again.

"I'm glad this is behind Logan and all of us, for that matter. We have an album to finish. I'm sure you must be relieved. You should be able to see him soon," Alan remarked, giving me a huge hug.

Sitting down, I whispered a prayer of thanks. Logan and I had just gotten over our first major hurdle. Anything else would be a cakewalk, I thought. Then, finally, after another wait of almost an hour and a half, a nurse walked in.

"If you're waiting for Logan James, he's out of recovery and back in his room. Wow, I never thought I'd make that announcement," she laughed. "I'm a huge fan," she added. "Sorry, only two people can go in."

"Jade and I will go first," Alan stated. "Afterward, the rest of you can go in for a few minutes."

Entering Logan's room, I didn't know what to expect. Walking over, I noticed he was awake. Taking his hand, I leaned over the bed, giving him a quick kiss.

"Hey Babe, the doctor said it went well. So I told you not to worry. I love you."

"Hey doll, are we married yet?" Logan questioned drowsily.

"Married?" Alan questioned, walking over.

"Alan, when did you get here? It looks like a florist shop threw up in here."

"I've been here the entire time. Brian, Zoey, and the guys are all in the waiting room. I'm relieved you're out of surgery, and everything went according to plan. The doctor said you should be back on stage in about six weeks. Now," Alan hesitated. "Is there something else I don't know?" he smiled curiously.

"Yes. Godfather, there is something you should know. We're getting married as soon as I can walk," Logan blurted out. "On the beach, we're getting married on the beach before we leave Hawaii," Logan mumbled, slightly incoherent.

"Wow, you guys work fast. I guess congratulations are in order for the second time. When you're ready, just give me the date, and I'll arrange everything. Don't worry. I'm not going to say a word."

"Thanks, Alan. I had no idea Logan was going to make the announcement this way. He sounds like he's drunk."

"Oh, I'm sure it's the pain meds talking. But, Jade, just so you know, if Charles isn't available, I'd love to take that walk with you."

"Alan, you have no idea how much that means to me," I smiled unexpectedly, becoming a sobbing, emotional wreck.

"Jade, it's okay. I've got you," Alan whispered, pulling me into his arms. "Sweetheart, it's been a hard day. It's okay to cry. I love you like a daughter. You're getting a great guy."

"Thanks, Alan. I'm sorry. I didn't mean to lose it. I don't know what's wrong with me.

"Sweetheart, it's alright," Alan reiterated. "I can think of a few reasons why your emotions would be all over the place. Why don't you let me take you back to the bungalow? You should rest for a while."

"No. I'm not leaving. I promised Logan I would stay. So I'll be alright."

"Jade, he's asleep. There's nothing you can do. Let me take you home for tonight. I'll have the driver bring you back in the morning."

"No. I'm not going anywhere. I'm staying."

"Okay, sweetheart, suit yourself. I'll have the staff bring in a cot. If you need anything, let the staff know. If you change your mind later tonight, call me, I'll send the car back for you. I'm going to ask the guys and Zoey to come back tomorrow. Logan is asleep, and he needs his rest. So try to get some sleep. I'll see you tomorrow. Oh, let Zoe know what you need from the bungalow, clothes, toiletries, whatever," Alan reminded.

"Thanks, Alan. See you tomorrow."

Alan, along with the guys, and Zoey left the hospital, leaving me alone with Logan. There was no other place I wanted to be than next to the father of my baby. Needless to say, I never left the hospital until Logan was discharged four days later.

Finally, Logan was back at home, and our small bungalow took on the feel of a nursing home. After two weeks of nurses coming and going, along with walkers and an assorted sundry of medical devices, Logan finally entered the rehabilitation phase of his recovery. At last, after six long weeks of rehab, we were finally ready to continue a normal life. We had a wedding to plan while Logan and the guys finished recording their third album. But first, we needed to make our announcement official. We decided to host a Hawaiian Luau with the help of Alan's staff. It would be the perfect occasion. We scheduled it for the following weekend. While Logan and the guys worked on the album, my days became hectic with a whirlwind of activities focused on our official wedding announcement. Then, all too soon, the day arrived.

"Geez, Babe, I've never seen you in a colorful Hawaiian shirt before. You look sexy," I complimented as Logan walked out of the bedroom.

"Thanks, Sweetheart, you don't look half bad yourself."

Wearing a bright floral muumuu disguised my growing baby bump.

"Come over here and give Daddy a kiss before we leave," Logan winked mischievously.

"Logan, I love you, but we're going to be late. So let's go," I demanded.

"Jade, wait, there's one thing missing. I promise it will be worth your time."

Walking toward Logan, I couldn't imagine what would be so important that we couldn't leave. We were definitely going to be late for our party. Then it hit me like a bolt of lightning. I knew."

"Jade, considering the fact this our engagement party, I think you're missing an essential accessory. You will marry me, right?" he questioned, opening a tiny blue box.

"Yes, of course, I believe I already asked you, remember?" I smiled. Taking my left hand, Logan lovingly placed a five-carat heart-shaped diamond ring on my left hand. I was breathless. I couldn't wait to marry this incredible, handsome guy.

"Oh my God, Logan, it's gorgeous. I love you. You have no idea how much I love you," I cried once again, entirely consumed with emotions.

"Sweetheart, please don't cry. I think we have a party to attend," he grinned, attempting to kiss away each tear.

The past six weeks had been so debilitating, filled with stress and worries, that not having an engagement ring had never entered my mind. However, staring at my left hand, I was thrilled Logan didn't forget.

"Let's go show it off. Shall we? After all, it was a substantial purchase," Logan smiled. Then, locking the door to the bungalow, he took my hand, leading me towards the golf cart. Pausing for a moment, Logan softly caressed my face with his hands. Then, gently lifting my face upwards to meet his, he kissed me with such passion it left me weak in my knees. "Geez, Babe, maybe we should make this party private, just the two of us," he whispered.

"Not on your life. Alan has his staff working overtime for us tonight. So we're going," I demanded. "However, another kiss like that might quickly change my mind."

A huge bonfire was glowing on the beach as we arrived. Alan's staff had left nothing to chance. Tiki torches lit a path from the main house down to the beach. Everyone was in a festive mood, the album was almost finished, and Alan swore it was the best embodiment of work the band had ever recorded. When Alan was happy, everyone was happy. He had a complete bar set up on the beach under a thatched roof palapa. Booze flowed freely, and it was time to party.

"You both look great," Zoey complimented as we stepped out of the golf cart. "Oh my God, Jade, does this mean what I think?" Zoey screamed, grabbing my hand to closer inspect my glistening six-carat diamond.

"Yes. We're making it official tonight. Logan is going to announce our engagement later this evening."

"Congratulations," Zoe beamed excitedly.

"Thanks. I can't wait to marry this handsome guy."

"Ditto," Logan smiled. "Let's get this party started. I've endured a long dry spell, but it ends tonight."

Walking over to the palapa bar, Logan joined the guys. Tossing back shots of whiskey and shooting shots of tequila with salt and lemon, the festivities were getting off to a fast start.

Finally, the roasted pig, which had been cooking for several hours, was unearthed, revealing a heavenly aroma. Everyone was served the delicious pork delicacy, poi, pineapple, Hawaiian coleslaw, and rice.

"Guys, as you're served, please take your plate and find an open beach chair near the fire pit," Alan interjected in the middle of the guy's laughter

Sitting close to Logan under the brilliance of the night sky, the evening was perfect. The sound of waves gently washing ashore, along with the cool ocean breeze, added to the ambiance.

"Guys, I have a few announcements, then I'm going to turn the evening over to Brian and then Logan. First, I have to say how excited I am to be releasing the band's new album, *Chain Reaction*. It's by far the best compilation of material we've ever recorded. I expect it to hit number one on the charts within the first week. Second, the Pacific Rim tour is selling out faster than we can book the venues. Thank God, I wasn't sure how well we would be received across the Pacific. I think it's safe to say you're well-loved, and the fact you will be introducing songs from the new album, well, it's just the icing on the cake. Brian will fill you in on the schedule. Enjoy yourselves. It's well deserved."

After Brian hurriedly went over the scheduling and the logistics of the tour, he acknowledged that Logan's surgery was a success which meant the band would soon be back on tour.

"Finally, guys, we're grateful to have Logan's knee replacement behind us. We're ready to head out on tour again and introduce our new album to the millions of fans who are waiting to hear it for the first time. It's going to be a hell of a ride. Thanks for all your hard work," Brian added, taking a seat.

"Thanks, Brian," Logan smiled. "Yes. I'm totally relieved to have the surgery behind me. However, the reason we invited everyone here tonight besides my surgery and celebrating the album is that Jade and I have an announcement. We actually have two announcements. First, Jade and I are getting married next week, right here on the beach."

"Right on!" Ethan yelled as the guys whistled their approval.

"I always knew it would happen. Then, of course, I saw the ring. Congratulations," Zoey eagerly shouted.

"Thanks, everyone."

"Of course, you know you're all invited. It's going to be a simple ceremony, nothing formal, no written invitations. Our second announcement is," Logan hesitated. "Babe, why don't you come up and explain the reason you were sick in the limo a few weeks back," Logan grinned, pulling me up from my chair.

"Logan, really, why don't you?" I hesitated, slightly embarrassed by the sudden attention. Then, reluctantly standing, I put my arms around Logan. I never liked being singled out, even among friends.

"Okay. We're pregnant, and we couldn't be more excited. Riot Storm is having their first baby, and on tour, I might add," Logan smiled, rubbing my tummy like a proud papa as he gave me a quick kiss.

"Wow, you guys don't waste any time," Noah laughed.

"Just name it after me," Jarrod yelled, totally inebriated.

"I guess that's all I had to say. Thanks for being with Jade and me through the surgery and, as a result, our time in Hawaii. I hope you enjoyed your time in the water. Let's face it. The north shore is truly the mecca of the surfing world. I hope to make it into the water before we leave."

Jarrod, Noah, and Ethan thundered their approval with earsplitting whistles as the staff brought out fluted glasses filled with champagne.

"Let's toast to Logan's recovery, the completion of the album, our first wedding, baby, and finally the upcoming tour. Hell, you guys are a busy lot. Let's party. You've earned it!" Alan toasted.

Partying until the wee hours of the morning, I was the only one sober. The guys got rambunctious before the night ended and tossed Alan and Brian into the ocean fully clothed. It was only the beginning. Before the party was over, each of them had been dunked into the water, some more than once. Even Zoey was no longer wearing dry clothes. I began to think our wedding might be bathing suits optional. Finally, getting tired, I went to retrieve Logan, who was three sheets to the wind by this time.

"Babe, I hate to be a party pooper, but it's late, and I need to get some sleep. Can we go? I love you."

"Hey Jade, where have you been?"

"Logan, I've been here the entire night watching you drink yourself silly. It's late, and we should go. I'm tired."

"Okay. Where are we going?" Logan stammered.

"Home. We're going to the bungalow. Goodnight everyone," I smiled. "Thank you for an unforgettable evening. Zoe, I'll call you tomorrow."

"Do you need help with Logan?" Ethan stuttered, completely intoxicated.

"No. He can walk. We're good. Thanks."

Helping Logan back to the golf cart, I knew the next time I walked on this beach, it would be to say, I do."

Arriving at the bungalow, I managed to get Logan inside and to the bedroom just before he passed out on the bed. Removing his wet clothing, I put him under the warm covers. Changing clothes, I turned out the lights and slipped into bed next to him. Kissing him goodnight, I knew the past six weeks had been incredibly difficult. Hopefully, tonight the party and mischief with the guys released any remaining stress from the surgery and finally put it all behind him. We were ready to move on with our lives. We had a wedding to plan, and I couldn't wait to become Mrs. Logan James.

Chapter Ten

The Wedding

Waking up before Logan, I sat up. Our wedding day was less than two weeks away. Opening the curtains with the remote, the morning sun streamed inside the room. The view revealed a picturesque panorama of the sandy beach and turquoise waters of the Pacific. Oahu would be the perfect location for a wedding. Staring at my soon-to-be husband, his scruffy appearance, tousled bed hair, and day's growth of dark stubble took my breath away. His sexy appearance was irresistible. I couldn't resist caressing his handsome face as I softly kissed him awake.

"Awe, it's the future, Mrs. Logan James. Good morning gorgeous," Logan smiled, slowing opening his mesmerizing blue eyes. "Did you put me to be bed last night?"

"Yes, and I love that you called me Mrs. Logan James."

"Wow, Sweetheart, someone made out like a bandit," he winked playfully, reaching for my left hand. "That's a substantial rock. I love you, Mrs. Logan James," he whispered, pulling me into the warmth of his embrace. "Babe, thanks for taking care of me last night. Let me thank you properly," Logan smiled naughtily, reaching for the remote as he closed the curtains. Pinning me against the bed, he covered every inch of my body with delicate kisses. Each magical kiss sent shivers of rapturous pleasure racing throughout my body. I loved Logan with every fiber of my being. I was truly where I wanted to be, wrapped inside the comfort of his arms, as the world simply faded away.

Bolting upright later that morning, I panicked.

"We've got a wedding to plan, and I need a dress. So I'm calling Zoe to see if she can go shopping this afternoon."

"Geez, Babe, slow down. We've got about two weeks."

"Logan, two weeks isn't nearly enough time, but trust me, I'll make it work."

"Sweetheart, you've got nothing to worry about. Alan's staff did a great job last night with our impromptu engagement party."

"Oh, I know. It was fun, but there's more involved with a wedding. You guys are going to need tuxedos."

"Jade, really, tuxedos, we're getting married on the beach. Shouldn't it be more relaxed and casual?"

"Not on your life, and miss a photo opportunity with you and the guys in tuxedos. Are you crazy? The band lives in tee-shirts and frayed jeans. This is my one chance to have formal photos. You and the guys will look amazing on the beach at sunset. I can't wait."

"Okay, sweetheart, if you insist," Logan reluctantly agreed. "You're my forever, and I'm only doing this once, so make it the wedding of your dreams. I'm sure with the help of Alan and Zoey, you shouldn't have any problems."

"Thanks, Babe. I love you."

Later that afternoon, Zoey and I hit all the prominent wedding boutiques on the island. Logan insisted on paying for my dress, and Alan gave us the use of the limo.

Finally, after hours of shopping, I knew I had found the perfect gown as soon as I stepped onto the pedestal in front of the dressing room. The image reflected in the mirror was breathtaking. Zoey and I both cried. I chose a white Chantilly lace and Tulle gown in a fit-and-flare design. It featured a strapless, heart-shaped neckline with Swarovski crystal buttons down the back bodice. Even with my barely noticeable baby bump, it was sheer elegance. Choosing not to purchase a veil, I decided to wear my long blonde curls down and swept back with fresh flowers.

The guys purchased tuxedos and accessories by the end of the week. So the design of the cake and menu was now my main focus.

Logan and I spent the next few days sampling cakes at local bakeries and menu choices with Alan's staff. Finally, we decided on a three-tier Pink Champagne cake with raspberry mousse and vanilla buttercream. As expected, the top of the cake was the silhouette of a couple with an acoustic guitar. The chocolate groom's cake was designed to emphasize rock and roll. Regarding our menu, it was simply the best of surf and turf.

At last, our wedding day arrived, and not a moment too soon. It was Saturday, November Seventeenth, and I had waited for this day my entire life. Opening my eyes, I felt Logan's intense stare.

"Good morning, Sweetheart, today's all ours. I can't wait to marry you. You're my forever," he whispered.

"How long have you been awake and staring at me?" I smiled.

"Longer than I care to admit without sounding crazy. I love watching you sleep. How did I ever get so lucky? But, Jade, before our day starts, I have a little something for you," he grinned, pulling out another blue velvet box.

"Oh, my God, what is it?" Opening the box, it contained a diamond eternity necklace. I melted. Logan, you must have spent a fortune. It's breathtaking."

"Jade, you're breathtaking. But, unfortunately, these are mere stones."

"Logan, I didn't get you anything. I feel stupid. I'm so sorry," I cried, wiping tears from my eyes.

"Oh, but you have, Sweetheart," he smiled lovingly, caressing my growing belly. You're giving me something which I recently lost and to be honest, I thought I might never have, our baby. Jade, I don't think I could be more in love with you and this little girl or guy. Today, you're both making my world complete."

"Oh my God, Logan, I'm the lucky one," I cried.

Pulling me into his arms, Logan gently held me near his heart while my emotions consumed me.

"Jade, please don't cry," he whispered, wiping away my tears. "I love you."

Hearing a light knock at the door, neither of us expected anyone this early. Logan grabbed his robe and walked into the living room to answer the door.

"Champagne and breakfast compliments of Mr. Zimmerman," the young man smiled, pushing a cart laden with silver chafing dishes into the room. The aroma of hot coffee and bacon was delectable

"Thanks." Quickly tipping the room service attendant, he was on his way.

"Who was it?" I asked from the bedroom.

"Breakfast and champagne compliments of your godfather, Alan," Logan laughed. "Damn, Babe, we have a bottle of Dom Perignon."

Grabbing my robe, I was starved.

Lifting the lid from the chafing dishes revealed scrambled eggs, hash browns, bacon, toast, and blueberry pancakes.

"Wow, he thought of everything, even blueberry pancakes," I remarked, filling my plate as Logan popped the cork on the champagne. Then, taking my plate over to the sofa, Logan filled his fluted glass with the sparkling beverage.

"Here's to the future, Mrs. Logan James," Logan grinned, handing me a glass of milk from the fridge."

"Orange juice, please. I hate milk, I reminded. "Here's to our future and a house full of healthy, rambunctious children," I snickered.

Really, Jade, and how exactly would that work on tour? If their old man was a rock star, just saying," Logan laughed, handing me the orange juice.

"Oh, I don't know. I think our kids might enjoy seeing their dad on stage," I smiled, stuffing myself with pancakes. Then, watching as Logan walked over to get more bacon, he suddenly stopped.

"Oops, I forgot. Is the bacon making you nauseous?"

"No. I'm finally past those early queasy weeks?"

"Thank God," Logan smirked, stuffing strips of bacon into his mouth.

Hearing another knock on the door, Logan grumbled. "Geez, suddenly it's the grand central station?"

"Flower delivery for Ms. Dupree," the young man announced, handing a large bouquet of red roses to Logan.

"Wow, those are gorgeous. Is there a card?" I asked, walking over for a closer inspection.

"I think they're from the guys."

"Geez, the flowers smell heavenly. There must be two dozen long stem roses in this vase. They're gorgeous. Babe, come over and sit down. I want a few moments to relax with you before my day starts spinning wildly out of control," I smiled.

"Whatever, the future Mrs. James wants," Logan winked.

"Logan, we have no family members here today. How do you feel about that? I'm having a hard time. I'm not saying I'm back on good terms with my parents. That might never happen. I guess it's just the fact my dad will never walk me down the aisle. I'm a little sad," I mentioned as my eyes watered.

"Sweetheart, I'm sorry. I wished I could make your world entirely perfect, especially today," Logan smiled, pulling me into the warmth of his muscular arms. "Jade, you might not have your family here, but Zoey, the guys, Brian, and especially Alan are family. They became my family when I signed on with the band. Remember, my parents were killed when I was very young, and I was an only child. Thank God I was raised by my Aunt Grace in Upper New York. Unfortunately, I haven't seen her in years. One day, I'd love to retire in Dutchess County. It's been a dream of mine since I signed on with Riot Storm," Logan paused, reflecting on his life. "You forget the most important part about today, us. We're becoming husband and wife. We're starting our own family, and we have a new little member on the way. Now, please, no more waterworks. Sweetheart, how will you ever make it through the day. No more tears. I love you. Now, let's get this day started," Logan grinned, giving me a quick, passionate kiss.

Once again, hearing a knock at the door, I walked over. It was another stunning arrangement of local flowers, bright yellow Hawaiian Hibiscus, intermingled with colorful Bird of Paradise and Red Ohia Lehua. The card simply read as follows:

To my dearest goddaughter, On your special day, know that you are wished a lifetime of happiness. I've watched you grow into a beautiful young woman. I know Charles will not be here to walk you down the aisle. However, I feel truly honored to take his place. See you soon. Love, Alan.

"Wow, Logan, the flowers are from Alan. This card means the world to me. How did I get so lucky? I have two wonderful men in my life. I feel so blessed."

"I told you," Logan mentioned giving me another quick kiss. I promised the guys I would hang out with them this afternoon. We're getting dressed at the main house. I love you. I think we have a date this evening. I'll be waiting for you on the beach."

Less than an hour after Logan left, Zoey arrived to stay with me until the wedding. She walked in with her bridesmaid's dress, a stunning navy blue chiffon halter gown safely enclosed in a zippered bag. After hanging her dress in the bedroom, we drank orange soda, popped popcorn, and lounged on the sofa in the living room. We watched old movies and reminisced about our high school days. Then, deciding to order pizza, we figured it was best to eat before getting dressed. The afternoon passed in a fun, dizzy blur. Eventually, the hairdresser and cosmetologist arrived.

"Well, let's get you dressed," Zoe giggled like a schoolgirl.

"Oh, I almost forgot. I have to show you what Logan gave me this morning. Follow me into the bedroom for a moment while the hairdresser and cosmetologist set up in the living room.

Reaching for the box, I opened it as Zoey gasped.

"Geez, Jade, I think these are over ten carats. It cost thousands of dollars. Seriously, I'm sure this necklace easily cost over sixteen thousand dollars. I think you're going to need a bodyguard," Zoey laughed, closely scrutinizing the brilliance of the diamonds.

Next, the hairdresser adorned my hair with a Hawaiian Haku Lei, a small crown of delicate local flowers. I decided on white rosebuds, with white butterfly ginger intermingled with orchids. It was the perfect compliment to my white Chantilly lace gown. Zoey's red auburn curls were loosely swept back with a silver hair clasp and adorned with pink plumeria. Zoe's petite frame, sculpted facial features with a hint of freckles made her the perfect bridesmaid. Finally, done with hair and makeup, the two ladies gathered up their belongings. Zoe held the door as they exited with everything in hand. Now, all that remained was getting dressed. Unzipping our garment bags, Zoe and I removed our beautiful gowns. Zoe dressed first. She looked incredible in her navy blue chiffon halter gown. Now, it was my turn. Slipping into my fit-and-flare Chantilly lace gown, Zoe buttoned all the tiny Swarovski crystals down the back bodice. Staring at my reflection in the mirror, I felt regal in my elegant lace gown wearing a Haku Lei. Gently caressing my small baby bump, I smiled. "Daddy's waiting for us."

"Wow, Jade, you're breathtaking. You look stunning. Logan is a lucky guy," Zoey smiled.

Suddenly, there was an unexpected knock at the door.

"Are you expecting someone?" Zoey asked.

"No."

Walking over to the door, it was another delivery.

"Hello. I have a package for Ms. Dupree."

"Thanks. Wait just a moment." I ran for my purse and quickly returned, giving the young man a generous tip. Closing the door, I was shocked by the surprise of another delivery. Anxiously ripping into the small package, Zoe watched in anticipation. It revealed a small satin box and card.

"Wow, I can't imagine what's inside?"

"Well, open it," Zoey smirked. "I'm dying to know."

"Okay, don't rush me. First, let me read the card. I have to know who sent it. Wow, it's from Logan."

Sweetheart, I think this will perfectly complement your necklace. I love you. See you on the beach. Yours forever, Love Logan.

Opening the box, we both gasped. It held a pair of diamond earrings.

They perfectly matched the eternity necklace. Their flawless brilliance reflected a fiery kaleidoscope of colors.

"Oh my God, Jade, those are exquisite. You're one lucky girl."

"Zoe, I'm lucky because I found Logan for the second time, and I'll always have you to thank for making that happen. You're the best, and I love you like a sister."

"Jade, stop, you can't go there. We'll become blubbering idiots, and it'll ruin our makeup," Zoey laughed with tears in her eyes.

"I love you, Zoey Zimmerman," I smiled, putting on the diamond earrings. "Can you help me with the necklace?"

"Sure. Isn't that my job as maid of honor?"

Finally, I was elegantly accessorized with sparkling diamonds, thanks to my soon-to-be husband, famous rock star Logan James.

"Okay. Let's go. I think you have a date."

"Wait. I have a little something for you too," I smiled, handing Zoey a small, delicately wrapped box.

"Jade, this isn't necessary."

"Awe, but it is."

Anxiously, Zoey ripped the wrapping away, exposing a small blue box from Tiffany's. It held a pair of flawless diamond earrings.

"Oh my God, Jade, you shouldn't have. They're beautiful. Thank you," Zoey remarked with moist eyes. "You're making me cry."

"Now we can go," I smiled.

Zoey drove us over to the main house. Parking under the entrance, I carefully managed my long, lace gown as I stepped out of the golf cart. Walking inside the foyer, an amazing aroma infused the air with a heavenly fragrance. The living room was covered in fresh flowers and bathed in a warm glow of lit candles. The ambiance was wonderfully romantic. Alan waited for us at the back of the living room near the massive sliding glass doors. He looked debonair in his black tuxedo with his hint of salt and pepper hair.

"You both look gorgeous," Alan smiled, giving us a quick kiss. Then he handed me a bridal bouquet of fresh gardenias and Zoey a miniature replica of the same flowers.

Instantly, my heart stopped as I got my first glimpse of Logan waiting on the beach. I melted at the mere sight of him wearing a black Armani tuxedo. Even from this distance, he was extremely handsome. His long blonde curls were pulled back in a ponytail, giving him an edgy, sophisticated appearance. Logan not only had one best man, he had three. They were each dressed elegantly in a black tux. Ethan, of course, was closest to Logan. Then Jarrod and Noah completed the trio.

"Well," Alan paused with a smile, looking down at his watch. "It's 6:00 p.m. Are you ladies ready to take a walk?"

"Yes," I smiled.

"Zoe, honey, I believe you go first."

"Thanks, dad. I love you," Zoey smiled.

"I'll meet you on the beach," Alan winked.

Taking my arm, Alan grinned. "Jade, sweetheart, thanks for allowing me the honor to walk with you. I think someone is waiting for you."

"Wait, just a moment," I smiled, carefully removing my Christian Louboutin stilettos. "I want to walk in bare feet. I love the feel of the sand." With tears welling within my eyes, I took my first step towards my future. The path to the beach was covered in rose petals and lit with glowing tiki torches. With just the sound of waves washing ashore, I walked towards the love of my life. I didn't need a symphony playing to make this moment better. It was surreal, more than I ever dreamed was possible. Reaching Logan, my heart melted.

"My God, sweetheart, you're stunning. I see you received the necklace and earrings," Logan whispered.

"Thanks, Babe. I love you."

"I want to thank Alan for flying me over from Los Angeles. It's indeed an honor and privilege to unite you in marriage this evening," Reverend Schumann smiled. "Who gives this woman in marriage?"

"I do," Alan smiled, giving me a quick kiss before he stepped back to sit with Brian.

There were only a few staff members in attendance. However, Alan was nervous regarding news reporters and paparazzi. Even though he had tightened the security, there was always the off chance they might manage to get past the gates.

Handing my bouquet to Zoey, I felt breathless as I stared into Logan's mesmerizing blue eyes.

"Logan, please take Jade's hand and repeat after me. Afterward, place the ring on Jade's finger."

"I, Logan James, take thee, Jade Dupree to be my wedded wife, to have and to hold from this day forward, for better, for worse, for richer, for poorer, in sickness and in health, to love and to cherish, till death us do part, according to God's holy ordinance, and thereto I pledge thee my faith.

Logan smiled, repeating the vows. Then afterward, he took my left hand, placing the ring on my finger.

"Jade, please take Logan's hand and repeat after me. Afterward, place the ring on Logan's finger.

"I, Jade Dupree, take thee, Logan James to be my wedded husband, to have and to hold from this day forward, for better, for worse, for richer, for poorer, in sickness and in health, to love and to cherish, till death us do part, according to God's holy ordinance, and thereto I pledge thee my faith."

I smiled, taking Logan's hand, repeating each word as I placed the ring on his finger. "You're my forever," I whispered as tears welled within my eyes.

"As an ordained minister, it's my privilege to pronounce you husband and wife. You may kiss your bride."

Pulling me to his chest, Logan kissed me with intensity and desire. I thought my heart would burst as the guys applauded and whistled their approval.

"You're my forever," Logan whispered.

As the photographer snapped dozens of photos, abruptly, out of nowhere, the sound of helicopters buzzed overhead.

"Well, at least we made it through the ceremony," Logan smiled, scooping me into his arms.

"Everyone inside. Hurry," Alan demanded. "The party's over out here. At least, until those crazy reporters are out of the area, they can't get their photos from inside the house."

Walking into the dining room, Alan's staff had eloquently arranged his extended Asian-inspired dining table with the best of everything. It was beautifully executed. Popping the corks from bottles of Dom Perignon, the staff placed fluted glasses of champagne at each table setting.

"I like to make a toast to the happy couple. Everyone, please raise your glasses," Alan announced. "Jade, first of all, welcome to the family. Logan, you're a lucky guy. I want to wish you both the very best in life, but looking at you, I'd say you already have the best. We love you, and we're looking forward to the birth of this little one. Congratulations."

"I'd like to add to that, Brian," interjected. "Here's to the best damn vocalist this band has ever had and his lovely new bride. Congratulations."

The staff served appetizers of bruschetta, smoked salmon bites, and glazed chicken wings, Logan's favorite, along with a varied selection of salads. Finally, the main course was served. It consisted of lobster with filet mignon and twice-baked potatoes with asparagus. We were stuffed.

Suddenly, a beautiful lace-covered table containing our elegant three-tiered wedding cake was brought into the dining room. Finally, it was time to cut the cake. Looking at Logan, my expression implored him to be nice. However, knowing Logan, I knew this wouldn't go my way.

"Babe, be nice," I laughed.

Taking the knife in our hand, we sliced into the delicious Pink Champagne Cake. Flashes of light from the photographer's camera caught Logan in the act of shoving cake not only into my mouth but my face. Quickly, cutting another piece, I figured turnabout was fair play, as I good-humoredly pushed cake in his face.

"Oh, wow, someone is asking for it," Logan laughed, kissing away the remains of cake from my face.

"I have one last announcement," Alan spoke up, lightly tapping his glass. "Jade, Zoey has a change of clothes for you in the bedroom, and we've packed your bags. However, I believe a swimsuit is all that's required. The jet is waiting at the airport. You're on your way to Tahiti.

We'll meet you in Tokyo next weekend. Have a fabulous honeymoon. We love you both," Alan grinned.

"Thanks, Alan," Logan smiled.

"Alan, that's unbelievable. Thank you," I added.

"Now, you kids, get out of here. The limo is out front. We'll see you in Tokyo next weekend."

Arriving at the airport, Logan managed to carry me up the steps and onboard the aircraft. Taking our seats, it felt odd that we were the only passengers. Logan held me in his arms as the jet lifted skyward. This day held many memories. The most important was seated next to me. At last, I was Mrs. Logan James.

Chapter Eleven

Japan

rriving in Tokyo, the band was staying at the exquisite Imperial Hotel. Unlocking the door to our suite, it was total elegance and offered unparalleled views of the city. Riot Storm was performing at the Tokyo Dome. Its capacity held over forty-two thousand, and it was sold out due to the recent release of the band's third album, *Chain Reaction*.

"Wow, Alan never disappoints when it comes to accommodations. I should call Zoey and let her know we're here."

"Zoe can wait until tomorrow. It's late, and the flight was grueling. Remind me again why we had to fly commercial?" Logan whined, immediately pouring himself a shot of bourbon.

"Babe, calm down. It wasn't that terrible. Alan took the jet to Singapore. I think you'll live."

Suddenly hearing a knock at the door, Logan walked over. "Well, it appears someone knows we're here. I'll bet it's Zoey."

"Flower delivery for Mr. and Mrs. James," the room service attendant smiled. Walking in, he sat a gigantic bouquet of fragrant pink peonies with baby's breath on the credenza. Tipping the young man, he was instantly on his way.

"Pink peonies have always been my favorite. My curiosity was heightened as I reached for the card.

Jade & Logan, Congratulations, Love, Charles and Amanda

"Wow, these are from mom and dad. How in the world did they find out?"

"I believe this will answer your question. Take a look at these," Logan gasped, holding copies of newspapers and tabloids which carried extensive coverage and photos of our wedding. Alan must have left these to make us aware that the pictures were everywhere.

"Oh my God, I didn't think any photos would have leaked to the press. I'm sure my parents are furious. They didn't even bother to sign the card as 'mom and dad.' The flowers are just their way of letting me know they saw the photos."

"Sweetheart, I'm sorry. I guess I should have warned you this might happen. Remember the helicopters?" Logan grimaced. "I'm afraid it was probably unavoidable."

"What am I going to do?"

"Jade, there's nothing we can do," Logan frowned, pouring himself another shot of bourbon. "We need to talk." Taking my hand, he pulled me over to the sofa and removed my shoes. Lounging back, he pulled me into his arms. "Jade, when you married me, unfortunately, you married into the business. I'm afraid our lives, at least some of it, will always be fodder for the tabloids. Remember the paparazzi outside the Westin and how your parents saw those photos. Sweetheart, I'm sorry. I know you're new to all of this, but trust me, I've learned to deal with it for the most part. Alan and Brian do a great job with our security. They work hard to keep as much of our lives private as possible out of the newspapers and rag tabloids. But, Babe, I have to tell you, unfortunately, sometimes even their best efforts aren't enough. Do you hate me?"

"Logan, where did that come from? I could never hate you. I love you. I knew coming into this relationship, the dynamics of our lives would change. I guess I was just caught off guard tonight with the flowers. Poor Alan, I'm sure my father is going to make his life a living hell."

"Sweetheart, I wouldn't worry about Alan. Trust me. He can take care of himself."

"My dad and Alan have been friends since college. I'll feel responsible if this causes a rift between them."

"Jade, you worry too much. Influential men such as Alan and Charles have ways of getting past disagreements. However, if it were your mom and Joyce, that might not end so well. However, once your mom discovers she's going to be a grandmother, she'll be begging to be involved in your life. Trust me. You sound tired. I think Mrs. James could use some rest," Logan winked. Scooping me into his arms, he carried me into the bedroom.

"Geez, Logan, don't you ever think of anything else?"

"What? I'm tired," he laughed wickedly, pretending to yawn.

"Really. Logan, you're lying."

Turning out the light, it was apparent he wasn't tired. Helplessly, I fell into his arms again, a willing victim of his shenanigans. What started as playful fun always ended in a long night of passion, and I wouldn't change anything.

Waking the following day, we had a full day ahead. Alan was arriving from Singapore, and I wanted to speak with him regarding my parents. Apparently, they knew which hotel we were in, which meant my dad had probably talked to Alan. The guys had a sound check at 4:00 p.m., and I wanted to shop. Unfortunately, my expanding belly demanded larger clothes.

"Good morning, sweetheart," Logan smiled, rolling over to give me a quick kiss. "What are your plans for today?"

"I want to talk to Alan regarding my parents and shop for clothes. My jeans are fitting a little snug."

Laying his hand over my extending belly, Logan tenderly whispered, "Hey, you, little person, I hope you have your mommy's gorgeous looks. I can't wait to see you. Daddy loves you."

"Babe, that was sweet, but you're not too shabby yourself. Somehow, I don't think the baby has to worry about their appearance, but inheriting your wicked sense of humor has me concerned."

"Really, Sweetheart, I thought it was my sense of humor that attracted you. But, please, don't tell me it was the fact I'm a famous rock star."

"Logan James, you're conceited, but I'm totally in love with you," I smiled, kissing his forehead. "How did I ever get so lucky?"

"Awe, but I'm the lucky one," Logan smiled, pinning me against the bed as he passionately returned my kisses.

"Babe, you always respond with those words. If this continues, we're not going to get out of bed this morning."

"And, what's wrong with that?" Logan smiled with a wink.

Hearing my cell phone was the perfect distraction. Quickly checking the caller ID, I sat up in bed. It was Zoey.

"Hey, when did you get in? I didn't hear from you last night."

"Oh, we got in late. I was going to call, but we were exhausted from the flight."

"Did you see the newspapers? You looked amazing."

"Yes. Zoey, what time is Alan getting in this morning? I need to talk to him?"

"Funny, you should mention it. It's why I'm calling. Dad got in earlier this morning, and he's on his way over to your room."

"Thanks. I have to run. We're still in bed. I need to get dressed."

"Geez. It sounds like you're still on your honeymoon. Call me after he leaves."

"Okay."

Hanging up my cell, I instantly jumped out of bed.

"Logan, quick, get dressed. Alan is on his way over," I demanded.

"What's the rush? Maybe he would like to join us."

"Don't be silly. Get dressed."

Hurriedly, I dressed just in time to answer the door.

"Hey, Sweetheart, how was Tahiti?" Alan smiled.

"Fabulous. Come in. I'll have coffee brought up to the room."

"Coffee? I think we both need a drink," Logan smiled, walking from the bedroom with tousled bed hair and pajama bottoms, exposing his buffed tattooed physique.

"Awe, honeymooners, sorry for interrupting," Alan grinned.

"Geez, Logan, you should have gotten dressed," I blushed.

"Babe, I think Alan has probably seen the guys and me in a lot less," Logan laughed, walking over to the bar to pour them each a glass of bourbon.

"I suppose you've seen the newspapers and tabloids. I had them brought up to your room after Charles called. I'm truly sorry. Your wedding photos were leaked to the press. As the band's manager, I try to keep your lives private and out of the media. Still, as you've discovered, it's not always possible," Alan explained, taking a sip of his drink.

"Yeah, well, I think we discovered that last night," Logan frowned, tossing back his entire drink as he reached for his cigarettes.

"Alan, how did my parents take the news? It's clear they're upset. They sent the arrangements of peonies with a card simply signed by Charles and Amanda. It was their way of letting me know they were upset when they saw the photos."

"Jade, I'm truly sorry. Naturally, your parents were not happy about the fact they were not invited to your wedding. Charles stated he was disappointed not to have been the one to walk you down the aisle, and you are his only daughter. Is there anything I can do to make things better? I feel responsible," Alan explained, finishing his drink

"No, you're not to blame. I saw the photos. My parents will have to accept that Logan and I are married. After that, I'll deal with them."

"Jade, I don't mean to pry, and I'm not trying to tell you what to do regarding your parents, but what about the fact you're pregnant. Don't you think they have a right to know?"

Walking over to the sofa, Logan refilled Alan's glass with bourbon. He knew Alan felt terrible and was now caught up in Jade's deceitful relationship with her parents.

"No. I've involved you in my problems, and I'm sorry. I know you feel like you're caught in the middle, but I do not want my parents to know about the baby. At least, not yet. I hope you can respect my wishes, even if you disagree."

"Sweetheart, you have no worries where I'm concerned, regardless that I'm close friends with your parents. I do respect your right to privacy, and my loyalty is with you and Logan," Alan remarked, throwing back his entire drink. "Sorry, I've got to run. I have a couple of appointments before the concert tonight. No worries. We're good, right?" Alan grinned.

"Yes, Alan, we're good. I feel like you've been more of a father to me than my own," I frowned.

"Well, I'm your godfather, and I love you. See you at the venue."

"Love you too, Alan," Logan jested.

"Watch your mouth," Alan laughed. "I'm expecting one hell of a concert from you tonight. It's the release of our new album. So don't disappoint me."

"When have we ever disappointed you? It's why we get paid those huge salaries." Logan smirked.

"Right."

After Alan left, I suddenly felt sick.

"Geez. I feel dizzy."

"Jade, it's because you haven't eaten this morning. How could I have been so stupid? So I'm ordering blueberry pancakes with extra bacon and juice."

I knew it was only nerves. Receiving the flowers and talking with Alan brought back memories. Memories that I had hoped to keep hidden in the recesses of my mind. Memories that had been responsible for me leaving home. Even though I was thousands of miles away, they continued to haunt me.

After breakfast, I decided to stay in rather than shop. Taking a nap seemed like a better idea. Logan was right. The trip from Tahiti had been exhausting. I managed to sleep the entire afternoon while Logan worked out at the gym.

"Hey, sleepyhead, sorry to wake you, but we only have an hour to dress before we meet the guys downstairs. How are you feeling?"

"I'm better. The baby and I just needed a little downtime this afternoon."

"I picked up a couple of burgers and fries from the restaurant downstairs. Don't worry. I demanded their entire inventory of ketchup. I'm going to jump in the shower," Logan smiled, pulling my messy, blonde bed hair away from my eyes. Lovingly kissing my cheeks, he whispered, "I love you, Mrs. James."

Waiting for Logan to exit the shower before entering the bathroom, I wasn't up to his usual antics. Hurriedly, getting ready, we devoured our burgers and were finally on our way downstairs. Stepping out of the elevator, Zoey immediately ran over.

"What happened? You never called."

"Oh, I slept in this afternoon. I felt exhausted."

"Understandable, you're pregnant. Next venue, we'll get in some girl time and shopping," Zoey suggested as we walked out to the front entrance of the hotel.

"Sounds good," I smiled as Logan took my hand, helping me and my expanding belly inside the limo.

Entering the car, the guys began their usual routine. Jarrod immediately opened a bottle of Jameson. Then, taking a huge sip, he passed the bottle. Alan and Brian had arrived earlier at the venue, so Noah instantly pulled out a reefer.

"Hey, man, not inside the limo. I can't have my baby inhaling pot," Logan sternly demanded.

"Geez, Logan, would you prefer we hang a *baby on board* sign in the back window of the limo. For heaven's sake, we're a damn 'rock band,' or have you lost your freaking mind?"

"Noah, I don't care what the hell you do at the hotel or the venue, just not inside this car. We don't have the luxury of rolling down the windows."

"Thanks, Noah," I smiled.

"Okay, but only because I happen to like your wife," Noah smirked, putting his joint away for the moment.

Reaching the venue, the guys went through sound checks as Zoey and I helped with the band's merchandise booth. Grabbing a few of the band's extra-large tee-shirts, I knew they would suffice until I could find time to shop.

Within hours, the arena began filling up with fans who were anxious to hear the band's new material. Searching for a place to watch the concert, Alan called us over. He put us in a hidden small corner behind the guys where the lights wouldn't expose us. Then, watching the guys take their place on stage, the fans thundered out their love and support. It was exhilarating.

"Good evening, Tokyo. Thanks for coming," Logan yelled, taking the microphone. "Hope you like our new album. We're going to perform several of our new songs."

"It's great to be in Japan," Ethan screamed.

Opening with *Chain Reaction*, their new single, the fans went crazy. It was apparent their new album was destined to top the charts. Over the next two hours, the guys poured out tremendous love for their fans in Tokyo. Watching from backstage, it felt the concert was over way too soon. Perhaps Logan was half-right when he asked if I married him because he was a famous rock star. Maybe I did, I mused. His charm and magnetism on stage were alluring and heart-stopping.

Even though I had missed my chance to explore the historical city, Logan and I vowed to return, leaving Tokyo the following day.

Over the next three months, Riot Storm performed in the Philippines, Taiwan, and Australia. We were on our way to Jakarta, Indonesia, when the unthinkable happened.

Chapter Twelve

Indonesia

California

We had been on tour for twelve long weeks, and things had gone according to schedule. The new album received rave reviews thanks to an aggressive marketing campaign. Alan and Brian were ecstatic as the venues continued to sell out weeks before our arrival.

As the Lear jet approached the runway at the Soekarno-Hatta International Airport, I was excited to be in Jakarta. Not only was it the capital of Indonesia, but it was also modern, having forty-seven museums and trendy malls to appease my desire to shop. The band was finally getting their first week of total respite, which meant no soundchecks, no concert performances, or appearances after the concert at the Arena Pekan Raya. As predicted, it was sold out before our arrival.

Unfortunately, the Pacific Rim tour required grueling hours of air travel. Even though we had the luxury of a private jet, it was exhausting at best. Grabbing our carry-on items from the overhead bins, we were anxious to be on our way downtown to the Ritz-Carlton. As the jet taxied across the tarmac, the mere sight of the waiting limo represented a comfortable bed and the fact I would soon be relaxing under its warm covers.

Suddenly, Alan and Brian's cell phones began blowing up with incoming calls and texts, entering the limo. No one thought it unusual. It was common for them to be bombarded with calls and texts upon arriving at a venue. However, those calls would soon change my life forever.

Arriving at the prestigious Ritz-Carlton, everyone hurriedly exited the limo. We were all anxious to receive room keys and stretch our legs. Entering the elevator, I thought it strange that Alan and Brian were turning in a bit early. Their usual ritual included hitting the lounge upon arrival to discuss the venue while tossing back a few drinks to relax.

"Logan, Brian, and I need to speak with you. Why don't we follow you to your suite?" Alan asked in a subdued voice.

With my head leaning against Logan's broad shoulders, I was falling asleep in the elevator and entirely oblivious to their discussion.

Unlocking the door to our suite, I apologetically made my way to the bedroom. I was exhausted. Changing clothes and slipping into bed were the only thoughts on my mind. I was almost five months pregnant, and I knew the guys would easily understand my need for extra rest. Slipping under the comfortable duvet, I was out like a light bulb, entirely unaware of the ongoing conversation in the next room. When Logan came in to gently wake me, my whole world turned upside down.

"Jade, Sweetheart, I need you to wake up," Logan insisted, gently pulling back strands of my hair. Then, wiping my face with a warm towel, it appeared odd that he would go to such extreme measures to wake me. After all, we had just arrived at the hotel. "Babe, please, we need to talk. I'm afraid it's serious," Logan added.

"Quick, give me your hand. The baby just moved. You have to feel her," I insisted, totally unaware of his last comment. Then, reaching for his hand, I laid it over my belly. "Isn't that amazing?"

"Yes. Sweetheart, that's beyond amazing. But, Jade, your father called Alan, and I'm afraid the news isn't good."

At this point, it began to sink in that something was wrong. However, nothing could ever have prepared me to hear what was coming next.

"Jade," Logan hesitated. "I love you with all my heart. This is by far the most difficult thing I've ever had to do.

"Logan, I love you too. You're scaring me. What's going on?"

"Sweetheart, Alan just informed me that your mom and Charlie were involved in an auto accident. They were both taken to the hospital. Unfortunately, Amanda was injured, but she's expected to make a full recovery. I'm so sorry. Charlie wasn't as fortunate. Jade, he's on life support, and sadly, his diagnosis is grim. He sustained numerous internal injuries, and your dad wants you home immediately."

Sitting up in bed, I wiped my eyes in disbelief. Admittedly, I had misunderstood Logan. I was undoubtedly having a nightmare, and I would wake up to discover none of it was true. Evidently, I was merely fatigued from the long flight.

"Jade, have you heard a word I've said?"

"What?" I asked, not wanting to make a connection to anything I'd heard.

"Sweetheart, I'm so sorry. There's been a terrible accident. I don't even know how to begin. Your mom and Charlie are in the hospital. Charlie is on life support."

"Oh my God, Logan, what are you saying? You must have been misinformed. Charlie can't possibly be on life support. I'm calling Dad, I'm sure this is all a huge misunderstanding," I replied in complete shock. "You're scaring me."

"Babe, I'm so sorry. Trust me, I hate myself for giving you such tragic news."

Reaching for my cell, I called dad. I was sure there was no truth to any of it. However, he answered almost immediately.

"Jade, I need you to come home. Your mom and Charlie were involved in a serious car accident."

"What happened?"

"Your mom had been drinking all day, and we got into one of our usual heated arguments. Finally, she said she was leaving and that she was taking Charlie. Jade, you have to know that she always threatens to leave and take Charlie. I had no way to know her threat was any different from all the others, but I feel responsible," Dad cried softly.

"Are you okay?"

"As good as can be expected under these circumstances," he paused. "Honey, it wasn't until an officer from the County Sheriff's Department came to the house with the devastating news that I realized what had happened. Amanda ran a red light at a high rate of speed, and a delivery truck hit their car broadside. The impact was on the front passenger's side of the car where Charlie was sitting. I'm so sorry," Dad sobbed.

"Dad, how is Charlie?" I interjected.

"He's on life support, and the prognosis isn't good. I'm afraid they aren't giving me much hope. Your mom sustained minor injuries, but she's expected to make a full recovery. Jade, Charlie suffered numerous internal injuries. My precious boy is in critical condition. Charlie is my whole world, and I can't lose him. I need you. Alan is making arrangements for you to leave immediately."

"Oh my God," I screamed, dropping my cell phone as I fell into Logan's arms. "Not Charlie, it should have been Mom," I cried hysterically. "Why wasn't it, Mom?"

"Jade, calm down. Sweetheart, you have to calm down for the sake of the baby. I love you, and I'm so sorry. Please don't cry. We'll get through this, I promise. I'm sure Charlie is going to make a full recovery."

"Logan, you can't possibly know that. I'm leaving as soon as I get dressed," I sobbed relentlessly. "I knew I should never have left Charlie behind, but he was so young. There was nothing I could do, and now he might not make it. I feel responsible. Mom and dad have never been accountable for their actions, and they should never have had children. I hate them. Are you coming?"

"Jade, I'm so sorry. I can't go. The concert is tomorrow evening. It's completely sold, and Alan asked me to stay behind, but he's arranging for Zoey to go with you. Do you understand? I hate the fact I can't leave with you, but Alan has arranged for me to fly out immediately after the concert."

"Yes. I understand," I cried, becoming an emotional wreck. "It doesn't mean I like it, but I know the band is performing tomorrow evening. So you promise to leave immediately after the concert?"

"Of course. Alan and I are flying out tomorrow night as soon as I walk offstage. I'm so sorry that I can't leave with you right now. The jet is being serviced to fly you both to the states. The limo is arriving at any moment to take you to the airport. The band is getting some down days after tomorrow night, and Brian is going to hang back with the guys until we return."

"Logan, I can't lose Charlie. I just can't. You have no idea how much I love him. I've always tried to protect him from mom and dad, and now I failed him," I wept bitterly as I hurriedly gathered up what few things I had brought into the hotel. Quickly, throwing everything back into my suitcase, I was utterly devastated.

"Jade, you haven't failed Charlie. Trust me. There was no way you could have taken him when you left. He was too young and in school. You did the best thing by leaving."

"Logan, I never said goodbye to Charlie before I left. I only wrote a note for mom and dad. I never personally explained my reasons for leaving or that I loved him."

"Jade, you're too hard on yourself. I'm sure he understood why you had to leave."

Hearing a knock at the door, Logan ran into the other room to answer it.

"Hey, where's Jade? I'm so sorry to hear about the accident. How is she taking the news?" Zoey inquired sympathetically.

"Jade's in the bedroom gathering her things. She's as good as can be expected. Zoey, I need you to take care of her until I arrive. Alan and I are leaving tomorrow evening as soon as the concert ends. Zoe, I'm trusting you with Jade and the baby. Please don't let anything happen to either of them. I hate the fact I can't go, but I promised your dad that I would stay behind."

"Logan, calm down. I would never let anything happen to Jade. For heaven's sake, I know she's pregnant. Don't you think I'm worried about her, but she's stronger than you think? Just promise me that you and dad will be on a flight tomorrow night. I've never liked Jade's parents. I can't believe Amanda would get behind the wheel of a car after she'd been drinking. Poor Charlie, he didn't deserve this. I'm sorry if anything happens to Charlie, Amanda is the one who should suffer. I hope they put her in prison and throw away the key."

"Zoe, please keep your thoughts to yourself. How is that supposed to help Jade? Your job is to keep her calm. Promise me that you won't allow her to cry all the way to the states. If she's an emotional basket case, she won't be the support Charlie or Charles needs. Zoe, please keep your cell phone close, in case Jade doesn't answer when I call."

"Logan, don't worry. I love Jade like a sister. I'll call you when we get to Marin. Just keep Charlie in your prayers."

Walking into the living room, I was ready to go, even if it meant leaving Logan behind.

"Hey, Zoey, I guess you know about the accident. Oh, Zoe, I can't lose Charlie. I just can't." I completely broke down sobbing. Once again, I was becoming entirely unglued.

"Babe, please don't cry. This is killing me. I want to leave right now with you, but I promised Alan to stay behind," Logan explained, reaching for more tissues. "Jade, I love you, and I know how hard this is for you, but you have to take care of yourself and our baby. I'm counting on you to be strong. I'll be there as soon as I possibly can. I can't even imagine going on stage tomorrow night under these circumstances."

Hearing another knock at the door, it was Alan.

"Logan, why don't you ride with us out to the airport. So we can see the girls off. I'm sure Jade would like that," Alan requested.

"Yes, of course. Babe, are you ready?"

"I suppose. I'm not sure if I could ever be ready for something like this," I cried, reaching for another Kleenex.

Putting his arm around me, Logan held me as we made our way downstairs and out to the entrance where the limo waited. As we rode to the airport, there were no words, only moments of emotions. Logan held me in his arms as I cried uncontrollably.

Exiting the limo, Logan briefly pulled me into his arms before I boarded the jet.

"Sweetheart, I love you, and I love this little one," he smiled softly, placing his hand against my pregnant belly. I'll be there as soon as possible."

"I know. I love you too."

"Zoe, you take care of yourself and Jade. I'll be there soon," Alan solemnly promised.

"Thanks, Dad. See you soon."

Boarding the jet, Zoey and I had the entire aircraft to ourselves. Quickly finding a seat, we lounged back, trying to get comfortable for the long flight. As the plane lifted skyward, I found it impossible to believe that we were leaving Jakarta after arriving only two hours earlier.

Watching the skyline of San Francisco come into view, I had been gone almost a year. So many beautiful things had happened in such a short period. However, I never envisioned returning to Marin under such harsh circumstances. Upon arrival at the San Franciso International Airport, Alan had arranged for a limo to pick us up and drive us the short distance to Marin.

Driving across the Golden Gate Bridge, memories of the day I left flashed across my mind. In only a few short minutes, I would be home where my journey had begun. Yet, as we entered the circular drive, its massive stucco exterior remained the same. The only thing that changed was the lives of the individuals who lived inside.

"Jade, you're shaking. Are you okay?" Zoey asked in a concerned voice.

"Just nerves. This house contains too many memories, and most of them aren't pleasant."

Ringing the doorbell, Fran answered almost immediately.

"Oh my God, Jade, you're home. I've missed you. Let me look at you," Fran smiled, giving me the once-over before embracing me a huge hug. "Oh, my, you've finally gained some weight. That's good."

"Fran, I'm pregnant," I smiled. "Is Dad at the hospital?"

"Yes. Mr. Durpree hasn't been home since the accident. I'm praying for Charlie. I know he's going to be alright. Please come inside. Are you hungry?"

"Fran, this is Zoey."

"Yes, I remember Zoey. Why don't you both come into the kitchen? I've just baked some chocolate chip cookies. They're Charlie's favorite. Perhaps you can take some to the hospital."

"Thanks, Fran, maybe later. I'm going to run up to my room for a moment, and then I'm sorry, but we're going to the hospital to see Charlie."

Quickly running upstairs, I opened the door to my room. I gasped. Nothing had changed since the day I left. Everything was in its place. It felt sad and depressing as if they expected me to return at any moment. Quietly closing the door, Zoey and I went downstairs to let Fran know we were leaving. It was evident she hadn't received the complete details regarding the accident or the severe nature of Charlie's condition.

"Fran, we're leaving for the hospital. It was nice to see you," I yelled as we closed the front door. "We'll be back later."

I don't know why I chose to go by the house before the hospital. I knew in my heart Dad wouldn't be there. But, I suppose in a strange way, I just needed to reconnect with the feeling of my home before I saw Charlie. I needed to remember the better moments of my life in Marin. The ones which included Charlie. I was hoping against all odds that I could will him to live.

Entering the limo, Dad called to say that Charlie was transferred to the Children's Hospital in San Francisco. However, Mom remained at Marin General. Thoughts of visiting her before driving over to the Children's Hospital never entered my mind. I had no empathy for her. I would never be able to forgive her if Charlie didn't somehow miraculously pull through.

Arriving at the Children's Hospital, Zoey and I checked in at the information desk in the lobby and received our identification badges. Making our way up to the ICU and Charlie's room, nothing could have prepared me to see my little brother hooked up to so many tubes, lines, and medical devices. Undoubtedly, they were keeping him alive. The low continuous hum of the ventilator brought tears to my eyes as we walked into his room. At first, Dad didn't notice as we entered. He was standing over Charlie's bed holding his hand. Walking over, I lovingly wrapped my arms around him. Then, with tears flowing down my cheeks, I hugged him.

"Hey, Dad, I'm so sorry," I cried. "I'm here."

"Jade, darling, I'm so thankful you came. I've missed you." Pulling me into his strong arms, we quietly wept. The smell of cigars and his cologne instantly felt comforting. I merely needed to be held. I was speechless as my emotions totally consumed me. There were no words that could ever convey the depth of sadness and despair we felt. Words could never express how heavy our hearts were at this very moment.

Walking over to take Charlie's hand, his small, fragile body was covered in bruises. His head was completely wrapped in white gauze. Tears streamed from my eyes. Staring at the ventilator, which pumped oxygen into his lungs, his chest expanded with each thrust of the machine. I only wished it had been me lying there instead of Charlie. He was so young. He didn't deserve a death sentence due to my mom's drinking and poor judgment.

"Hey, Charlie, it's me, Jade. I'm home. I love you, and I've missed you," I softly whispered as a myriad of tears flowed down my face. "Charlie, please forgive me for not saying goodbye before I left. I never meant to hurt you, and I only hope that you can forgive me. Charlie, I need you to fight to stay alive. Do you hear me? You're the strongest little boy I've ever known. Please, Charlie, you can do this. I'm not leaving. I love you." Kissing his hand, I gently placed it under the stark white sheet. Then, leaning over the bed, I kissed his beautiful face. Taking another glance at his delicate lifeless body, I turned to walk away. Suddenly, my legs buckled from underneath me. I could no longer support myself. Just before I hit the floor, I felt my dad's strong arms catch me.

"Zoey, quickly get a chair and call for a nurse."

"Mr. Dupree, Jade's pregnant. It was a long flight, and she's probably just exhausted. But, seeing Charlie, I'm sure overwhelming."

"I had no idea. Please call for a nurse," Charles reiterated in total shock.

Hurriedly, a young lady came running in to evaluate my condition. After checking my vital signs, which thankfully were good, and applying a warm cloth to my forehead, I slowly came around.

"Sorry for the scare. I'm fine, just a little pregnant."

The nurse laughed. "Don't think I've ever heard anyone say they were a little pregnant," she smiled.

"So, I'm going to be a grandpa?" Charles interjected. "I think it's the best damn news I've heard," he smiled, walking over to give me a huge bear hug. "Jade, I didn't know. How far along are you?"

"Thanks, dad. I'm almost five months. Logan and I are really excited."

"Awe, that's right. You recently got married. Logan, that name sounds familiar. Is he, by any chance, the same guy you dated in high school?"

"Yes. The very same guy. I have Zoe to thank. She helped us reconnect."

"So, when do I get to meet this young man again?"

"Hopefully, tomorrow. Logan is flying in with Alan."

"Wonderful. Zoey, why don't you take Jade back to the house, and you both can get some rest. I'm not leaving Charlie."

"Dad, are you sure? I can stay. I don't want to leave Charlie."

"Jade, darling, there's not anything you can do. It would be best for you and the baby to get some rest. Please. I think you'll find your room just as you left it, and the guest room is available for Zoey. Fran can help you girls with anything you need. I'll call if there's any change with Charlie."

"Okay. I'll be back first thing tomorrow morning, and you can go home and get some sleep. I love you."

Walking over to Charlie, I wanted to tell him about the baby before leaving.

"Hey, little brother, you're going to be an uncle. We need you. I'll be back tomorrow. I love you," I whispered, kissing him softly on his cheek.

"Dad, try to get some rest. I'll see you tomorrow. I love you," I smiled, giving him one last hug before I left.

"Wow, your dad sure handled the news well regarding your pregnancy," Zoey smiled as we walked out into the hallway. "I pray Charlie gets better."

"Thanks, Zoe. I don't think I could handle it if he doesn't. I'm extremely worried about him. He looks so pale, and he has so many bruises."

Reaching the house, Fran had already prepared the guest room for Zoey. After munching on chocolate chip cookies and downing a glass of milk, we were ready for bed.

"See you in the morning," I smiled as we reached the top of the stairs.

"Get some rest. We'll talk tomorrow."

Just as I was about to lay my head down on the pillow, my cell phone rang. My heart stopped as I glanced down to identify the call. It was Logan. Instantly, a feeling of relief swept over my entire body.

"Hey, Sweetheart, how's my little mommy?"

"Tired. Zoey and I just got back from the hospital. Charlie doesn't look good. He's hooked up to all kinds of machines. I'm so worried about him."

"Jade, please try to think positive. I'm praying that he'll recover. I just wanted to let you know that we'll be leaving for the airport in a few hours. We're almost ready to go onstage. I love you."

"I love you too. Dad is looking forward to meeting you. He's excited about becoming a grandfather."

"Really, that's great. I'm glad Charles doesn't hate me."

"Logan, how could anyone hate you. I love you. I'm exhausted and falling asleep. Enjoy your concert, remember, the baby and I are your biggest fans. See you tomorrow."

"Babe, get some sleep. I'll see you soon."

Putting down my phone, I was asleep as soon as my eyes closed.

Waking the following day, I checked my phone to ensure I had no missed phone calls during the night regarding Charlie. Then, opening my closet, I reached for my robe and walked down to the kitchen. Pouring myself a cup of coffee, Zoe walked in.

"Good morning. We're you able to get any sleep?" she inquired.

"Yes. Logan called, and afterward, I was completely out. It felt good."

"What would you ladies like for breakfast?" Fran asked, walking in from the laundry room.

"Oh, I'm not really hungry, and we should leave for the hospital."

"Jade, you're not going anywhere without eating. I promised Logan that I would take care of you and the baby.

"Okay. I suppose it's Blueberry pancakes," I reluctantly smiled.

"Great. Blueberry pancakes it is," Fran replied, grabbing her apron.

After enjoying a delicious breakfast of pancakes and sausages, we dressed for the hospital. Then, deciding to call for a taxi, we were soon on our way to San Francisco.

Reaching the hospital, once again, we checked in at the information desk and received our badges. Making our way back up to the ICU unit, I was surprised to find dad talking with a doctor in the hallway. Dad looked despondent. Immediately, a feeling of dread overtook me, and I felt extremely nervous.

"I'm truly sorry, Mr. Dupree. You have my deepest sympathy." Overhearing the doctor give my dad the devastating news, I felt nauseous. Every part of my being wanted to scream, but words refused to come.

"Jade, we need to talk. Why don't you and Zoey follow me to the waiting room? Dr. Evans assures me the room is empty, and we can be alone."

"No. I can't. I can't do this. It's Charlie, isn't it?" I cried.

"Jade, please, you need to sit down. Follow me," dad said, gently putting his arm around me. Reaching the end of the hall, he led me into the waiting room. Closing the door, his eyes moistened.

"Sweetheart, sit down. I know this will be hard to hear. Earlier this morning, I asked Dr. Evans to perform an electroencephalography test on Charlie. Unfortunately, the results didn't turn out as I had prayed and hoped," Dad paused, wiping tears from his eyes. "The test conclusively determined that Charlie is brain dead. Sweetheart, I'm so sorry. We've lost Charlie. I've lost my only son." Dad trembled, entirely overwhelmed with sadness and heartache, as he pulled me into his arms. Together we sobbed bitterly, no longer able to contain our emotions. I felt as if my entire world had collapsed. Holding me in his arms, we quietly cried rivers of tears. There were no words. No words of comfort could ever bring Charlie back to us. Finally, Zoey reached for a box of Kleenex. With tears flowing down her face, she handed us the tissues. I had lost my brother, my only sibling, and dad had lost his precious son. We were consumed with heartbreak. Our world had been rocked by tragedy, and we would never be the same.

"Jade, I've agreed to donate Charlie's organs which are still viable. We need to walk back to his room. It'll be the last time we can see him. Soon he'll be taken to surgery and afterward the morgue." Dad led me back to Charlie's room with his arms around me. Walking in, I once again felt faint. However, I was determined to say goodbye to my brother. Dad held me in his arms next to Charlie's bed.

"Oh, Charlie, my sweet brother, I've lost you way too soon. I'll never get to see you grow into the handsome young man I knew you would become. I'm so thankful God let us have you for twelve years. You have no idea how much you're going to be missed. I love you. I'll always love you."

Feeling extremely dizzy, dad sat me in a chair while saying goodbye. I was in no condition to ever remember what he said. However, I will never forget the memory of watching him pull Charlie into his arms. Holding his precious son, he sobbed. Later, we were utterly devastated as we walked out of my brother's room. Grief consumed us.

Arriving back at the house, Fran met us at the door. Hearing the news, she was overwhelmed with heartache. Dad held her as she cried. We had a funeral to plan, and my mother wasn't even aware Charlie had passed. Later that morning, Dad went to the hospital to give her the news. I knew then I never wanted to see her again. Charlie's funeral would be the last time I ever saw her.

Three short days later, we had my brother's services. It was private. Only the immediate family and a few close friends were in attendance. Logan held me close as we walked into the small chapel. It was overflowing with an abundance of floral arrangements, and the fragrance of fresh-cut flowers infused the air. A warm glow streaming through picturesque stained glass windows filled the tiny sanctuary with a somber ambiance.

"Babe, are you okay?" Logan whispered, handing me a tissue.

"Yes. I suppose."

Wiping my moist eyes, Logan and I took a seat next to dad and Fran. Mom, Joyce, and Alan sat across the aisle. Looking at mom, I was filled with rage. She should have been the one who paid the price for her actions, not Charlie. He was merely an innocent victim because she was inebriated and driving under the influence. I prayed she would receive the maximum sentence allowed under the law in California.

As the eulogy ended, my visceral disdain and hatred for my mother were suddenly unleashed as we stepped outside the chapel.

Breaking away from Logan's arm, I lunged toward her. With all the force I had within me, I slapped her in the face. "It should have been you that died as a result of the accident," I screamed. "It should have been you, not Charlie," I reiterated. "It's all your fault," I raged as Logan and dad attempted to pull me away from her. "I never want to see you again. Never."

Charlie was laid to rest in our family mausoleum. After that, I never saw my mother again. Her alcohol blood level at the time of the accident was higher than the 0.08 necessary to charge her with vehicular manslaughter. Nevertheless, she was sentenced to only three years in the state prison, and my dad finally filed for divorce.

Once again, it was time to leave Marin. This time I knew that I would never return. However, I was leaving with everything I needed, a loving husband and a new life which I carried close to my heart. It was time to rejoin the guys of Riot Storm.

Chapter Thirteen

Thailand

*L*eaving San Francisco, we were on our way to Bangkok. Falling asleep on Logan's broad shoulders, I was finally able to put the funeral behind me for a few hours and get some much-needed rest. Soon, the impending arrival of our first child would fill our days with joy and happiness. Alan was undoubtedly correct when he said the Pacific Rim tour would involve a lot of air travel. It seemed the confines of the jet had become our home. We lived onboard the plane.

Brian, Noah, and Jarrod were already in Bangkok waiting for our arrival. Riot Storm was performing at the open-air Rajamangala National Stadium, which held over forty-nine thousand seats. The venue wasn't entirely sold-out out upon our arrival. Still, Alan and Brian expected the arena to be near full capacity by the night of the concert. Brian had arrived early to methodically prepare the groundwork for the band's mass media marketing campaign. It appeared to be working as ticket sales soared each day.

Entering the flight approach into the airport, Bangkok appeared to be a sprawling metropolitan city with a modern landscape of high-rise structures and historic temples. I had always wanted to visit Thailand.

Unbelievably, I was finally getting my chance to experience the culture and cuisine of Bangkok.

Arriving at the luxurious Mandarin Oriental Hotel on the Chao Phraya River, we were again bombarded by the paparazzi. Blinding lights flashed in our eyes as we exited the limo. Apparently, the media had leaked the name of the hotel where the band was staying, and numerous reporters were camped outside the main entrance.

"Smile," Alan teased, grabbing Zoey's hand as he hurriedly pulled her inside the safety of the lobby. "Sorry for the inconvenience. I know you're exhausted from the flight. Brian should have had this under control."

Checking in at the legendary hotel, it was the epitome of luxury. Its classic contemporary design was breathtaking. However, after being confined for hours in the cramped cabin of the Lear jet, we were ready to enjoy the comforts of a king-size bed where we could relax. Unlocking the door to our suite, we were immediately drawn to a wall of sheer glass at the back of the room. It exposed the city of Bangkok and its famous nightlife along the river.

"Wow, the view is incredible," I gasped, immediately removing my shoes. Then, walking over for a closer look, I was mesmerized. The Chao Phraya River sparkled under the bright lights emitted from the numerous tall buildings as boats ferried passengers across its shimmering waters. As usual, Alan never disappointed the guys when it came to lodging. He always reserved the best. "Geez, the view is truly breathtaking," I remarked, taking in the magnificent panorama.

"You know Alan. The man has exceptional taste," Logan smirked. Walking over, he gently put his arms around me as we stood awestruck by the scenery below. "He only knows one rating when it comes to accommodations. It's always five-star elegance," Logan added. Giving me a quick kiss, he smiled, changing the subject. "I think my girls could use a good night's sleep." Walking over to the bar, he poured himself a nightcap.

"Logan, speaking of the baby. I think it's time we find out if we're having a little girl or boy. I know we discussed not having an ultrasound, but I'm anxious to know. What are your thoughts?"

"Jade, you've always felt that we're having a little girl," Logan questioned with a grin.

"I know, but I could be wrong. Why don't we get an ultrasound?" I suggested.

"Okay," Logan agreed, tossing back a shot of bourbon. "When?"

"Tomorrow."

"Tomorrow?" Logan repeated, almost choking on his drink.

"Yes. I don't want to wait any longer. I'm sure the hotel connoisseur could help us make the arrangements."

"Geez, babe, I've had them arrange a lot of things for me, but never an ultrasound," Logan laughed. "But if it means that much to you, let's do it."

Tossing back his second shot of bourbon, Logan grabbed my hand and pulled me towards the bedroom. "Daddy's ready for bed," he winked mischievously.

Waking up the following day, thoughts of finding out the baby's sex consumed me. After enjoying breakfast, the concierge called to inform us that arrangements had been made for an ultrasound at a nearby medical clinic. I was like a kid on Christmas morning waiting to open their first gift.

Exiting the hotel through the employee's entrance, Logan and I managed to escape the paparazzi and enter the limo without being seen. Arriving at a small medical clinic, a young woman greeted us. Without making us wait, she immediately escorted us into a room near the back of the clinic. I felt anxious, laying back on the table as she prepared my belly for the test. Staring intently at the screen, Logan winked, giving me a quick kiss.

"Babe, you know it doesn't matter. All I want is a healthy baby.

"I know."

Taking Logan's hand, the room was instantly filled with the sound of the baby's heartbeat. It was music to my ears. Then suddenly our little one appeared on the screen. Tiny arms and legs moved amazingly fast across the screen as we fixated on the image of our baby. Finally, after what seemed like an eternity, the technician smiled. "It's a boy."

Totally surprised, I looked up at Logan. Then, smiling as my eyes moistened, thoughts of Charlie overwhelmed me.

"It's a boy," I beamed.

"I see," Logan grinned proudly.

"The baby is completely healthy and appears to be twenty-four weeks. Congratulations," she smiled, printing our first baby photos.

Thoughts of a baby girl were entirely erased from my mind discovering our first child was indeed a boy. Perhaps next time, I thought as a huge smile crept over my face.

"I suppose I can no longer refer to you both as my girls," Logan laughed.

"Maybe next time," I smiled.

"Geez, Sweetheart, slow down. Our first one hasn't arrived yet," Logan winked with a proud smile. Then, leaning over to kiss me, his eyes glinted the hint of a tear as the young lady handed us the baby's photos.

"We have a couple of hours before sound check. Is there anything you would like to do?" Logan asked as we were driven back to the hotel.

"Yes. I want to go to the Sampeng Market. Why don't we ask Zoey and Ethan if they would like to go?"

"Sounds like a plan."

Arriving back at the hotel, I immediately called Zoey.

"Hey, this better be important," Zoe answered with a flustered voice.

"Oops, you sound busy," I giggled. "Sorry, I forgot you and Ethan haven't seen each other in a few days. Logan and I are going to the Sampeng Market and wanted to know if you would like to join us?"

"No, we're sorta busy, but thanks for asking."

"Carry on," I laughed. "Oh, we're having a boy."

"Oh my God, really?" Zoe questioned. "That's fantastic. I thought you said it was a girl?"

"I know. There was always a fifty percent chance I was wrong. We'll talk later tonight at the concert," I added, quickly hanging up.

"Well, are Ethan and Zoe joining us?" Logan asked.

"Nope. They're a little tied up," I laughed.

"Oh, got it," Logan smirked. "Maybe the market is a little overrated. Perhaps we should stay in as well," Logan winked playfully.

"Logan James, you're a bad boy. You're taking me to the market. Right now," I demanded. "You know that I've always wanted to visit Bangkok. Let's go."

"First, I have to find my disguise," he laughed. He looked hilarious, wearing a dreadful black wig with a baseball cap and sunglasses.

"Okay, Babe, after you," he laughed, opening the door.

Walking through the Sampeng in Chinatown was overwhelming. Vendors of all descriptions lined the alleyways. We strolled past colorful stalls selling fabrics, clothing, electronics, jewelry, and dried foods, just to name a few. Slowly making our way farther into the market, it came alive with the smell of Thai cuisine. The unforgettable aroma of Moo ping (barbequed pork), fish cakes, mangoes, sticky rice, spring rolls, and crispy tacos with sweet filling infused the air.

"Let's try the barbequed pork with sticky rice," Logan suggested as we approached a food vendor. Stopping to enjoy the delicacy, it was delicious. Picking up the sticky rice as the locals, we formed it into small balls with our fingers and dipped it into the barbeque sauce.

Noticing a stall in the distance, it sold unique embroidered baby blankets. Reaching for Logan's hand, I pulled him the short distance to the vendor. Finally, after thoroughly inspecting each one, I purchased a blue satin blanket with embroidered giraffes.

Next, Logan led me to one of the jewelry vendors.

"Sweetheart, pick out a charm bracelet. You can add a charm for each city we visit."

"Okay," I smiled without hesitation. Then, acting like a crazed jewelry fanatic, I meticulously picked out a twenty-four-carat gold bracelet. It was breathtaking. Adding a Buddhist Temple charm completed our purchase. "Thanks, Babe. I'll always remember Bangkok as one of my favorite places. It will always hold the memory of discovering that our first child will be a little boy. I hope he has your handsome features and incredible blue eyes."

"Oh, I'm not so sure about that. I happen to think his mom is pretty amazing as well," Logan grinned, pulling me closer as he quickly kissed my forehead.

Logan realized it was time to call it a day, glancing down at his watch.

"Sorry, we've gotta run. It's almost 2:00 p.m. Just enough time to get back and shower before sound check."

Taking my hand, we raced back to the limo. We had enjoyed a fantastic few hours at the impressive Sampeng, and never once had anyone questioned Logan's identity.

Later that evening, under a bright starry sky, the guys gave a stellar performance. The Rajamangala Stadium was finally sold-out. Over forty-nine thousand screaming fans echoed their love to the guys. As Logan walked on stage, he effortlessly transitioned into a rock icon, giving his fans everything they expected from him plus more. He never left anything on the stage. Logan was an exceptional performer. Regardless of that fact, his antics were sometimes a bit dramatic. But, it only made his loyal fans love him even more.

"Good night, Bangkok, it was a riot," Logan yelled, holding his guitar high into the night sky.

"Thanks for having us. See you next time," Ethan screamed.

Watching my handsome guy walk off stage, I couldn't wait to be alone with him. I felt like the luckiest girl on earth to know he belonged to me.

"Hey, Babe," Logan grinned, catching sight of me as I waited for him backstage. "I feel wired. That was a hell of a concert."

"Great performance," Alan smiled, lightly slapping Logan on the back as he walked past.

Following Logan backstage to the guy's dressing room, I didn't feel like sharing him. However, the room was filled with news media. Zoe and I sat on the couch as reporters surrounded the guys. Finally, after giving numerous interviews and posing for photos, Logan called us over.

"Hey, girls, over here," Logan demanded. "Don't you want your photo's taken with a legendary rock band?" he laughed.

Walking over, Logan put his arm around me. Not knowing exactly where these photos would wind up, I quickly pushed back my hair. Zoe and I stood proudly next to our guys as bright lights flashed in our faces. Standing next to my famous husband, I felt giddy, like a young schoolgirl at her first prom. Staring up at Logan, it wasn't possible to be more in love with him than at this very moment.

After the press finished their photos and interviews, Alan and Brian ushered us outside to the waiting limo. I was anxious to get back to the hotel. It had been a long day.

"Who would like to experience the famous nightlife of Bangkok?" Alan inquired, entering the limo. Making himself comfortable, he lounged back in his seat, pouring himself a scotch. "I think we could do with a little fun this evening. You guys certainly didn't disappoint tonight, and I think you deserve some downtime," Alan added, savoring a sip of his drink. "I've reserved a private room downtown at the Nara Thai Restaurant."

"Oh, you don't have to ask me twice," Jarrod spoke up. "I've heard they have the best Thai food in Bangkok."

"Count me in," Noah grinned, pouring himself a shot of bourbon as he passed the bottle to Logan.

"Sounds like a phenomenal evening, but I think the little lady and I are going to call it a night," Logan laughed. "Just in case everyone hasn't heard, we're having a boy," he announced with pride.

"Congratulations, here's to the newest member of Riot Storm," Alan beamed. "Well, Sweetheart, are you and Ethan going to join Jarrod, Noah, and me for a fabulous dinner?" he questioned.

"Definitely," Zoey acknowledged. "I didn't come all the way to Bangkok to not enjoy a delicious dinner at the Nara Thai Cuisine. I can't wait to taste everything."

"Sorry, Alan, I know Jade needs to rest," Logan interjected.

"Completely understandable," Alan grinned. "No worries."

Arriving back at the hotel, we wished everyone a wonderful evening.

Unlocking the door to our suite, Logan, as was his usual custom, walked over to the bar to pour himself a nightcap. Taking off my shoes, I looked forward to a quiet evening. However, I had tremendous guilt for keeping Logan away from the guys and an exotic dinner which I'm sure we both would have enjoyed. Unexpectedly becoming emotional, I wiped my moist eyes, hoping Logan wouldn't notice.

"Hey, little momma, are you ready for bed?" Logan teased seductively. Walking over, he noticed. "Sweetheart, are you crying?"

"I'm sorry. Raging hormones, I suppose."

"Jade, what's wrong?"

"Logan, I feel like I kept you from having a fun evening with the guys," I sniveled.

"Oh my God, Babe," Logan smirked, pulling me into his arms. "Sweetheart, you've not kept me from anything, not even an evening with the guys. Trust me, there's only one place I want to be right now, and that's next to you. Let me show you why I declined dinner," Logan smiled with a wink. Scooping me into his arms, he carried me into the bedroom. Laying me on the bed, he turned out the lights. Needless to say, sleep never entered our minds.

Waking the following day, the sun slowly crept in under the curtains bathing the room in a soft radiance. Turning over to face Logan, I kissed him awake.

"Good morning, sweetheart, wow, last night was incredible," he smiled, slowly opening his dreamy blue eyes. "I love you, Mrs. James."

"Yes. It was unbelievable. I love you too, Mr. James," I whispered, caressing his face, which was covered in a five-o'clock shadow. You look sexy with bed hair and dark stubble," I smiled, staring at his handsome profile. "Logan, I think we should give our baby a name. Do you have any suggestions or favorites?"

"No. To be honest, I guess I've not given it much thought. Do you have any names that you like?"

"Well, not really."

"Jade, my father's name was Alexander. What do you think of

Alexander Charles? I think it's a strong name and pays respect to my father, your father, and Charlie. Do you like it?"

"Oh my God, I love it. Alexander Charles is perfect, and I love the nickname, Alex."

"Okay. I think we've chosen his name. I'm afraid this little one already has a lot to live up to. What if he doesn't like it?"

"Logan, there's not a chance. He'll love it. Don't be silly."

Later that morning, we finally got out of bed, ordered breakfast, and packed. Riot Storm was scheduled to perform in New Zealand two days later. The band performed to sold-out crowds across the Pacific throughout the next few months. Riot Storm continually made headlines in all the local and national news media. Their popularity grew with each venue, and I simply expanded like a blimp. I was nine months pregnant and fast approaching my due date. Finally, the band was put on 'baby' watch. The guys were now placing bets on which venue would welcome our first child. It appeared Singapore might be the winner and possibly the birthplace of Alexander Charles James.

Chapter Fourteen

Singapore

$\mathcal{A}$pproaching the flight path into Changi International Airport in Singapore, Alan's worst fear had been avoided. He had ongoing nightmares that I would unexpectedly go into labor onboard the jet, and even worse yet, the baby would be born in the air. Alan panicked every time I boarded the plane. Zoey and I thought he was hilariously funny and overdramatic. I suppose his worst fears were possibly realistic and not without merit. However, we were only moments from landing in Singapore, and I felt fine.

Entering the limo, we again had reservations at the prestigious Mandarin Oriental Hotel. We often stayed in their exclusive hotels when they were in close proximity to a venue. Alan loved the hotel and its amenities. The band was performing at the Singapore Indoor Stadium, which held twelve thousand seats and had quickly sold out before our arrival.

Arriving at the hotel, it was the last week of July, and I was due any day. Alan had scheduled a two-week break for the band after their performance in Singapore. He graciously offered to fly me back to the states for the birth. However, there was no way that I would leave Logan, so he arranged for me to deliver the baby at one of the local hospitals. Alan also had ulterior motives for our two-week hiatus in Singapore.

It was common knowledge to the guys and even Zoey that Alan had an ongoing relationship with a young woman in Singapore for years. His marriage to Joyce was on paper only and meaningless. Alan, like Charles, had always intended to file for divorce, and like myself, Zoe had learned to live with the fact her parents were no longer madly in love. Zoey knew from an early age that not all marriages were made in heaven, and she tolerated her dad's infidelity. There was enough distance between Los Angeles and Singapore to have sustained this relationship for years. As the limo parked under the brilliantly lit entrance of the hotel, Alan gave the guys explicit instructions.

"Guys, I'm going to be unavailable for the next two days. Brian will be in charge. Brian, you can reach me through my cell phone. Logan, please call me immediately if Jade goes into labor, and I'll meet you both at the hospital," Alan explained, tossing back a shot of Blanton's Bourbon. "The last thing Jade will need is to be bombarded by the media and reporters. There will be plenty of time for photos after the baby arrives. Brian, I expect you to stay on top of things regarding the paparazzi, no surprises. I'll be at the concert on Saturday. Enjoy the next two days. Guess we're all on 'stork watch.' Wow, that's a statement I never thought I would make as manager of Riot Storm," Alan grinned as the guys exited the limo.

Reaching for my hand, Logan helped me out of the car. It was a good thing travel was suspended for the following weeks. I was huge and wobbled like a penguin. I no longer fit comfortably in confined spaces. Slowly making my way inside the well-designed lobby with Logan's assistance, he picked up our room key. My feet and ankles were swollen from the long flight, and I was looking forward to a nice long nap in a comfy bed. We left the guys and Zoey in the hotel lobby. Then, we made our way over to the elevator and up to our floor. They were headed to the lounge with Brian to relax and toss back a few drinks before they called it a night. Unlocking the door to our suite, it was once again luxurious. The Mandarin was never disappointing.

"Hey, Sweetheart, I'm going to order room service. What would you like?"

"I'm not hungry. I ate on the plane."

"I think you should have something before going to bed. Would you like milk and cookies?"

"Logan, really, will you ever stop with the milk?" I laughed. "Okay, I relented. You can order a glass of milk and chocolate chip cookies."

"That's my girl."

After enjoying a late-night snack, and a couple shots of Jack Daniels, Logan reached for my hand. Pulling me up from the sofa, he led me into the bedroom. Even changing clothes at this point took effort. It appeared my expanding belly made everything more difficult. Finally, helping me into one of the band's oversized cotton tee-shirts, Logan pulled back the comforter and tucked me under the warm blankets. Then, stripping down to his black boxers, he slipped into bed. Pulling me next to him, I could sense his worries regarding the fact I could go into labor at any minute.

"Babe, are you worried?" I asked.

"About what? Labor and delivery?"

"Yes."

"Honestly, Sweetheart, I think the right word here is petrified."

"Logan, you're funny. I'll be the one doing all the work. You're not going to faint, are you?"

"God, I hope not, but I'm not making any promises."

"Logan, as long as you're with me, I think we're going to be just fine, all three of us," I whispered, trying to put on a brave face. Then, unexpectedly, my eyes moistened, knowing no family members would be present to support us or share in our joy.

"Jade, I would never leave you to go through this alone. What's wrong?" Logan asked, wiping my face with the back of his hand.

"Oh, it's the fact that once again, we'll have none of our family with us to share in the excitement. Of course, I would never want my mom here, and besides, she's in prison. I don't have anyone to give me advice on newborns. We only have my dad, and he's thousands of miles away."

"Jade, somehow I think you're going to do just fine. This little guy is one lucky dude to have you as his mom. Kids are resilient, and if you want a houseful of rambunctious children, it would be my pleasure. I'm confident I can make that happen," Logan teased. "Sweetheart, trust me, everything is going to be fine regardless of the fact we have no family with us. We're starting our own family."

"Awe, thanks, Babe." Laying my head against Logan's chest, I could envision us with a houseful of kids, and chaotic holidays, birthdays, and everything that makes a family unique. Logan was right. We had each other, and it was all we needed to create our own family.

Waking early the following day, sleep was becoming elusive. Staring at Logan, he was out cold. Finally, deciding to let him sleep, I slowly made my way into the bathroom. Alan had made arrangements for us to be given a VIP tour of the birthing suites at a nearby hospital. Quickly taking a shower and getting dressed, I walked over to wake Logan.

"I hate to wake you, but we have to be at the hospital at 10:00 a.m. this morning," I smiled, kissing him awake.

"Hospital, did you say, hospital?" Logan blurted out in a state of panic as he bolted upright.

"No. Relax. I'm not in labor, at least, not yet," I laughed.

"Oh my God," Logan froze. "Don't scare me like that."

After ordering a large breakfast of blueberry pancakes, eggs, bacon, and hash browns, we sat in the living room, devouring our food. Lounging back on the sofa, we were enjoying a second cup of coffee when we heard a knock at the door.

"Good morning. Alan wanted me to go with you to the hospital. I promised to speak with the staff and make sure everything was secure. We certainly don't want their complex besieged by news media," Brian smiled. "The limo is waiting downstairs if you're both ready?"

"As ready as we'll ever be," Logan grinned once again, helping me up from the sofa.

Arriving at the Gleneagles Hospital, it offered an unparalleled level of luxury. It was far superior to most stateside maternity hospitals. It even offered a cocktail party and a complimentary massage. After touring their medical facility, I felt it easily provided a safe environment to deliver our son. The medical staff was accommodating, and I knew they would make our stay pleasant and worry-free. Thanks to Alan everything was finally arranged.

The following two days came and went without me going into labor. Alan returned, and the concert was scheduled for 8:00 p.m. this evening at the Singapore Indoor Stadium. It was one of the smaller venues and completely sold-out. I was determined to be there regardless of the fact I could hardly walk. I knew Alan would be relieved to have this evening's performance a thing of the past. He worried I might go into labor just before the band's performance or, worse yet, while Logan was performing. Alan's luck held as I sat in a comfy chair just off stage next to Zoey and watched my incredibly handsome husband deliver one hit after another. Logan continually made eye contact with me during his performance. I knew he was worried I might go into labor. I smiled, giving him a thumbs up. I certainly didn't want to become a distraction, even though I felt like a giant blimp

Walking off stage, Logan immediately ran over to check on me.

"How's my girl? Any contractions?" Logan grinned, giving me a huge kiss.

"No, not yet. I don't think this little guy is in a hurry to make an appearance."

Helping me up from the chair, Logan took my hand. He held me securely as we slowly made our way down to the guy's dressing room.

"Another great concert," Alan smiled as he rushed past us in the narrow corridor.

"Thanks, Alan."

The room was once again crowded with reporters as we entered. Helping me over to the couch, Logan brought me a glass of water before he began mingling with the news media and the guys. Noticing that I was sitting alone on the sofa, Zoey walked over.

"How are you feeling?"

"Geez, I wished everyone would stop asking that question? Other than feeling larger than an elephant, I feel fine."

"Jade, I need you to have this baby soon. I want to be here for the birth, but Dad is going to let Ethan and I take the jet to Bora Bora during our hiatus."

"Really, Zoe, you'd rather be on a tropical island than support your best friend through childbirth?"

"Jade, that's not what I meant, and you know it. I'm not leaving until after the baby is born. So relax. I'm going to be your labor and delivery coach if, God forbid, Logan faints."

"Zoe, please give him a little credit. He's stronger than you think. However, the other night he was somewhat worried."

"Jade, Logan gets squeamish at the mere sight of a hangnail, and the guys are already taking bets that he's going to pass out."

"Oh, really?" Logan laughed, overhearing Zoey's remarks. "Zoe, you and Ethan can leave tomorrow. You're not going to be needed."

"Geez, Logan, how long have you been standing there?" Zoey blushed, unaware that he had walked over.

"Long enough."

"Sorry."

"You can let the guys know they're acting like petty children. Jade, sweetheart, everyone is leaving. I came to help you out to the car."

"Thanks."

The conversation between the guys was subdued as we entered the limo.

"Wow, it's awful quiet. If I didn't know better, I would think something is going on between you guys," Alan mentioned pouring himself a drink.

"Yeah, well, these idiots think I'm going to pass out in the birthing room," Logan vented.

"Oh my God, really, that's hysterical," Alan laughed, choking on his drink. "That's too funny." Then, grabbing a napkin to wipe his mouth, he regained his composure. "Guess it's possible."

"Thanks, Alan. I love your vote of confidence."

"Logan, relax. Guys, I'm afraid you're getting way too involved. I know having a baby isn't the norm for a group of guys on tour, but I think you're overlooking someone important. It can't possibly be easy for Jade. Sweetheart, I honestly don't know how you put up with these guys," Alan grinned, taking another sip of his drink. "Jade continues to put up with the lot of you when she's the one who's nine months pregnant."

"Awe, thanks, Alan. Guess I fell in love with one of them. They're not so bad. I suppose they are the older brothers I never had."

"Dysfunctional brothers, maybe?" Alan smirked. "Listen, we've all been on tour for months now, and the routine is getting old. Trust me, I understand. However, we're family. This little one is part of our family, so let's pull together to support Jade and Logan. I'm giving everyone two weeks to relax. But, of course, that might not be the case for you two after the baby is born. If memory serves, I believe there are a lot of sleepless nights involved," Alan winked, staring at Zoey. "I love you."

"I love you too, Dad. How did you get so smart?" Zoey smiled.

"Age," Alan grimaced, lounging back in his seat.

Reaching the hotel, Logan and I called it an evening while Zoey and the guys continued to the Clarke Quay for a night of fun.

"Call if anything changes," Alan mentioned dropping us back at the hotel.

"Will do. Try to keep those guys out of trouble tonight, if that's even possible," Logan smiled, helping me out of the car.

Unlocking the door to our suite, we settled into what had now become our nightly routine, a late-night snack and then falling into bed. However, by the following evening, things were slowly beginning to change. I think I felt my first contraction around 6:00 p.m. Trying to keep the pains under wrap for the first hour, I kept quiet. Then things progressed rather quickly. I was literally holding my breath as the unrelenting pains took control of my body.

"Logan," I screamed, trying to breathe. "We need to get to the hospital."

Running in from the other room, Logan's expressions depicted panic.

"Oh my God, I'll call Alan. We need to get you to the hospital. We need a car."

"Babe, this isn't a good time to lose it. Please call Alan or Brian."

They were just two floors up from our suite. Alan had been expecting the call and wasn't surprised by the degree of terror he heard in Logan's voice. Calling for the car, he was immediately on his way down to our room. Alan called Zoey on his cell, and Zoe called everyone. Hearing a knock on the door, Logan ran over to let Alan in.

"The car will be here in a few minutes," Alan smiled. "Everyone, stay calm."

Within moments, Zoey, Ethan, and Brian were at the door.

"Oh, my God, this is it," Zoey yelled, walking into the room.

"Zoe, get a grip. You and Logan are both losing it."

"Jade, sweetheart, can you walk, or do you need a wheelchair?" Alan inquired.

"Alan, for God's sake, I'll carry her," Logan interjected in a state of panic.

"I can walk," I laughed, getting a short reprieve from the contractions.

By the time we reached the hotel entrance, the entire gang had arrived, and we were all acting like crazed freaks in a circus sideshow. It wasn't our finest hour. Looking around the limo, I laughed in between bouts of the worst pains I'd ever felt. Finally, Jarrod popped the cork on a bottle of champagne and began pouring everyone a glass.

"Everyone, calm down," Alan laughed, quickly downing his entire drink. "I'm not sure the hospital is expecting our entire entourage. But, whatever, I suppose they'll just have to deal with it, with us," he laughed.

Reaching the hospital, the staff was expecting our arrival and not surprised by the fact the entire band was in tow. Parking at a back entrance, Alan didn't want to draw the attention of any news reporters that might have been camped out or lurking in the immediate vicinity.

As the limo stopped, a nurse was waiting outside with a wheelchair.

"Awe, Mrs. James, we've been expecting you. I'm Amelia, and I work in labor and delivery. I'll be taking you to your birthing suite. The rest of you are welcome to stay in the waiting room."

"Thanks," I gasped as a wave of intense pain held me in its grasp.

"Zoey, I want you to stay with Logan and me. Can you handle it?" I asked as I was wheeled into the hospital.

"Of course."

"Sweetheart, I'll be in the waiting room with the guys," Alan remarked. "If you need anything, send Zoey out to get me. I love you."

"Thanks, Alan."

Entering the birthing room, Logan was surprisingly calm despite the fact he'd melted down earlier at the hotel.

"I need you to change into one of our gowns, and afterward, I'll come in and hook you up to the fetal monitors. The doctor will be in soon," Amelia explained.

"Thanks," I moaned.

"Babe, I love you. You have no idea how much I love you at this very moment," Logan smiled, helping me into the hospital gown.

"I know. I love you too," I cringed in pain.

Quickly returning, the nurse hooked up the monitors. All eyes were instantly on the screen, which registered each contraction's strength and the baby's heartbeat and vital signs.

"Wow, this is amazing. Did you feel that contraction?" Logan grimaced, totally involved with the intricacies of the equipment.

"Really, Logan, you don't need a machine to tell you that I'm in pain. Just look at my facial expressions."

"Geez, Jade, you're becoming a little grumpy."

"Logan, I think I'm going to need drugs, major drugs, lots of drugs," I laughed, catching my breath.

"Mrs. James, it's nice to meet you. I'm Doctor Huett, one of the obstetricians here at Gleneagles. I'm told this baby has a famous father," he smiled, glancing at Logan. "Don't worry. We're going to take great care of them," he added.

"Thanks," Logan smiled, grasping my hand.

"I'm going to do a quick check. So just bear with me," Doctor Huett explained.

"As expected, you're in the early stages of labor," Doctor Huett stated after the exam. "First babies can often take a while. However, that's not to say things might not progress faster. Amelia will keep me posted. Also, please let one of our staff know if there's anything we can do to make you more comfortable."

"Drugs, my wife is going to need heavy-duty pain meds," Logan insisted.

Doctor Huett smiled. "I understand your concern. We can help with that. However, our main goal at Gleneagles is to deliver a healthy baby. We can provide pain medications up to a certain point in labor. For the moment, try to relax and practice breathing through each contraction. Do you have a birthing coach or someone to assist you?"

"Yes, my friend Zoey."

"Great. The nursing staff will keep me posted. I'll be receiving updates on your progress. It was nice to meet you."

"Damn, Babe, Zoey isn't even close to being a birthing coach. She doesn't have any experience," Logan worried as Doctor Huett left the room.

"Logan, speak for yourself. Seriously, how hard can it be?" Zoey laughed. "Jade, what do you want me to do?"

"I don't know, maybe help me breathe through the contractions."

"Okay, just let me know when you're having one."

"Now, Zoey, now."

"Jade, look at me and focus. Try to relax."

"Oh my God, this is like the blind leading the blind. I don't think you need a breathing or birthing coach until you're fully dilated and ready to push. Neither one of you knows what you're doing. I need a cigarette," Logan vented.

"Logan, she needs a birthing coach now. Would you please go and have a cigarette? This is women's work. We can handle this," Zoey demanded. "Women have been birthing babies since the beginning of time."

"Wow, Zoey, is that your extent of medical knowledge. I'm afraid you're in over your head. I'm sure the next words out of your mouth will be to boil some water. Geez."

"Guys, stop arguing. We're in a hospital, and trust me, they do know what they're doing. Thank God. Neither of you has a clue how to help. If you can't get a grip on yourselves, I might ask you to leave."

"Sorry, Babe."

"I'm sorry, I never said I was an expert," Zoey remarked, becoming emotional.

"Oh my God, you're both acting crazy. Please, try to keep it together. This isn't helping."

"What can I do?" Logan sympathized.

"Please, get the nurse. I think I just accidentally wet the bed."

Quickly, returning with Amelia, she smiled. "Let's take a look and see what's happening. Your water broke. It's completely normal. Things might begin to progress a little faster from this point. I'll check back in a half-hour. If you get too uncomfortable, ring the buzzer for the nurse's station."

At this point, it appeared the tiff between Zoey and Logan had calmed. Dimming the lights, Logan pulled a chair next to my bed and lovingly began massaging my back. Zoe was curled up in the fetal position in a lounge chair. It appeared we were all doing alright for the next hour except for the intense contractions. Then suddenly, my pain level jumped significantly.

"Logan, please buzz for the nurse."

"What's wrong?"

Grabbing Logan's hand, I held tight, trying to breathe, as the worst contractions ever completely overwhelmed me.

"Babe, get a nurse. Now," I begged, writhing in pain.

"Mrs. James, what can I do for you?" Amelia inquired, walking into the room.

"The pain is intolerable," I groaned.

"Let me check to see if you're still a candidate for an epidural? I know you're in a lot of pain, but just bear with me for a minute," she explained. "Okay, it looks like your going to get an epidural. I'll call for the anesthesiologist."

After getting the epidural, I felt relaxed. It was amazing to get some relief finally.

"Babe, how are you holding up? How's your pain level?"

"Much better. I actually feel sleepy," I smiled in a state of bliss.

Gently brushing back my long curls with his hands, Logan leaned over, kissing my forehead. "Sweetheart, I love you. I wished I could have taken the pain from you. But, you're a strong girl."

"I love you too," I said, nodding off.

The room fell quiet. Everyone was asleep. Logan had dozed off with his head leaning against my bed. Zoey never moved from her position in the recliner. The nurses came in and out, trying not to disturb us. Then about four hours later, I unexpectedly woke up feeling an excessive amount of pressure.

"Logan, something feels weird. Please, call for the nurse again," I asked, waking him from his slumber.

"Babe, what is it?" he smiled drowsily.

"Get the nurse. I feel a lot of pressure."

"Are you sure?"

"Logan, get the nurse," I demanded.

"Okay. I'll be right back. Don't go anywhere," he teased.

"Hurry."

Walking in and quickly checking my progress, Amelia smiled. "You're about to meet that little guy you've been carrying for nine long months" Turning on the lights, the room was once again a beehive of activity. I'm going to call Dr. Huett."

"Oh my God, I think I fell asleep," Zoey smiled as the bright lights came on.

"Don't we need blue paper gowns and booties," Logan asked.

"Logan, we're in a birthing suite, not the operating room," Zoey laughed.

"Good morning," Doctor Huett smiled. "Jade, we're going to drop the end of the bed down, and I need you to give me a few strong pushes. Dad, why don't you stand at the head of the bed for right now. Then, in a moment, I'll let you cut the umbilical cord. Okay, young lady, I'm going to need you to give me some strong pushes."

After my fifth push, the cries of our newborn filled the room. "Congratulations, you have a healthy baby boy. Dad, would you like to cut the cord?"

"Yes." With tears in his eyes, Logan did precisely as the doctor instructed. The nurse swaddled our son a moment later and handed him to Logan. The guys were wrong. Even though Logan was a bit crazy at the beginning of my labor, he never fainted.

"Mommy, meet Alexander Charles James," Logan smiled, laying our son in my arms. His eyes glistened with pride.

"Babe, he looks just like you," I paused, staring at his blonde curly locks. "Oh my God, Logan, he's gorgeous," I cried. I knew Charlie was in the room. I could feel his presence. "Charlie, you're an uncle," I whispered silently. "Somehow, I believe you already know. I love you."

Twenty-four hours later, we left the hospital. The paparazzi snapped endless photos as we entered the limo. Arriving back at the hotel, Logan carried his newborn son up to our suite. Opening the door, I gasped. The room was overflowing with blue balloons, a giant stuffed giraffe, and flowers. Alan and Brian had lovingly taken care of everything. A wicker bassinet, stroller, car seat, everything a newborn could possibly require filled the room. I was completely overwhelmed.

"Welcome home," Alan smiled.

"Nothing but the best for the newest member of Riot Storm," Brian added.

Hearing a knock at the door, Logan walked over.

"Congratulations, Papa," Ethan grinned, giving him a massive hug as he walked in.

"Yes. Congratulations. Where's my handsome godson?" Zoey laughed.

"Congratulations, Daddy," Jarrod and Noah smiled, following behind Zoey and Ethan.

Looking around the room, I stared at the guys and Zoey. We were indeed family. I discovered home wasn't a stucco mansion in Marin. It was a hotel room in Singapore. Logan was right. Families are not necessarily the people who share your genes, but rather those who share your life.

I left home at eighteen, and my entire life changed. Would I change a thing? No. Sometimes our lives are directed on impulse. I took a chance and found everything I ever dreamed was possible. Follow your heart. It will always lead you home.

New York

$\mathcal{M}$any years later, after endless tours with the band, Logan and I finally retired in the rolling hills of Dutchess County in Upper New York. Suddenly, our lives became much simpler. The years of travel and living in hotels had come to an end. Instead, we were now permanently settled in our sprawling, custom-built log home. We purchased over three hundred acres and added horses, chickens, goats, and every farm animal imaginable. However, most importantly, we added the love and laughter of our five children and eighteen adorable grandchildren.

It was late Christmas Eve. Snow had been falling relentlessly for hours, covering everything in a glimmering, white, pristine blanket. Despite the frigid temperatures outdoors, inside our home was warm, cozy, and teaming with merriment. Our children and grandchildren were home for the holidays. It was chaotic, loud, and boisterous. Then, unexpectedly, the doorbell rang. Logan and I both ran over to see who would be out in such horrid conditions.

"Merry Christmas," Alan smiled. "I would like you to meet, Jordan Kensington."

"Excuse me. I'm not sure I heard you correctly? What was your name?" Logan and I both froze in complete disbelief. We were face to face with a ghost on Christmas Eve.

"Jordan Kensington."

"That's impossible. Jordan passed before he was born and was laid to rest in the Kensington mausoleum," Logan answered in total shock. We were both utterly speechless.

"May we come in? We need to talk."

"Yes, of course," Logan replied, inviting them into the living room. "Please have a seat." At a complete loss for words, Logan was visibly shaken to his core. Trying to comprehend that Alan might have spoken the truth, we could only stare at the young man who appeared to be about the same age as Alex. However, his trademark blonde hair and piercing, sapphire blue eyes were a dead giveaway. He easily resembled his brothers.

"Jordan is your son."

"How is this even possible?" Logan questioned with a ragged breath.

"Unfortunately, Kelsey never told you the truth. She didn't lose the baby," Alan hesitated. "Several years ago, before she passed from injuries she sustained in the auto accident, she admitted to her father, Edward, that Jordan was your son. Kelsy had always led Edward to believe Jordan's father was a drummer in another band. Edward never told another person until a few weeks ago. You know Edward and I have always been close, and I guess he just needed to get it off his chest before he passed away."

"My son," Logan slowly acknowledged trying to comprehend Alan's explanation. Then, taking a few minutes to let the facts sink in, we only had to look at him, and we knew without hesitation he was indeed Logan's son. Walking over to embrace Jordan, with tears in his eyes, Logan pulled his son into his arms. It seemed the perfect occasion for Jordan to meet our entire family. Christmas Eve had arrived with a miracle.

"I hate to run, but I'm on my way to Singapore for the holidays," Alan grinned. "After Joyce passed, I decided to buy a home in Singapore. I spend a lot of time in that part of the world. So give me a call sometime.

We have a lot of catching up to do. Jordan is the sole heir to Edward's music empire, Kensington Entertainment. It's a multi-billion dollar conglomerate," Alan added with a whisper. "Merry Christmas."

"Welcome home," Logan smiled, wrapping his arms around Jordan. The moment felt surreal as he led Jordan into the next room. "You have a huge family. I'm sure they would love to meet you."

Walking into the expansive, vaulted family room, the entire family was gathered around a roaring fireplace and an enormous Christmas tree that towered upward into the ceiling.

"I'd like you to meet my son," Logan smiled.

www.ingramcontent.com/pod-product-compliance
Lightning Source LLC
Chambersburg PA
CBHW031018190726
48286CB00003BA/901

9 781955 177801